Kerry Katona

Kerry was born in Warrington in 1980. She came into the limelight when she joined the hugely successful band Atomic Kitten, but left in 2001 when her first daughter was born. As well as winning *I'm A Celebrity ... Get Me Out Of Here!* she has been a regular presenter on *Loose Women*, starred in the successful Irish TV series *Show Band*, and has been the subject of a prime time ITV documentary, *My Fair Kerry*. Most recently she and her husband Mark have starred in *Crazy in Love* on MTV. Her memoir *Too Much, Too Young* was a *Sunday Times* Top Ten bestseller.

www.randomhouse.co.uk/minisites/kerrykatona

D0762453

The Footballer's Wife

Kerry Katona

EBURY
PRESS

1 3 5 7 9 10 8 6 4 2

Published in 2008 by Ebury Press, an imprint of Ebury
Publishing
A Random House Group Company

Copyright © Kerry Katona 2008

Kerry Katona has asserted her right to be identified as the
author of this Work in accordance with the Copyright, Designs
and Patents Act 1988

The Random House Group Limited Reg. No. 954009
Addresses for companies within the Random House Group
can be found at www.randomhouse.co.uk

A CIP catalogue record for this book is available from
the British Library

The Random House Group Limited makes every effort to ensure
that the papers used in our books are made from trees that have
been legally sourced from well-managed and credibly certified
forests. Our paper procurement policy can be found on
www.rbooks.co.uk/environment

Printed in the UK by CPI Cox & Wyman, Reading, RG1 8EX

ISBN 9780091923242

To buy books by your favourite authors and register for offers visit
www.rbooks.co.uk

The footballer's Wife

chapter one

Charly Metcalfe asked her driver to drop her as near as possible to Harvey Nicks in the centre of Manchester. He pointed out that it was pedestrianised but lately she did what she always did when someone gave her an objection – she offered him money. Flashing a fifty pound note in his direction she said, 'Here you go, Terry. Just see how far you can get, don't worry if it's not to the door.'

'Put your bloody money away. What d'you think I am, a lap dancer?' Terry chided. Charly smiled. Terry wasn't into taking money from her, but she still offered; she thought it rude not to.

Charly checked her reflection in her compact; her MAC make-up was perfectly applied to her sunkissed skin. Her green eyes were framed with the slightest hint of mascara and her cheekbones had a dash of pink blusher. Charly didn't need much more to enhance her features; she was naturally pretty. Terry drove around the back of the cathedral and up towards the giant, flower-shaped windmills in the Triangle. 'This is as far as I can get you without carrying you in.'

Charly smiled. 'Thank you.'

Terry raised an eyebrow in his rearview mirror and shook his head.

'What?' Charly asked with a cheeky smile. She knew *what*. She was pushing her luck, as always, but she knew that Terry liked her and that he'd drive her to the counter if he could. Charly and Terry got on well. It was as if they both knew how lucky she was. He liked her cheekiness and seemed to appreciate her kindness – not her financial kindness, he wasn't buying any of that – but her thoughtfulness; she would often buy him little gifts from town or cook for him. Charly liked Terry because of his humour and warmth. A lot of people who worked for Charly's boyfriend didn't seem to notice her but Terry did. She was glad to have him around. The fact that Charly had a driver at all wasn't lost on her. Only a year ago she had been living on the Bolingbroke council estate wondering where her next pair of fake Rock & Republic jeans were going to come from. And now she was living the life that she, and thousands of other girls like her, could have only dreamed of. Well, almost. She and her footballer boyfriend Joel Baldy had been arguing a lot lately but Charly just told herself that it went with the territory. They had recently decided to move from their Cheshire home into their Manchester penthouse to see if a change of scenery would improve things. If nothing else, Charly thought, Terry wouldn't have to drive her to Harvey Nicks. She could walk the 100 yards from the apartment to the store herself.

Charly stepped out of the Lincoln Navigator, throwing her Balenciaga bag over her shoulder, and headed for her favourite shop. The doorman tipped his hat and said, 'Hello, madam,' as he did every Thursday when Charly came shopping. The first area of the shop was the bag section. The woman serving at one of the well-known designer bag counters gave Charly a tight smile as she perused the wares.

'Hello, Ms Metcalfe, can I get you anything today?'

Charly picked up a little blue number that was priced at one thousand and fifty pounds. 'No, I think I'm just looking,' Charly said, smiling back disingenuously. She was enjoying herself. This was the woman who, on Charly's first trip to the shop, had obviously taken her for a chav-on-tour and asked her to put the merchandise down if she had no intention of buying it. Charly had dropped the bag she was holding at the time and walked over to the Mulberry counter across the way and, in full view of the rude shop assistant, had spent in excess of five thousand pounds on three bags. She had given two of them away to her younger twin cousins, Anita and Tanita, and told them to sell them on eBay if they had any sense. Charly hadn't had any more *Pretty Woman* moments since. She knew she must be one of Harvey Nicks' best customers and that that particular shop assistant was wishing she had never been snotty with her.

Charly knew she'd get used to having money, but she hadn't realised how quickly. She thought nothing of spending two thousand pounds on a dress that would be worn once and cast to the back of the wardrobe. She didn't have much of a moral problem with spending Joel's money. She brought in enough money modelling and being in the occasional magazine to pass whatever she spent off as her own. Although she was doing less modelling these days – she wasn't a great fan of getting her top off in cold rooms and being told to look sexy. Glamour modelling needed renaming in Charly's opinion.

Joel was paid a fortune. He earned more in one week than most people earned in a year, two years even, as Charly had reminded him when his new contract was signed. He gave her money because he didn't know what to do with it and she spent it accordingly, but always made sure that whatever she spent on herself she spent the same on Joel.

Today she was going to buy Joel something special. But as she walked around the shop nothing grabbed her. Everything in here was something he could walk in and buy for himself. Charly slipped her shades on, popped her hair in a ponytail and ventured out into the street. Not that she was constantly mobbed by the press – she wasn't arrogant enough to place herself in the same league as Victoria Beckham – but she was often recognised, and she found it slightly disconcerting. She walked across to St Anne's Square and was contemplating buying something from the Disney Store when she saw a stall in the middle of the square selling hand-carved toys and door plaques. Charly smiled to herself, knowing that she had found Joel's ideal present.

*

A few hours later Charly let herself into the large detached house in Hale Barns that she shared with Joel. Charly had never quite got used to this place. It wasn't the house so much as the isolation she felt when they were there. It wasn't isolated in the strictest sense: they lived on a tree-lined street with other huge houses set back in their own grounds, but Charly was used to living shoulder to shoulder with her neighbours and here, nobody gave her the time of day. She was sure that she'd seen the snooty woman next door cross herself when she and Joel moved in.

There were a number of boxes and suitcases scattered around the entrance hall. The move to the Manchester apartment was taking place tomorrow and Gina, a woman from Manchester Rovers who seemed to help the players with anything they needed, was standing in the middle of Charly and Joel's belongings, checking each item off on a clipboard.

'Where's Joel?' Charly asked.

'Putting his feet up,' Gina said, nodding towards the dining room.

Charly wandered through to find her boyfriend

sitting engrossed in his XBox 360 game. She kissed him on the cheek but he didn't react, his gaze firmly on the soldier on the screen who was spinning round in a room, shooting into thin air.

'I've got you a present,' Charly said gently. When she and Joel had first become an item he had told her that as a child he'd always wanted a plaque for his door but because at the time his had been an unusual name he'd never had one. He was jealous of his school mate John who had his name plastered all over everything. Joel didn't take his eyes off the screen as Charly began to unwrap the paper bag containing the wooden room sign. *Joel's Games Room. Do Not Disturb*, the hand-carved sign said in bright letters.

'Here you go,' Charly said gently. Joel shut his eyes with rage and threw the control to the floor.

'I've just fucked that up now!' he shouted angrily.

'I've got you a present,' Charly said quietly. She heard the front door softly close. It was obvious that Gina thought it necessary to make herself scarce.

Joel's jaw set angrily. 'What?'

'It's a plaque for the spare room in the flat. You said you always wanted one when you were a kid.'

Joel looked down at the gift his girlfriend was cradling. 'Well, I'm not a kid now, am I? I'm a grown fucking man.' He stood up and walked out of the room.

Charly looked on after him, heartbroken. 'Where are you going?'

'Somewhere I can get some peace and quiet,' Joel said over his shoulder. Charly sat staring at the small gift; she felt foolish for even thinking of buying it now. She wrapped it back up in the tissue paper and put it in her bag. A door at the opposite end of the house slammed, and Charly stood up, determined not to cry. She walked into the hall and began to sort through hers and Joel's belongings; anything to distract herself from the feeling of foreboding that had crept over her.

*

Tracy Crompton was sitting flicking through the last-minute holidays on Teletext. Her blonde hair was scraped back harshly from her face, and her figure, which considering the sedentary life she led was still in great shape, was hidden from view by the stained towelling dressing gown she insisted on wearing around the house. She was due a break, she thought. It had been nearly a year since her ill-fated attempt to have the holiday of a lifetime in the Dominican Republic. And if that stroppy mare of an air hostess hadn't thought it necessary to wrestle her to the ground, sit on her back and have the plane diverted and Tracy arrested for being drunk and disorderly then she might have spent her two weeks on a white sandy beach rather than sharing a cell with a dangerous American lesbian called Brenda with Meatloaf's face tattooed on her arm.

This year she was doing things differently. She and Kent were going to get themselves to the Costa Del Whatever's the Cheapest, and she was going to lay off the rum until they were safely in their apartment. She heard Kent rustling around behind her. 'There's a week here in Magaluf, ninety nine pounds each. That's bugger all. What d'you reckon?' she shouted over her shoulder.

'Ninety nine quid? It'll be a rat-hole,' Kent said, his voice straining. Tracy turned around to see what he was doing. He was standing by the breakfast bar trying with all his might to zip up a white, rhine-stone-studded, all-in-one Elvis suit that was easily three sizes too small. He managed to get the zip as far as his belly button while simultaneously trapping his chest hairs. His eyes nearly popped out of his head with pain.

'What d'you think?' he squeaked, trying to put his arms up only to find he was unable to lift them any higher than hip level.

Tracy looked at him and shook her head. She wanted to bollock him for being such a fool as to own an Elvis jumpsuit in the first place, never mind trying to pour himself into it. But he looked like such an idiot she couldn't help but laugh. 'Lovely meat and two veg, Evel Knievel.'

'I'm the bloody King!'

'Which one? Henry the eighth?'

'You cheeky sod.' Kent tutted and tried to walk off but found that he was swinging his legs like John Wayne.

'Where d'you dig that up from?'

'It's the one I won Butlin's Skegness "Elvis of the Year 1989" in.'

'Well, I think you might want to have a look at a picture of Elvis just before he slumped off the toilet with a burger in one hand and a handful of Temazepam in the other and get yourself another suit made up.'

'D'you think I've put on weight?' Kent asked, self-consciously stroking his portly belly.

Tracy rolled her eyes. 'When was the last time you saw your feet? Year after Skegness I reckon,' she said, without a thought for Kent's bruised feelings. 'So am I booking this holiday or not?'

'What's the date?'

'Next week.'

'I can't next week. It's the competition.'

Tracy spun around in her chair, finally listening to Kent. 'What competition?'

'The Bolingbroke Lane Working Men's Club Elvis competition,' Kent said as if it was his thousandth time saying it. 'Winner goes through to Blackpool. Then Blackpool winner goes through to Memphis. And that's what I'm talkin' 'bout.' Kent finished his sentence with his best Elvis impression, not realising that Tracy was staring at him agog.

'No fucking way!' Tracy said, sparking up a cigarette and jabbing it in the direction of her common-law husband.

'What you on about, "No fucking way"? I've been looking forward to this for months!'

Tracy glared at him. She knew that he had been rattling on about some competition that was coming up but she hadn't really been listening. Now she knew it was at Bolingbroke Lane Working Men's Club she was all ears. 'Anywhere but there, Kent. Over my dead body.'

'It's just a club.'

Tracy jumped to her feet. 'How can you say that? Any place that has Len Metcalfe running it is not just a bloody club. That man is poison.'

'Just because his daughter chucked Scott.'

'Get your facts right. That little slag bled our Scottie dry until the first opportunity she got to jump ship and shack up with that nob-head footballer. I told our Leanne not to introduce her to anyone famous but did she listen? No. And now she's in every frigging paper I open, rubbing our Scott's nose in it. And I wouldn't mind but he's still paying off Fat Paul at the warehouse for all the bags he had nicked for her, while she swans around the place dripping in money. No morals, any of them Metcalfes.' Tracy shook her head indignantly.

'That's her, not her dad. He's just a fat get who calls the bingo every Sunday; he's hardly Don Corleone, is he?'

Tracy's face clouded over and rare angry tears welled in her eyes. 'I hate him!' she yelled. The ferocity of her statement took Kent aback. Tracy looked at Kent alarmed. She knew she was showing too much emotion about some bloke whose only connection to Tracy, as far as Kent was aware, was to be the dad of her son's ex-girlfriend. She took a deep breath. 'He's an arsehole, trust me. I know him from old.'

'What's he done to you?' Kent waddled over to Tracy in his spray-on jumpsuit and took her hand.

'He hasn't done anything,' Tracy said adamantly. She knew that she had to lighten the mood otherwise Kent would be grilling her about Len and that was the last thing she needed. She didn't like to think about that portly little man and his chavvy family if she could help it. 'Look, go to the competition if you want.'

'You don't have to come with me if you don't want to,' Kent said seriously.

Tracy arched an eyebrow. 'No way. If we're going we're going in force. I'll ring round and gather the troops. I don't want that Metcalfe lot thinking we do things by halves.' She sat down purposefully.

'Right.' Kent smiled proudly. 'Better get down the market and see if someone can run me up another jumpsuit.'

*

Charly Metcalfe was perched three seats back from the infamous manager of Manchester Rovers, Martin Connors. The ground was packed to capacity and she was sitting alongside her brother Jimmy. Jimmy had made a reappearance recently when it became obvious that his sister's new relationship meant free premiership tickets were on the cards. For the past few years he had been lying low on account of the fact that he had stolen anything valuable from his dad's house to fund a burgeoning heroin habit. He was now clean and seemed to be contrite – although he still couldn't look Len in the eye, Charly noted.

Len had accepted an uneasy truce with his son over the last few months, but Charly had a feeling that it would all come out in the wash at some stage. Although her dad had managed to keep his temper in check for a good few years, the legacy of the old Len was never too far away. A look or a pause was enough for people who knew him well to think that there was a possibility that he might blow. Not today, though. Today Len was as proud as punch, Charly could tell. They were in VIP seats with the rest of the Wives and Girlfriends and the TV cameras that were filming the game kept panning to Charly, who managed to maintain sphinx-like poise even when Joel, star player for Manchester Rovers, scored. The reality was that inside she was jumping up and down with excitement.

Charly couldn't believe sometimes how much her life had changed beyond recognition. When she and Joel had first met she had been living in a tiny flat with her then-boyfriend Scott Crompton who, although a lovely bloke, was too much of a pushover for Charly to see herself with permanently. She had met Joel at the opening of the Glasshouse nightclub in Bradington, where Charly had been out for the evening with Scott's sisters Leanne and Jodie. Leanne had signed Charly up to work as a glamour model for her recently founded agency and the three had gone out that night to promote the new enterprise. Joel had chatted to Charly and she knew immediately that there was a connection. When he asked for her number she hadn't hesitated. They had been together ever since.

A year on and Charly could pick and choose the modelling assignments she undertook and she didn't have to work if she didn't want to; Joel's huge salary took care of both of them. Leanne's modelling agency was doing well and Jodie was the one who was bringing in the most business. This didn't surprise Charly in the slightest; Jodie was a real grafter and would work her socks off to make sure she succeeded.

Jimmy cheered when he saw an image of his

sister flash up on the screen, which was more of a courtesy than the away fans were affording Charly. They had begun chanting a song speculating in which orifice she was most fond of having sex. Charly wasn't bothered; they might be making a joke of her but she'd be the one waking up in Egyptian cotton sheets in the morning, with freshly squeezed orange juice awaiting her prepared by the maid. Most of the chanting fans would be getting out of bed when their alarm told them to, next to a wife they never spoke to, to go to a job they despised. She knew where she'd rather be standing.

'What are that lot singing?' Len asked, straining to hear.

'Don't worry about it,' Charly said, putting her hand on her dad's large, tattooed arm.

A look of shock registered on Len's face as he realised what the away fans were chanting about his daughter. Soon his eyes were bulging out of their sockets with indignation. 'Dad, leave it,' Charly urged him.

'I'll leave nothing. That's a bloody disgrace!' Len said, flying off in the direction of the nearest steward. Charly watched as her dad protested vehemently, pointing at his daughter then pointing to the away crowd. She wanted to curl up and die but thankfully she had her Christian Dior shades on which helped keep her expression inscrutable.

'What's he showing us up for?' Jimmy asked. Charly thought this was particularly rich coming from someone who'd spent his life showing his family up. Other people in the area where they were seated were now craning their necks to see what was going on. Len jabbed his finger at the steward who in return went to grab Len to throw him out. Len quickly pulled away and followed this move with a lightning punch that sent the steward reeling. Suddenly he was surrounded by six policemen. Charly couldn't see where they'd come from but they were wrestling her father to the ground and pulling him out of the stadium. She felt her jaw fall open and quickly shut it again, knowing that was the photo any long-range lenses that were trained on her were waiting for. She grabbed Jimmy's arm. 'Come on, we've got to go after him.'

'But it's not even half time!' Jimmy complained.

Charly slid her glasses down her nose and eyeballed her brother. 'Get your arse out of that chair, now!' she said menacingly. Her brother did as he was told.

*

Len was sitting in a police cell somewhere on the outskirts of Manchester, holding his head in his hands. He hadn't wanted any aggro, especially not today. Charly had tried to do something nice for him and Jimmy by bringing them to the game and what happens? He gets slung out on his backside for all to see and ends up in the cop shop. *Nice going, Len*, he thought. He had sat quietly in the back of the police van on the way to the station. Gone were the days when he would wax lyrical about the arresting officer's wife or make a meal out of asking if the coppers in the front of their van enjoyed their jobs – invariably they did and it wouldn't get him anywhere being mouthy.

The door opened and a young policewoman asked Len if he'd like to follow her. He was being released now that the match crowd had been dispersed in their different directions and he was no longer a threat. They were not going to press charges this time; they were going to let him off with a caution and some friendly advice to not attend a Rovers match for the foreseeable future.

Len walked out of the police station onto the anonymous road in South Manchester. He didn't know how he was meant to get home. He had a mobile phone but he'd forgotten it – he didn't really like the things and only used them for emergencies – forgetting that emergencies rarely announced themselves and that he should probably keep it with him rather than placing it next to his landline as if that was where phones lived.

'Dad!' he heard Charly shout, and looked up. She was getting out of her sports car, quickly followed by Jimmy. Len smiled, shamefaced.

'Sorry, love,' he said, and he genuinely was. He knew that it was a big thing for her and he was meant to be meeting her boyfriend, Joel, after the game for the first time; something Len had managed to put off until now simply because he wasn't so sure of this flash young super-stud.

'Get in the car.' Charly's voice was stern. Jimmy was standing next to her doing his usual impression of a useless lump. Len opened his mouth to try and apologise to her again when a round of flashes went off in his face. He turned to see two photographers standing with their cameras flashing away. Len could feel his blood boil, and angrily turned on the men.

'What the bleeding hell do you think you're doing?' he asked menacingly.

Charly grabbed his arm.

'That's a right temper you've got on you, Mr

Metcalfe,' one of the snappers goaded. Len lurched forward but he felt a far stronger pull on his other arm. Jimmy had hold of him and was pulling him towards Charly's car.

But Len wasn't finished. 'And who the bloody hell are you, you twat? This how you make a living?' Len spat.

'Dad!' Charly shouted. 'Get in the car now!'

Len glared at the photographers before pulling his gaze away and allowing himself to be bundled into the car.

Charly and Jimmy jumped in quickly after him, Charly turning the key in the ignition and pressing the accelerator to the floor. 'Jesus Christ, Dad,' was all she could muster as the car shot away from the still-snapping paparazzi.

chapter two

Len Metcalfe had a job, which was more than could be said for the rest of his family. He took great pride in his work. As the club steward of Bolingbroke Lane Working Men's Club, Len had a fair amount of responsibility. He oversaw the draymen, making sure they delivered the right amount of beer – a shortage of bitter on a busy night could easily lead to a riot. He booked the turns, and more importantly turned people away that he didn't think were suitable. That woman who pulled light bulbs out of her whatnot who turned up to audition the other week, for example; he had sent her packing, but not before asking her how on earth she thought that passed for family entertainment. He cashed up and made sure that no one had their fingers in the till: he could tell a thief a mile off, coming as he did from a long line of them. Len's brothers were both in prison doing a long stretch and his dad had spent more time inside than out by the time he died five years ago. Len himself had spent two years in Strangeways when he was in his early twenties. He had believed his dad's stories about the camaraderie in prison; how everyone looked after one another. But he found out first-hand that these were just stories that his dad made up so that his boys weren't worried by the truth. Len's two years had been long and violent, although he'd managed to keep himself to himself. He tried not to think about those times. It was nearly thirty years ago and since then he had kept his nose clean and made sure that he didn't spend any more time at Her Majesty's pleasure.

Len was cleaning the optics and checking the drinks invoice for that week. He liked the order and routine of his work. It kept him focused and calm. All in all, Len was very proud of what he did. It wasn't Caesar's Palace but it was alright, and although it was named Bolingbroke Lane, it wasn't actually in Bolingbroke, which was a godsend. Bolingbroke might be where Len lived, but he didn't need the hassle of running a place there; it'd be easier to run a bar in Basra. It was on the outskirts between Bolingbroke and the marginally more upmarket area of Bilsey, so it drew a more mixed crowd than the Beacon, the hell-hole of a pub perched on the top of the estate.

Len liked being defined by his job. He liked to be thought of as The Steward. The title felt right, like it had some weight behind it; some responsibility. But lately he wasn't known for what *he* did, he was known for what his daughter did, and it was beginning to trouble him.

Yesterday's display wasn't something he was particularly proud of. But he didn't think the punishment fit the crime. He wasn't Joel Baldy, he was plain old Len Metcalfe and he'd never seen himself in the paper before. Had he been presented with the scenario, he would have hoped that his tabloid debut hadn't seen him frothing at the mouth. He had avoided getting his usual *Sunday Globe* today. It was one of his small pleasures: a coffee, a smoke and a scan of the Sunday rag. But he just had a feeling that he might be making a rather unpleasant appearance in it today and, as such, had avoided the newsagents. It didn't matter, though, there was no shortage of people who wanted to show him today's issue. Marge the cleaner had been the first. 'Bloody hell, Len, you look like a madman!' she had said gleefully as she threw the paper down on the bar that morning. Len had looked at it with abject mortification. She was right; he looked like a man possessed. Marge read the opening lines aloud: 'Madman Metcalfe, father of Joel Baldy's WAG Charly, was chomping at the bit yesterday moments after being released from police custody without charge after a fracas at the Manchester Rovers game …' As Marge went on, Len hung his head. The rest of the day saw a steady stream of punters coming in armed with the paper, ready to tell him something he already knew: he was a national laughing stock.

Charly had called him earlier. After his appalling showing yesterday she was ringing to rearrange introducing him to her boyfriend. She said that she wanted them to meet sooner rather than later and had suggested that evening. Len had decided that he was going to agree to anything his daughter wanted – he'd brought enough trouble to her door as it was without being all huffy about meeting her famous other half. But he wasn't sure about Joel. There had been rumours in the papers about him playing away using more than just his feet, and the fact that they'd been together for so long and he'd never met him made Len suspicious. Len tried not to worry too much, he knew that Charly had gone into this relationship with her eyes open, but he was still fiercely protective of her and the last thing he wanted was some silly pretty-boy footballer upsetting her.

He looked up to see Fat Paul, a dimwitted wheeler-dealer from the area, heading towards him with the day's papers under his arm and a stupid grin on his face. Before he had time to say anything Len fixed him with a glare. 'Shut it, Paul, or I'll tear you another arsehole.' Paul put the papers behind his back as if he didn't know what Len was referring to.

'Bloody hell, I was only after a quick pint,' he said.

*

Markie was sitting at the bar of the Glasshouse, the nightclub that he co-owned with his business partner Mac Jones, in the centre of Bradington. He was sipping sparkling mineral water and looking at the guest list for this evening – more for his own amusement than anything; he liked to see who thought they were special around town – when his phone began to ring. 'Mum?' he said out loud, looking at the caller ID. *What did she want?* His mum had been keeping her head very much down over the last year, since it had been discovered that she was selling stories to the tabloids about her daughter, his sister Leanne, who'd had a career as a well-known glamour model.

'Yes?'

'Well, that's nice, innit?' Tracy snapped. 'When was the last time you came round to see me or called me and then I call you and I get "Yes?".'

'Hi Mum, long time no see. God, I've missed you,' Markie said sarcastically.

'Lovely. I bend over backwards for years for you lot and all I ever get in return is lip and sarky comments.'

Markie wasn't rising to the bait. 'Alright, Mum, what can I do for you?'

'I've been thinking …'

Markie waited for it. Whatever it was would somehow serve Tracy. She never did anything that didn't directly benefit her.

'Thursday night. Let's have a get-together. When was the last time we did that? Me, you, our Jodie, our Scott, our Karina, our Leanne …'

'The last time was before you decided that selling stories about our Leanne and your granddaughter was a normal way of making some extra cash.'

Tracy tutted; she hated being reminded of her

misdemeanours. 'And am I ever going to live it down? Anyway, it's just been blown out of proportion now. I'm being painted as the wicked witch of the west when all I was trying to do was earn a bit of cash to take us all away somewhere nice.'

Markie burst out laughing. 'Pull the other one, it's got fucking bells on! This is me you're talking to.'

'Right,' Tracy said, 'if you don't want to come then fine. Suit yourself. I'm not begging.'

Markie finished his water, stood up from his stool and walked across the floor of the VIP area to the spiral stairs that led down to the main part of the club. 'So what's the occasion?'

'Kent's entering a competition; I thought we could give him some moral support.'

Markie's eyes narrowed. *What did she need them for?* 'What sort of competition?' he asked, seeing his business partner, Mac, walk in. Markie nodded to him.

'Elvis.'

Markie stifled a laugh, 'You *what*?'

'You heard. So you coming or not?'

Markie hung up as Mac approached. 'What's so funny?'

'That dipshit my mother lives with is entering an

Elvis competition and she wants us all there like the Waltons to give him moral support.'

Mac laughed and shook his head. 'She's a rum 'un, isn't she?'

'That's one way of describing her.'

'Saw her the other day, in town. She was in Super Cigs. I've not seen her look so well in years.'

'My mum?' Markie asked incredulously.

'Yes, *your mum*. She used to be a looker when she was younger.'

Markie glared at him. Mac held his hands up to placate his business partner. 'I'm just saying …'

Markie relaxed and half smiled. 'Really?'

'Yeah, but it was always hard to see past that gob of hers.'

The smile turned wry. 'I can well believe that,' he said, passing Mac a breakdown of the takings for the week.

*

Jodie had spent the past three days in Majorca on a photo shoot for a leading men's magazine. In the past year she had seen her stock rise. When her sister Leanne, herself a successful glamour model, had signed her to her new management company

Jodie didn't really think that she could be successful at it. She *dreamed* she might, but she was a realist and years of living on the Bolingbroke estate didn't automatically fill a girl with hope that there was a great life to be had out there. A year ago she thought that she was going to spend the rest of her days pulling pints at the notorious Beacon pub, but she hadn't touched a pint pump in nearly a year and she was making good money as a model. The difference between Leanne's career as a model and Jodie's was that Jodie had Leanne guiding her, whereas Leanne had had a manager who didn't really care what happened to her once she earned her cut. Leanne was ensuring that Jodie was saving half of everything she received. The temptation to go and blow everything had been great when she'd first had some money but she didn't have that option with her sister around, thankfully.

She was living in an apartment near the city centre, using the money she earned from her first few months as a model as her deposit. It wasn't Trump Towers, and it was in Bradington, but Leanne had warned Jodie away from getting starry-eyed and thinking that she needed to move to London just because a lot of her work took place there. Leanne advised Jodie to stay at home and dip into the London life for parties and premieres; that way it would always seem exciting and yet she wouldn't find herself stranded, as Leanne had, if work dried up. Not that Leanne was going to let Jodie's work dry up; she was finding work for her daily.

Jodie was standing in her kitchen leafing through the post and waiting for the kettle to boil when her phone began to ring. No one ever rang the landline. She was going to ignore it, thinking it was probably a sales call, but curiosity got the better of her.

'Hello.'

'Don't put the phone down …' the familiar voice said quickly. Jodie's face registered shock; it was her mum.

'What d'you want?'

'To stop all this bollocks. I'm fed up with us all not speaking; it's time to let bygones be bygones.'

Jodie took a deep breath; anyone else's mum and she might have believed them, but not her own. Whatever it was that Tracy wanted it was for herself, not because she really wanted reuniting with her family. 'Is it money?'

'Is what money?' Tracy asked.

'What you're after?'

'You cheeky sod. I don't need your money.'

'Right,' Jodie said, trying to sound neutral. The fact was, as much as her mum was the worst example of motherhood that Bradington had to offer, she was still her mum and no matter how many times Tracy let her down, Jodie always hoped that one day she'd stop acting like a sneaky overgrown kid and start acting like the parent she was supposed to be.

'Right, nothing. Don't think just because you've been asked to go on *Celebrity Breakdance* you're a cut above, because you're not.'

How did she know about that? Jodie wondered. She'd quite liked the idea but Leanne had told her she wasn't doing anything that didn't involve modelling. Those types of shows were fine to do when you had something to promote or your career was in the doldrums, she'd said, but as Jodie was doing fine and was doing all the promoting she needed by just being in magazines, she didn't need to spin on her head and be marked out of ten just yet.

'I don't think anything of the sort.' Jodie was about to snap at her mum but caught herself; she knew this could descend into a full-scale slanging match very quickly if she wasn't careful. 'OK, Mum, go on, what's up?'

'I've arranged a night out for us all. As a family.'

'Have the others agreed to this?' Jodie asked with surprise.

'Markie has. Scotty has, but then again he's not seen his arse with me the same way the rest of you have …' Jodie bit her tongue. Her brother Scott was too soft with Tracy in hers and everyone else's opinion. '… and I'll ring Leanne and Karina when I've finished talking to you.'

'So what's the big occasion?' Jodie asked.

'Kent's entering a competition and I thought it'd be nice if we were all there.'

'What sort of competition?'

'Elvis.'

Jodie snorted laughing. It came out involuntarily; she couldn't help herself. The thought of stupid Kent up on stage doing one of his terrible Elvis impersonations was too much to bear.

'What you laughing at?' Tracy sounded indignant. 'You're as bad as Markie.'

'What do you think I'm laughing at? Kent as Elvis. Brilliant. Put my name down.'

'I don't want you taking the piss out of him. He takes it very seriously.'

Jodie rolled her eyes. 'Would I?'

'Yes, you would. Right, Bolingbroke Lane

Working Men's Club; Thursday night, half seven. Don't be late.'

'Bolingbroke Working Men's Club!' Jodie began to protest about the pipe-and-slippers venue but Tracy had already put the phone down.

*

Charly was nervous. She was standing in front of her full-length mirror in the city centre penthouse, scrutinising her reflection. Her blonde bobbed hair was perfectly straight, her petite size eight figure was poured into a muted silver Body Con dress that didn't give her any room to breathe, and her feet were encased in a pair of leopard-print Dolce and Gabbana shoes that matched her handbag.

'You look fit,' Joel said, sliding his arm around her waist, his hand making its way down her skirt and between her legs.

'Thanks,' Charly said flatly, taking his hand off her leg. 'You don't look half bad yourself,' she added without really looking at him. Things had been tense between them since he stormed off the other day. The move into town couldn't have been described as fraught, as Gina had organised everything, but the tension had remained in the air.

Charly knew that the last thing Joel wanted to do tonight was meet her father. But he also wanted to make his peace with Charly. He often did this, sulked for days and then decided, *when he was ready*, that they should act as if nothing had happened.

'Suit yourself,' Joel said at the rejection. 'Shall we go then?' He waved the keys to his Lamborghini Murcielago.

'I hope you like my dad,' Charly said anxiously. And she meant it. She was fraught enough as it was, trying to keep up the paper-thin veneer of civility between her and Joel, without having to deal with him not liking her father.

'What's not to like? Other than the fact he twats stewards and ends up getting arrested,' Joel said sarcastically.

Charly smiled tightly at the ill-judged joke. Joel pulled her into his arms.

'Don't worry. I'm sure he'll be like a pussy cat,' he said, kissing Charly on top of her head. *Let's hope you are too*, Charly thought grimly.

'Do I need to keep it buttoned about your old dear?' Joel asked. Charly felt a sudden shudder run through her. It was one of those moments where she wanted to go back to just before he'd opened his mouth and say, 'Please Joel, don't say what you're thinking.' She had impressed upon Joel on a number of occasions how distressing it was to her that her mum was not in her life and how it had affected her. But it seemed that Joel, as ever, wasn't thinking about her feelings. He was just saying the first thing that came into his head. This to Joel was probably the height of compassion, Charly thought; actually remembering to think that she even had a mum who was still floating around somewhere.

Charly had last seen her mother, Shirley, when she was eleven. Her mother had taken a job in a factory about two miles away from Bolingbroke. As Charly remembered it, Shirley had never been the most confident woman, but suddenly she had a personality that shone out from under Len's larger-that-life persona. She went from being just plain old 'Mum' to a woman with her own money and as a result her own small bit of independence. At first Shirley had used the money just in the home, spending it on Charly and Jimmy. But the more Len seemed to dislike his wife going out to work the more Shirley pushed back and she began to spend her hard-earned cash on herself. She wasn't prepared to just spend it on washing powder and tea towels any more.

Charly remembered the first time that her mum had got dressed up to go into town without her dad. There had been an almighty row. Len was shouting about not having his wife going out dressed like a prozzie and Shirley was saying she could go out in just her knickers and bra if she felt like it, seeing as she'd paid for them. Charly hadn't known what her dad was complaining about: she thought her mum looked really pretty. But she remembered the anger in the room and it hadn't felt normal. Ever since she had tried to avoid conflict although when it came her way the Metcalfe gene did have a tendency to raise its head.

Things at home had gone from bad to worse with the arguments occurring daily and Len spending more and more time out of the house just to avoid Shirley.

Charly remembered the last argument they had clearly. It was a bright summer evening and Shirley had been washing up. Len had come into the house and demanded to know where his tea was. Shirley had wiped her hand on the tea towel and said, 'Make your own sodding tea.'

Len had hit the roof. But Shirley didn't seem interested in arguing with him. It was as if she'd given up. Charly had hid in her bedroom listening to music, hoping that the noise would drown out her dad's shouts.

Her mum had opened the door and walked into the room and asked if she still fed her Tamagotchi. Charly had laughed and told her mum not to be daft, she was eleven. She'd got her Tamagotchi when she was nine; they were for babies. Shirley asked if she could have it. Charly didn't like it when her mum cried, so if it meant giving her one of her old toys to make her stop then that was fine. She'd put her arms around her mum. Shirley had taken the toy, kissed her daughter quickly on the head and then stood up quietly and walked out of the room.

That was the last time Charly had seen her mother. No one had heard from her since then. She walked out of her life, out of *their* life, and never returned. At first Charly blamed herself, then she blamed her dad. But ultimately she had to arrive at the conclusion that the only person who made Shirley leave her family was Shirley herself. To begin with Charly thought that her mum had died. Why else would she leave them without even saying goodbye or ever getting in contact? But then they found out that she had been spotted in London. One of her sisters had tracked her down and spoken to her on the phone. Len didn't say much about the whole episode but from what Charly could gather her mum hadn't been keen on the idea of returning to them or to Bradington. It was as if Shirley had walked out of her own life and blocked out her past.

After her initial contact with her aunt, Charly had tried to contact her mother a few times, but Shirley had moved by the time Charly wrote to her and her sister never heard from her again; or at least that was what she told Len and his family. After that Charly made a pact with herself to forget about her mum; she wasn't worth it but it was easier to *say* she was going to forget about her than to *actually* forget about her. Charly often thought about where her mum was now; she'd even thought she might come out of the woodwork when it became public knowledge that her daughter was seeing a famous footballer, but she'd stayed away. Charly was glad now, if she was honest. If Shirley could turn her back on her own children then she was better off staying where she was.

'Yes,' Charly replied firmly, turning around to look at Joel with a seriousness that was rare for her. 'Don't mention my mum. Not my "old dear", my mum.'

'Alright, keep your hair on.'

'My hair is on, Joel, you're just insensitive.'

'Your mum did a runner and *I'm* the insensitive one?'

Charly looked at him with ill-disguised disgust. 'You're a complete pig,' she said quietly. There was a lot more she wanted to say but she knew if she pushed it any further he'd pull out of dinner and she'd have to explain to her dad why he wasn't there, which would mean admitting to herself that things were far from rosy in the garden.

*

Charly had chosen the restaurant in the Manchester suburb of West Didsbury because she thought that it would make her dad feel comfortable. He hated fancy restaurants, but she knew that he would be able to have a nice well-done steak here and no one would bat an eyelid. She also knew that being with Joel meant that they got attention wherever they went but she liked this place; the staff treated them normally and didn't sneer at her when she asked for ketchup with her chips.

They were greeted at the door by the waitress and brought to their seats where her dad was already waiting. He was dressed in a suit that looked like it had been dragged out of mothballs and he had already tucked his napkin into the top of his shirt and thrown his tie over his shoulder as if it was proving a major inconvenience. Len jumped out of his seat when he saw his daughter and her boyfriend approach. He thrust his hand out. 'I trust you're looking after my daughter,' he said, trying to be affable but falling short of the mark.

A wry smile broke across Joel's face. Charly held her breath.

'I'm doing my best,' Joel said, shaking Len's hand. Charly noticed that her dad had taken her boyfriend's hand in a vice-like grip. He was obviously nervous. Joel kept eye contact with Len until he finally let go; it felt like an age to Charly.

They all sat down. 'Have you got a drink?' Joel asked amicably.

'They don't do bitter, so I've asked for a whisky,' Len said, as if the two drinks were similar.

Charly's eyes shot open in alarm. 'Whisky?'

'Yes, love, whisky,' Len said dismissively. Charly shifted in her seat. Her dad couldn't drink whisky. Correction, she thought, he loved whisky; it was just that on the odd occasion it could make him belligerent, and there was just no way of knowing if this was such a time.

Len scanned the menu before shutting it

decisively. 'It's all bloody fancy pants in here. Soup and a steak for me, I think.' Charly smiled awkwardly.

A little boy approached the table nervously. Charly looked at him; his hand was shaking as he held a piece of paper and shuffled his way towards Joel. Charly broke into a smile. She really felt for him. She'd seen this time and time again; little boys and girls, all their hopes, dreams and ideals about their hero bundled up inside their head, their faces begging Joel not to disappoint them.

'Could I have your autograph, please?' the boy's voice wavered.

'Ey, look at that. D'you want mine too, lad?' Len asked. Charly saw Joel shoot her dad a look.

Joel looked at the boy for a moment. 'We're in for a quiet meal, but if you get your mum to ring the club then they'll send you a signed picture no bother.' He said this as if he was being perfectly amicable. Charly's heart sank as the little boy returned to his table, evidently crushed. His mother glared over at their table. Charly hung her head.

'It wouldn't hurt to just sign something, would it?' Len asked, looking at Joel as if he couldn't believe how he had just handled himself.

Joel sighed. 'Len, if I stopped and signed

something every time a kid wanted an autograph I'd never have a minute's peace, would I, babe?' He turned to Charly, putting his hand at the back of her neck. It was a deliberate show of affection but had the odd effect of making her feel like he was puppeteering her answer.

'I know, but he looks gutted,' Charly said, trying to be diplomatic.

'Well, if he's so gutted why don't you go and sign something for him?' Joel asked tersely.

Charly could feel her dad shifting at the other side of the table. 'That's a daft thing to say if I ever heard one. You're a football star. He wants your autograph, not hers.'

'Jesus Christ, alright!' Joel said, jumping to his feet, scraping his chair noisily away from the table. Charly watched as he marched over to the table and turned on the charm. The little boy beamed from ear to ear as Joel signed his Rovers shirt and posed for a picture with him. Charly noticed that his mother wasn't quite as bowled over by the charm offensive as her son was. Joel knelt down beside the boy with a rictus grin as his mother took a picture on her camera phone. Charly looked at her father, who was watching the exchange with disapproval.

'He should be nicer to little 'uns; people like him are their bloody idols,' Len huffed.

'Alright, father of the year,' Charly snapped.

'What's that supposed to mean?' Len was evidently wounded by the comment.

Charly looked at her dad and knew she wasn't being fair. Her father had done a great job raising her, her brother and their twin cousins – who had lived with them since they were ten – despite the circumstances he found himself in. 'Nothing. Sorry, Dad,' she said as Joel sat back down next to her.

'Happy now, everyone?' Joel said, trying to sound jocular but missing the mark.

'Yes, and so's that little boy.'

'Len, Manchester Rovers is the biggest team in the world, always has been, and we're hassled every-where we go ...' Joel was about to go on with his poor-me, who'd-be-a-footballer speech but Len cut him off.

'Manchester Rovers?' Len said, shaking his head. 'Everyone forgets they were no good twenty years ago, scraping along, they were, then. That was when Bradington were in the first division. It was proper football then, mind.'

Charly squeezed Joel's knee, wishing that the meal was over and done with and that her boyfriend and father hopefully wouldn't have to set eyes on one another again until they got married, if that was ever on the cards. 'So it's not proper football now?' Joel asked.

'I'm just saying that it was in the days that men played for passion, not so they could see how many Porsches a week's wage would get them. And if some young kid asked for an autograph they'd be flattered.'

'Dad, don't have a pop …' Charly said quietly, smoothing down her napkin.

'Who's having a pop? I'm just saying …'

Joel leaned across the table. 'I play because I love football. And I happen to be good at it. Just because it pays well now and most lads would give their right arm to do it as a job is to me just an added bonus.'

'Course it is, son, I'm not suggesting any different.' Len nodded thoughtfully, and Charly breathed a sigh of relief, thinking that the conversation was coming to a close. Len turned his attention to his daughter. 'So then, our Charly …' he said with a smile, obviously about to try and lighten the mood. Charly winced; she could sense one of her dad's bad jokes brewing. 'What do you see in the millionaire Joel Baldy?'

'Dad!' Charly hissed.

'Len,' Joel said angrily.

'Mr Metcalfe ...' Len corrected.

'You weren't christened Mr Metcalfe ... Have you got a problem?' Charly knew that Joel was livid.

'I'm not the one with the problem, lad.'

Charly looked at her dad; how had things gone so badly? she wondered. Joel was just about to retaliate when the waitress arrived.

'Soup?' Joel looked away, a muscle twitching in his jaw as he restrained himself.

'Me, love. Thanks,' Len said, smiling. 'And grab us another whisky and water, would you?'

Charly stared at her starter. She had suddenly lost her appetite.

The rest of the meal continued in a similar if uneventful vein as the three ate their food and stuck as much to pleasantries as was possible.

After Len polished off a sticky toffee pudding and a large brandy, he asked for the bill. 'Hope you don't mind me giving you the third degree, lad. Just my little joke really.' Len smiled drunkenly at Joel, who was sipping water. 'Just want to make sure you're serious about this one.'

'We've been together a year, Dad, how much more serious can he be?' Charly asked angrily.

'Bloody hell, love, don't get your knickers in a

twist,' Len said, his eyes sparking, suddenly angry. Charly looked at him, worried what he might do next. His moods were unpredictable when he drank whisky. Len looked at his daughter and his face thawed; as if he was mentally bringing himself back from the brink. He patted her hand as the bill arrived. 'Good girl.' Len momentarily looked at the bill and took out his wallet. He was carefully leafing out notes as Charly looked on gratefully. Her dad shouldn't have to get this but she was proud that he was offering.

'I've already paid, Len,' Joel said.

'What do you mean? I wanted to get this.' Len looked almost wounded.

'It's done. Gave the waitress my card when I came in.'

Charly could tell her father's pride was hurt. He liked to pay his own way.

'It's alright, Dad, you can get the next one,' she said, praying to God there wouldn't be a next one. Len smiled weakly at his daughter.

'Thank you, Joel,' Len said humbly.

'No prob.' Joel got up from his seat. 'Shall we?' Charly looked at her boyfriend. He couldn't wait to get out of there.

Charly and Joel drove home in silence. She stared

out of the window, willing the angry tears that were threatening to overwhelm her to go away. Joel was trying to keep below the speed limit as his car was a police magnet but Charly could tell that he wanted to put his foot down and drive at one hundred and twenty miles an hour along the Parkway into town.

'What the fuck was all that about?' Joel asked angrily.

'What?' Charly asked, puzzled.

'I don't like being spoken to like a twat and your dad just made me out to be a prize one.' Joel threw the car around a roundabout.

'I don't like being spoken to like a twat either, Joel!' Charly snapped back.

'Let's call it a night, yeah? I don't want to talk about your cunt dad any more,' Joel said with real anger in his voice.

'*Cunt?*' Charly said, taking exception to the word. 'The only cunt in there was you.'

Joel slammed hard on the brakes and Charly flew forward. Her seatbelt cut into her as it pulled her back into her seat sharply and she gasped for breath before looking at her boyfriend in shock.

Joel pressed his face up to Charly's. She could feel his breath against her skin. 'Call me a cunt again and I'll show you what one looks like.'

Charly wiped the side of her face and looked out of the window as Joel pressed his foot on the accelerator, urging the car into life. She hated living like this but what could she do? She loved Joel, and she knew that if she left him there would be a line of women waiting to take her place. She didn't know what to do, so she'd do what she always did when faced with confrontation from Joel: nothing.

chapter three

Tracy was counting her blessings. To her complete shock Markie, Jodie, Leanne and Karina had all agreed to come to the Elvis competition tonight. She'd thought at least one of them would have had some moralistic hissy fit and told her where to shove it. Good, she thought, that stuff with Leanne last year was obviously all in the past for her kids. She wasn't quite so quick to forgive and forget, but their year-long avoidance of her was something she would deal with when she saw fit. Now wasn't the time. For the moment she needed her family on her side to show Len Metcalfe that the Cromptons were a family, unlike his rag-tag-and-bobtail mob. There was Jimmy Metcalfe, who had been in and out of the nick for petty criminality since leaving school. There were Anita and Tanita, the twins who sat on their fat backsides all day eating cakes and watching daytime telly, not bothering to converse with the outside world because they had that weird twin thing going on where they read each other's thoughts and knew if the other wanted a custard slice or a bakewell tart that day. And then there was Charly, who had been a thorn in Tracy's side for long enough when she had gone out with Scott. Now she was a bloody WAG, of all things. What a job, Tracy thought. As much as Tracy loathed Charly, she also had a grudging respect for her, one that she wouldn't be able to admit even to herself – Charly had found her meal ticket and had left Bolingbroke as quick as her sticklike little legs could carry her. Something that Tracy herself would have done years ago if she'd ever had the opportunity.

Kent came into the front room in his Y-fronts with what looked like a sandwich bag smeared with black paint stuck to his head. 'Am I done?' he asked nervously.

Tracy took a swig of the large vodka she had poured herself and walked over to Kent, pulling at the bag to inspect his hair. 'Give it another five minutes; you don't want to end up looking like Dickie Davies.'

'Don't say that!' Kent said, alarmed, scanning the back of the Nice 'n Easy packet.

Tracy began to cackle. 'It'll be fine; you're like a bloody woman.'

'I don't want to look like a prize nob tonight.'

'Yeah, dressed in a white catsuit down the working men's club, how could that happen?'

'I meant my hair!' Kent was stomping round the room with no obvious purpose.

'You're shitting yourself about it, aren't you?' Tracy said.

'Yes! And I don't need you taking the piss and making me feel uneasy.'

Tracy got up and went over to Kent and put her arms around him. 'You'll knock 'em dead, babe, don't worry about it.'

'Will I?' Kent asked forlornly.

Bloody hell, Tracy thought, *I bet Priscilla didn't have all this aggro.*

*

Markie walked into the foyer of Bolingbroke Lane Working Men's Club. The tatty cork board that was hanging on the wall informed him that all non-members must be signed in by a member and that women were not allowed in the pool room. He shook his head and laughed. *What year was it in this place?*

'Markie!' a voice said from behind him. Markie turned round, to see his sister Leanne. She looked stunning. Her long blonde hair was tied up in a ponytail and her skin was tanned from the two weeks she'd just spent in the Seychelles with her boyfriend Tony and her daughter Kia. Markie hugged his sister.

'Where's Tony?' he asked.

Leanne gave him a sarcastic look. 'He'd love to have come but he's washing his hair.' There had been a lot of bad blood in the past between Tony and Markie. Tony had been cold shouldered by Markie after what Markie saw as a total betrayal of friendship. When Tony had got together with Leanne, this had enraged Markie even further. But it seemed like a long time ago and there wasn't any sign of Tony and Leanne going their separate ways; they were stronger than ever. Markie knew that he needed to address this situation and be the bigger man about it. After all, he had been the one to cut Tony from his life, not the other way around.

Markie took a deep breath; he didn't want an argument with his sister. 'Is he looking after Kia?' he asked.

'Yes.'

'Mind if I phone him?'

'Why?' Leanne looked shocked.

Markie shrugged. 'Bridge building.'

'Be my guest,' she said, gratefully handing him her phone.

Markie waited for Tony to answer the phone.

'It's me, Tone. Markie.'

There was a moment of deafening silence on the other end of the phone before Tony spoke. 'Markie, what can I do for you?' he asked flatly.

'I just wondered if you fancied coming down here for the night. Bring Kia, give her some pop and crisps, watch Kent make a tit of himself and I can buy you a few drinks.'

Markie knew that Leanne was staring at him in disbelief but he chose to ignore her. 'Great,' he said, 'we'll save you some seats.' He ended the call and handed the phone back to Leanne. Tony didn't sound overly excited about the prospect of spending the night in his company but he thought it was time they buried the hatchet. Markie had enough enemies as it was without having a prospective brother-in-law that he never spoke to.

'So he's coming?' Leanne asked.

'Yep. What you drinking?' He didn't want to have a long, drawn-out discussion about why he had decided to offer an olive branch to Tony. He and Leanne had always been close and, although he knew she wasn't too impressed with the way he'd handled things with Tony, they had stayed close and Tony had taken himself out of the equation when it came to meeting up, just as he had done tonight. Markie knew that this couldn't go on for ever, and he and Tony had been good friends once. Besides, there was a little job that Markie thought Tony might be good for ...

Markie held the door open for Leanne as they walked into the main room of the working men's club. 'Don't be going in the pool room – no women allowed! Remember?' Markie whispered. Leanne giggled. There were a few of the usual neck-cranes and head-turns as Leanne took her seat. As a once-famous glamour model and one-time tabloid favourite, people still wanted to get a good look at her when she entered a room. It wasn't as bad now as it had been, Markie observed. There was a time when she couldn't step out of the door without being papped. Now that she was heading up her own successful model agency, people were more interested in the models she represented than her.

'Where's Mum?' Leanne asked.

'God knows.' Markie shrugged, heading for the bar. There was a rumble of excitement and Markie looked around from the bar to see Jodie walk in. Spotting Leanne and Markie, she made her way over to them.

'Large gin and tonic, Markie. And make it sharpish, will you, she'll be here in a minute.' Jodie looked around and anyone who was trying to get a good look at her quickly averted their eyes. Until Charly Metcalfe had started seeing Joel Baldy, Markie's two sisters had been the most famous faces in Bradington. Jodie had taken her rise to tabloid fame in her stride and, because she just wanted to model and didn't want to appear on every half-baked reality show she was offered, she had been left relatively untouched by the media.

'Don't you see much of her, then?' Markie asked.

'Mum? You're kidding. I've been round to the house twice since I moved out and both times she just wanted a slanging match.'

'So what's tonight about, then? No one other than Scott's paid her any attention for the last year and now she wants to play happy families.'

'Well, I'm sure it'll all come out in the wash,' Leanne said sagely. The door swung open and Markie's other sister, Karina, walked in. She was bone thin these days and her hair was scraped back. She wasn't wearing any make-up and the top and jeans combination she had plumped for Markie was sure she had been wearing five years ago. She headed straight over to the bar and lit a cigarette as she walked.

'Smoking ban!' Jodie said.

'Fuck. Keep forgetting,' Karina said, stubbing the cigarette out into her battered old handbag.

'Nice to see you made an effort,' Markie said sarcastically.

'It's hardly the fucking Ritz, is it?' Karina shot her brother a look. He looked back at her, taking in her sunken eyes.

'Are you still on the Charlie?'

Karina rolled her eyes. Markie knew she didn't want a lecture, but it was tough – she was his sister and she was getting one.

'It fucks you up,' he said.

'It's good fun, you want to try it, might make you relax a bit,' Karina retorted.

'Looks good fun, too. You used to look like these two,' Markie said, pointing at his two glamorous sisters. 'Now you look like a council estate skank.'

'Fuck you, Markie.' Karina shouldered past him to the bar. Leanne and Jodie said nothing, just stared in disbelief. Karina ordered herself a pint of lager. 'You two alright, then?' she asked, but she didn't look like she was interested in the response.

'Fine,' Jodie and Leanne said in unison.

Markie leaned across Karina to address the barmaid. 'I'll get that, love, and another pint of whatever the lady's drinking for me and whatever these two are having.' Karina sneered at him. As he waited for his drink and left his three sisters to chat, Markie looked around the club. *What a seventies throwback this place is*, he thought. He half expected some Bernard Manning lookalike to get on the stage and start telling close-to-the-knuckle century-old jokes.

*

Tracy was dressed to the nines. It wasn't often that she made this much effort but it wasn't often that she came face to face with her first boyfriend and the man she hated with a vengeance. It didn't matter that she'd gone on to have five children and two full-blown relationships since Len. When it came to Len Metcalfe, Tracy felt like the fifteen-year-old that she had been when he first asked her out. Things between her and Len hadn't lasted long but the way things ended had stayed with Tracy as if it had happened yesterday.

'You look bloody gorgeous,' Kent said as he stuck a rhinestone-encrusted leg out of Scott's car. Tracy looked down at her outfit. She was wearing a black satin pencil skirt and a black see-through blouse with a conservative – for her – black lace bra underneath. She'd wheeled out some silver stilettos that she'd found for a fiver in TK Maxx a few years ago and had had a spray tan done that morning at Tantastic, the sun-bed shop by the Beacon. Her hair, which she'd been growing out and getting re-permed since her twenties, was ironed straight courtesy of some straightners that had been left at her house by Jodie. All in all she looked, for once, what she was: the good-looking mother of two of the city's best-looking daughters. It made a change from her usual get-up of a velour tracksuit and trainers.

'Thanks, I could say the same about you ...' Tracy said, looking Kent up and down. He beamed, pleased with himself. 'But I'm not going to.' Tracy cackled. Kent looked crestfallen.

Scott finished parking the car and joined them. 'Come on then, Elvis, let's be having you.'

Tracy let Kent and Scott go ahead into the club.

She took a deep breath before entering the lounge of the working men's club. Once in, she looked around the room and there they all were: Markie, Karina, Leanne and Jodie, all staring at her. She knew they were still angry with her for selling stories to the papers about Leanne and the identity of her own granddaughter's father. But Tracy thought that enough time had passed for them to get over themselves; they were family, they shouldn't be arguing like some Jeremy Kyle scrubbers, she thought. And anyway, she was oddly proud to have them all there, not that she'd ever tell them. So Tracy decided to brazen it out. She wasn't about to apologise; she didn't think she had anything to apologise for. She walked straight over to where her family were sitting and gave Markie a hug. She knew he'd reciprocate and the others wouldn't have much choice but to follow.

Karina stood up next. 'Mum,' she said simply.

'Bloody hell, where've you disappeared to?' Tracy asked, looking at her daughter's gaunt face and sharp collarbones.

'Thanks. I was just about to say you look nice.'

'I'm just concerned, that's all,' Tracy said. Her daughter looked like a bag of bones.

Karina's eyes narrowed. 'Yeah right, Mum. Try

visiting your granddaughter now and again if you're so concerned.'

'For fuck's sake, Karina, you could get an argument out of the sodding Dalai Lama. Button it for now, will you?'

Karina huffed down into her seat.

Tracy turned to Leanne. 'Lee,' Tracy said, holding out her arms. Leanne edged nervously towards her. Tracy pulled her close. 'Good to see you.' As she nestled her chin into her daughter's neck, she opened her eyes to see Jodie eyeballing her.

'Good to see you too, Mum,' Leanne said.

'Are we mates now?' Tracy asked brazenly, pulling away from her daughter and holding her at arm's length to get a good look at her.

Leanne's eyes began to fill with tears. 'Course we are.' She looked relieved. Tracy smiled back but it galled her to be the one having to pass around the pipe of peace. This lot of hers, Tracy thought, they were all convinced that life was like it was on the TV: everyone gets their comeuppance and bad people have to say sorry for nasty things they've done and good people get to have nice teeth and neighbours without ASBOs.

Well, it didn't work like that. Life was hard and

you made your own way – she thought she'd taught them all that much. But seeing them all standing there like the Von Trapps made her realise that all they wanted was some mum they'd seen on an Oxo advert. Well, that wasn't her and it was never going to be her.

'Jode,' Tracy said, feeling in need of a stiff drink and a sit down. Jodie stepped forward and kissed her mum formally on the cheek. Of all of her kids, Jodie was the one who reminded Tracy most of herself. She was old beyond her years and used her acid tongue to make sure that no one challenged her. Tracy wouldn't be surprised if Leanne had told her to rein in her mouthy behaviour since she'd taken up the modelling thing, but it was there to draw on if she needed it. And Tracy quite liked that about her daughter.

'Drink?' Jodie asked.

Thank God, Tracy thought. 'Vodka and tonic would be lovely.'

'Right.' Jodie headed for the bar, obviously wanting this awkward moment to have passed. Tracy didn't really care what Jodie thought. As far as she was concerned her daughter had been a snotty-nosed self-righteous little madam over the whole Leanne thing. She had lived at Tracy's all her life and one whiff of bad feeling and she was off living somewhere else, badmouthing her around the place.

Tracy took a seat. She looked around to see where Kent had got to. There was no sign of him. She imagined that he was in the men's getting in 'The Zone', as he liked to call it. Jodie returned with Tracy's drink and plonked it in front of her.

'That's a double,' she said coldly.

'Should hope so,' Tracy said. She looked at her daughter. She knew that she should ask Jodie how her modelling was going; tell her that she was proud of her when she saw her in the paper or gracing the front cover of a magazine, but she couldn't be bothered. If Leanne's success in her younger days was anything to go by then she'd have enough idiots surrounding her telling her how great she was, and Tracy wasn't about to join in that game.

Someone poked their head from around the gold ribbons that created the backdrop of the small stage and Tracy froze. It was Len Metcalfe. He walked over to the microphone, tapped it twice and then said, 'Testing, testing.' Feedback suddenly screamed through the room and everyone winced. Len jumped back in surprise at the noise he'd created before readjusting the mike. As he went through his *testing* performance again, he looked up and caught Tracy's eye. Tracy felt a shiver bolt down her spine and suddenly she was seventeen again and fighting back tears. Len pulled his gaze away.

'Mum, are you alright, Mum?' Jodie asked, looking at Tracy to indicate that her face was giving away more than she hoped. Tracy barely heard her daughter as she flew out of her chair towards the ladies' toilets, where she promptly threw up.

'Mum?' Jodie said. Tracy could hear her outside the cubicle.

'Nerves.' Tracy exited the toilet, dusting herself down.

'Nerves? What for?' Jodie asked, looking at her mum – it was obvious that she wasn't buying this.

'Kent. It's not every day he goes on stage in front of everyone, is it?' Tracy said matter-of-factly. She could feel Jodie eyeballing her.

'At Bolingbroke Lane? It's hardly Wembley Arena, is it?'

'I'm just nervous for him, alright?' Tracy said in a manner that indicated that the conversation was definitely at an end.

Once back in the club, Tracy made her way over to her family. She sat down quietly next to Markie. 'First act's just about up,' Markie said.

'Good,' Tracy said, 'this place needs livening up.' The club was nearly full and people were getting the drinks in and taking their places expectantly. Tracy looked at Markie. He was a good-looking lad, she thought. He didn't look like her. He had dark hair and a Roman nose and was tall, unlike Tracy, who was five foot five in her heels. She must have been staring at him for too long because Markie turned to her and stared back.

'Want a picture?'

'Can't I look at my son if I want to?' Tracy asked.

'Course you can but you were taking the print off me.'

Tracy saw Tony walk in carrying Kia. He walked over to the group and said hello. Tracy had barely seen her grandchild or Leanne's boyfriend in a year.

'Come to your nana, Kia, I've missed you, chicken,' Tracy said, holding her arms out. Kia buried her head in Tony's chest, reluctant to follow Tracy's instructions. *Suit yourself then, you brat*, Tracy thought. Tony shook Markie's hand. Tracy looked on with interest. She couldn't be sure but she thought that the two men hadn't spoken in over a year, since Markie's wedding. He had only managed to be married to his bride for seven hours before he was citing irreconcilable differences on account of the fact that she'd shagged his friend. There was an awkwardness between Tony and Markie, but Markie soon got to his feet and came back with a drink for Tony. Leanne watched all this carefully but, once she realised Tracy was looking at her, trying to work out what was going on, she faced forward, turning her attention to the acts.

The PA crackled into life and a deep voice that was obviously Len putting on an American accent announced, 'Live, tonight from Bolingbroke Lane Working Men's Club, it's the Elvis extravaganza.' The music from *2001: A Space Odyssey* blasted out over the tannoy and a single light that wasn't quite plugged in correctly came on and flickered unimpressively. The stage setting wasn't living up to what the music promised.

A small squat man wandered out on stage dressed in a shirt with big collars and a pair of Farahs. He had a guitar slung around his neck. 'Uh huh huh,' he said in his best Elvis voice. Which wasn't good.

Tracy stifled a laugh. 'Fuck me, Joe Pasquale,' she whispered to Markie, who smiled.

The man's Elvis impersonation was terrible. He sang 'Blue Suede Shoes', which Tracy knew was a sure-fire way not to win. Kent had been droning on about it all day. 'Hound Dog' and 'Blue Suede

Shoes' were the two songs that made judges roll their eyes and want to shout 'Next!'

He was followed by two equally unimpressive acts. Tracy was happily lining up vodkas and keeping an eye on Len Metcalfe's whereabouts when a young man came on stage dressed in leather trousers and a leather jacket. He nervously approached the mike. As his backing music began, something happened. A look of calm confidence came over his face and as he sang the first line of 'Always On My Mind' people began to sit up and take notice. *Oh oh*, Tracy thought. *Kent's had it*. The young man finished his excellent rendition and received a standing ovation.

Kent was on next. Tracy didn't want him to make a fool of himself or, more importantly, her. She quickly threw a vodka down her neck and steeled herself for his performance. The music to 'It's Alright' began to play and Kent slid in from the side of the stage on his knees, jumped straight up onto his feet and burst into song. There were whoops and cheers from the audience. Tracy couldn't believe what she was seeing – it was like actually watching *Elvis*. Kent gyrated around the stage, flipping his pelvis towards the audience, causing screams from some of the women watching. Tracy looked around for a moment, making sure that she was right in thinking that Kent was pulling off the performance of a lifetime and then decided to relax into it; she even started clapping. As he finished he slid across the floor again, his arms raised in the air, and as the last beat of the song played he thrust his head and arms forward onto the floor as if praying to the audience. Everyone in the club was out of their seats, cheering and shouting.

'Bloody hell!' Markie shouted to his mum over the cheers and applause. 'He's a dark horse.'

Tracy nodded in agreement. 'Isn't he?' she said in wonder.

When Len Metcalfe came on stage and announced that Kent was the winner and would be going through to the Blackpool semi-finals to win a place in the Memphis grand final, everyone in the room stood up and cheered again. It made a nice change for Tracy to see Kent do something he was actually good at. In the four years they'd been together she had begun to have her doubts that he was good at anything. But something really didn't sit well with Tracy. Even though all her family were there and she was proud of Kent for the first time in living memory, the only thing that she could really think about was Len Metcalfe. And the fact that he and Kent were shaking hands on the stage and being all pally pally made Tracy feel sick all over again.

chapter four

'Shit!' Charly said as she burned the toast for the third time. It was their maid's day off and she was trying to make breakfast in bed for Joel. She put two more slices in the toaster and stood over it diligently until they popped out a golden brown colour rather than the blackened carcinogenic offerings she'd had to put in the bin.

She buttered the toast and cut it into triangles before neatly arranging it on the Alessi tray, next to the orange juice, tea and poached eggs she'd managed to make. Cooking wasn't Charly's strong point but today she had promised herself that she was going to surprise Joel. He'd been in a foul mood all week; since the whole debacle with her dad both at the football and the restaurant. She knew her dad could be an oaf; she didn't need her boyfriend constantly reminding her. But this week it looked like it was going to have to be her that held out the olive branch, as it often seemed to be these days.

Charly shimmied through into their bedroom. The view from the penthouse looked all the way across the city over to the hills near Oldham. To the other side the view stretched as far as Bradington, but Charly didn't look that way too often.

'Here you go,' she said chirpily. Joel threw the covers back and looked at his girlfriend and the tray she was carrying.

'I'm not hungry,' he said, burrowing back under the covers.

'But I've made it especially for you.'

'You've made it?' he sneered.

'It's Monika's day off,' Charly said, looking forlornly at the tray.

'Well, if you've made it, I'm definitely not eating it. Don't need food poisoning,' Joel said from beneath the sheets.

Charly felt wounded. She looked down at the small but lovingly made meal and then at the big lump in the bed. 'Well, I've put a lot of time and effort into this. The least you could do is say thank you,' she said, trying not to lose her temper.

Joel had turned and smashed the tray out of

Charly's hand before she realised what was happening. She looked down at the spilt orange juice and broken glass as Joel shouted, 'I didn't ask for any fucking breakfast, did I?'

Charly leapt up angrily. 'No, you didn't, but I thought I'd make you some because it's a nice gesture, not that you can even remember the meaning of the word *nice*.'

'Nice? I'll tell you what nice is, shall I?' Joel jumped out of bed. '*Nice* is putting up with your scumbag dad all night while he talks shit and badmouths me, *that's* nice. *Nice* is not losing my rag when your dad gets booted out of the match for all to see, *that's* nice.'

'That's my dad, that's not me!' Charly shouted.

'Yeah, well, the apple doesn't fall far from the tree,' Joel said, turning away from her.

'What's that supposed to mean? What have I done? What is wrong with you?' She didn't understand his moods.

'Just fuck off, Charly, yeah? You're doing my head in and I don't need it.'

'God, this is so typical. You start a fight then you twist things and make *me* out to look like the bad person then you won't even talk about it!'

'There's nothing to fucking say!' Joel spat angrily.

The veins on the side of his neck were bulging. He went to march off and walked straight onto a shard of glass that was sticking out of the carpet. He leapt in the air like a wounded animal. Charly's immediate reaction was to jump up after him. She grabbed his foot to inspect it. The cut was deep and the glass was protruding out at a right angle. Charly put her finger near the entrance of the wound. Suddenly she was knocked backwards with such force that she fell from the bed, narrowly missing the other pieces of glass that were scattered on the floor. She put her hand to her head in shock. This wasn't the first time Joel had hit her, but it was the first time he had used such force.

'Call a fucking ambulance – this could be my career over!' Joel screamed and to Charly's surprise she did exactly as she was told. She didn't scream and protest as she had in the past when he'd hit her, she calmly went over to the phone and dialled 999, trying to work out what she had done to deserve to be hit but thinking to herself that there must be some reason. It must be her fault in some way, otherwise why would her sometimes loving and caring boyfriend do such a thing? She looked at him as he rolled around the bed in agony. He didn't meet her eye once.

*

'Is he going to be OK?' Charly begged as she ran alongside Joel as he was wheeled through A & E. She knew they were drawing stares; any injury to Joel Baldy's foot was potentially big news.

'The consultant will be here any minute. Then we'll have a better idea. If you could take a seat in the waiting area, Ms Metcalfe, that would be a big help.'

Charly looked at Joel, who managed a smile through his obvious discomfort. 'Go on, babe, I'll be alright.' He winked at her. If Charly had been told about this situation before she had found herself sliding into it, she would have wondered why anyone would put up with such Jekyll and Hyde behaviour. But as it was, she clung to this display of positive attention like a sinking man to a life raft. 'But I don't want to leave you,' she said, grabbing Joel's arm.

'I'll be alright, babe. Go sit in the waiting room; see if we're in *Hello!* this week,' he joked. The orderly pushing the football star along the hospital corridors laughed at this self-deprecating joke. Charly smiled; the Joel that she loved was back.

'If you go to the counter you can give the receptionist your details,' the orderly informed Charly.

She quickly grabbed Joel's hand and mouthed *I love you* to him before setting off for the reception area of the casualty department. Joel winked at her.

Standing in line, Charly realised that the receptionist recognised her. 'Charly Metcalfe, isn't it?' The receptionist smiled.

'That's right,' Charly said, putting her hand to her head as she suddenly noticed the searing pain that was coming from the lump on her forehead. She hadn't had time to think about herself; she had been too busy trying to get Joel to the hospital.

'That looks nasty, what have you done?' the woman asked, poised to fill out a form to pass to a triage nurse.

'Oh,' Charly said, shocked, 'nothing. This? I banged my head. Really stupid. I walked straight into the fridge door this morning, can you believe it? But I'll be fine. I'm not here for me, I'm here because my boyfriend Joel has some glass in his foot and someone told me to come and give his details.'

The woman looked at Charly's forehead. 'You might want to have that looked at while you're here,' she said. Charly avoided her gaze – did she suspect that the fridge door excuse was a lie?

'OK, but I think it's fine, really,' Charly said reluctantly. *Should she say something?*

'Right. Well, tell me what your boyfriend has done to his foot. My husband's a big Rovers fan. I hope it's nothing too bad or my Keith won't sleep for a week.' She smiled again.

Charly returned the smile weakly. Everyone was a Rovers fan, she thought; she wouldn't get any sympathy from anyone if she started telling people where the lump on her head had really come from. Not that she wanted any sympathy. Right now, Charly couldn't see past her own certainty that everything that had happened that morning was all entirely her fault.

*

Jodie was sitting in Leanne's city centre office when Leanne offered her a sheet of paper for her approval. 'Why do I always get roped into these things?' Jodie wailed.

'Because a) you're my sister and b) you're my best model.'

'So shouldn't one of your up-and-coming I-need-to-please-my-agent models have to do all this?'

'Refer back to point a).' Leanne smiled at her sister.

'Bloody hell,' Jodie said, looking at the list of

models in her hand. Leanne had arranged for Jodie to take six of the newer girls signed to her agency for a night on the town. Leanne had made all the plans; they would be picked up from their hotel and whisked off to some beautiful-people cocktail bars.

'Why can't you take them?'

'Because then, my dear, it looks like what it is, a cynical PR exercise. This way it just looks like you all get on so well that you just have to go out together.'

'Genius,' Jodie huffed grudgingly.

'I try my best.'

'Have you recovered from the other night?' Jodie asked.

'What, Kent's encore? I don't think I'll ever recover from that.'

Jodie laughed. Kent had returned to the stage to accept his coveted Elvis prize and treated everyone to a performance of him doing the splits. The only thing was, his recovery wasn't quite as polished as his execution and he'd become stuck and had to be helped to his feet by Len Metcalfe. Kent had limped off stage triumphant. 'Yeah, brilliant. I thought Mum was going to kill him.'

'Talking of Mum, what did you make of it all, then? Why were we all there?' Leanne asked.

'Well, maybe she did really just want to make up with everyone,' Jodie said simply.

Leanne raised an eyebrow. 'Mum? You're kidding, aren't you?'

Jodie laughed in agreement. 'Yeah, you're right. We were all there for a reason. I've just not figured out what it was yet.'

*

Tracy looked in the mirror. She wasn't a fan of spending money on clothes, but she'd been to Peacocks and bought herself a skirt, a smart work shirt and some shoes for less than twenty pounds so she was quite happy with herself. Today was the day that she had finally decided to make herself useful. She had bumped into Mac Jones the other day and they had had a good chat. She'd always liked Mac. She wasn't the only one: there was a queue of women in Bradington who quite liked Mac Jones. He had the look of Ray Winstone and an attitude to match. But he'd been with his wife Candy for decades. Candy had died a few years ago. When she was alive there were rumours of other women; but not since her death. But now it seemed, as far as Tracy could tell from Mac's obvious flirting, he was finally coming out of the other side. And if he was coming out of the other side Tracy couldn't help thinking that it might be nice to get a piece of the action. Kent was OK but she'd already strayed from that path with her ex, Paul. So doing it a second time wouldn't seem so bad. Kent got on Tracy's nerves but she quite liked having him around – she knew that they had some shared interests, which was more than Tracy had with most people. Tracy checked her reflection in the mirror and headed for the door. The title music for *This Morning* was playing and Tracy smiled smugly to herself. This was the earliest she'd been out of the house in years.

She walked through the doors of Markie's office. Behind the reception desk was some snotty-nosed girl who looked like she'd had a rod inserted up her bum. 'Can I help you?' the girl asked superciliously.

'Tell Markie his mum's here.' The girl's face rearranged itself into something approaching humility and she smiled the only smile she could dredge up after having assumed that Tracy was something that the cat had dragged in. She pressed the buzzer and announced Tracy's presence in reception.

Tracy sat down feeling morally superior and

picked up the stray men's lifestyle magazine on the coffee table.

'I'm Tammy, by the way,' the girl said, swallowing her pride.

Tracy looked at her. 'Always thought that was a rough name to give your kids.'

The girl looked confused.

'Don't tell me they didn't call you Tampax at school.'

Tammy looked disgusted. 'No.'

'Must be the way my mind works then. Forget I said anything.' Tracy continued leafing through the magazine. Inside there was a picture of Jodie holding a mobile phone in as provocative a pose as it was possible to hold a mobile phone in. Had Tracy managed to remain silent she would have won her little battle with the receptionist, but she just couldn't help herself. She held the picture of Jodie up. 'See that, that's my daughter.'

'I know it's Markie's sister,' Tammy said with as much enthusiasm as she could muster.

'Pretty, isn't she?'

'Yes, she is.' Tammy nodded.

'Used to be a plain old ugly duckling when she was a bit younger,' Tracy said. Tammy looked on, obviously wondering where this conversation was heading; she was about to find out as Tracy continued nastily, 'So there's hope for that sour mush of yours yet.' Tammy looked as if she was about to burst into tears as Markie popped his head around the door.

'Mum. What you doing here? I see you've met Tammy.'

Tracy smiled sarcastically at the girl. 'Yes, we've just been having a lovely chat, haven't we, doll?'

Tammy glared at her.

'That cup of tea would be lovely. Three sugars. Ta,' Tracy said, waltzing into Markie's office.

'So then Mum, what can I do for you?' Markie asked, sitting back down behind his desk.

'I've come to offer my services.'

'What services?' Markie looked puzzled.

'Well, you said something the other day that made me think ...'

'What?'

'In the club, you were saying that some of the loan stuff you do, it's hard to lean on the women.'

'That was a conversation I was having with Tony.'

'It was a conversation that I was earwigging into.'

'I knew it. Your ears were flapping.'

'I thought you two had fallen out.'

'Well, we've made a truce.'

'And are you hiring him in again to sort people out?' Tracy asked. 'Because what you need is someone possessing what is known by the old bill as *soft skills*. Women have them, men don't. So that means you'd be better off sacking Tony and giving me a job.'

Markie snorted a laugh. 'Soft skills, you?'

'Yeah, me. Softly softly catchee monkey.'

'Fuck me, Mum, any monkey that you were trying to catch would think there was a foghorn up its arse before you got anywhere near it.'

'Listen, do you need a bird to go in and sort out the mither with women who aren't paying up or not, cos if you do, I'm saying I'll help.'

'You're not exactly qualified.'

'I didn't realise they did courses in extortion at the tech.'

Markie sighed and leaned back in his chair. He studied Tracy for a moment. 'I'll have to ask Mac,' Markie said.

'Ask Mac what?' Mac said as he walked into the office. 'Hello, Tracy, love, don't see you for ages then twice in one week.'

'Well, hopefully you can make this son of mine see some sense. Tell him,' Tracy instructed Markie.

'Mum wants to help out on the money collection

side. Overheard me saying we were struggling getting money out of women.'

Mac raised an interested eyebrow. 'Well, we can't go in all heavy-handed, not like the old days. Doesn't look professional.' He studied Tracy for a moment. 'But we really could do with someone who can dish out a good tongue lashing.'

'I'm your woman.' Tracy smiled.

'You've got that right,' Markie said wryly.

'And you're family, so there's trust there,' Mac said. Markie coughed behind Tracy, but she didn't bother looking at him. *Sarky get*, she thought.

'Is there any harm in giving your mum a trial run at a couple of the clients we've had no luck with?' Mac took down a folder and opened it. 'I can drive you round a few addresses. Saves us going through the courts: takes forever and we get fuck all in return.'

'So have I got a job?' Tracy asked Mac.

'You have for me, love.' Mac smiled. Tracy could see Markie rolling his eyes, but she didn't give a monkey's what he thought. She was interested in two things: one was earning some money and the other was Mac Jones.

chapter five

Len had a niggling feeling that something was wrong. He couldn't place it. He made himself a cup of tea and sat down. But the feeling wouldn't go away. He checked on the twins, Anita and Tanita, and they were both fine. The twins were his nieces but they had lived with Len for over ten years, since their mum and dad, relations from his ex-wife's side of the family, had been deemed unfit parents. Len didn't want to see the girls go into care so he had taken them in as his own.

Anita was organising her friend's hen do, and had been busy sewing luminous penises to a veil when Len had called round to the flat the girls shared around the corner from his house. Tanita had been at Tantastic topping up her year-round tan and had banged her head when her phone rang, meaning that Len got a mouthful as soon as she picked up the call. For someone with pale skin and strawberry blonde hair, Tanita was fighting a losing battle chasing a mahogany glow, Len would often think, but he didn't like to interfere. And anyway, she'd got an unlimited sunbed pass for fifty quid so you couldn't say fairer than that, he thought.

He called Jimmy. Len wasn't happy with Jimmy. He'd shown up like a bad smell the minute it looked like Charly might be onto something with this Joel Baldy character, but there hadn't been so much as an apology for stealing Len's valuables and pawning them. He hadn't seen Jimmy since the football match. He was shacked up with some rake-thin bird called Gemma on the other side of Bradington as far as Len knew, but he wasn't altogether sure where the house was. Jimmy answered the phone. 'Hello, Dad,' he said sheepishly. Jimmy's default tone was sheepish. It was from a lifetime spent being bollocked for being a dickhead.

'You've gone quiet. Again,' Len said disapprovingly.

'I've just been busy since the match.'

'Ask 'im!' a shrill rough voice squawked in the background.

'That's Gemma. She wants to know if you fancy

coming round one night to meet her. We can get some cider in.'

This was the most grown-up gesture Len could ever remember his son making. He was taken aback. 'Well, tell Gemma that would be very nice. I can come round tomorrow if you fancy.'

'Tomorrow any use, Gem?' Jimmy asked his girlfriend.

'Well, it's not like we ever bleeding go anywhere, is it?' she said. Finishing school obviously left a few rough edges with Gemma, Len observed.

'Yeah, come round about half seven, Dad. We're on Thorpecliffe estate. Near the offy. Give us a ring when you get there and I'll come and get you.'

'Will do,' Len said, putting the phone down. His feeling of foreboding was still there. He rang Charly's phone, and this time she answered.

'Hi Dad.' She sounded distracted.

'You alright, love?' he asked.

'I'm fine. Joel's been in hospital. He's out now but will have to miss a couple of games. He's got his foot bandaged – stood on some glass.'

'And are you alright?'

'God, Dad, why wouldn't I be?' Charly asked, exasperation in her voice.

'Just checking,' Len said gently before putting the phone down.

The next morning Len bought the *Sun*; he thought it was safe to bet that he wouldn't be featured snarling on page seven. He turned to the back page to see that the main story was all about his daughter's boyfriend and his injury. This wasn't news to Len and he was just about to look at his stars, something he'd never admit to reading but something he did every day, when a footnote caught his attention. As instructed, Len turned to page eleven and there on the showbiz gossip page was a picture of his daughter with a bruise blackening her left eye. The article was speculating on the origin of the bruise – Charly had claimed to have walked into the fridge – but Len didn't have to speculate, he knew full well where it had come from. He ran out of the house and jumped in his Allegro, heading for Manchester.

Len waited outside the apartment block where Charly had told him that she and Joel were now living, until someone was entering. There was no way that he was calling Charly, the temper he was in. He knew she wouldn't let him in. Who did this Joel Baldy think he was? Len thought beyond anger. Thinking he can thump his daughter? He wanted to stand up and fight like a real man, thump Len if he was going to thump anyone. He looked at the listing on the lift. They lived in the penthouse; that was easy enough to locate. Len stood in the lift, the blood coursing through his veins. He felt suddenly calm as he watched the numbers to the top floor fly by. He didn't know how he was going to handle this, and he certainly didn't know if he was going to be able to keep his temper in check.

Len stormed over to the door of the penthouse. He knocked and waited. The door opened and Charly stood staring at her father, as if at first she couldn't quite place why he was there. Len gently took her jaw in his hand and, turning her head to the side, inspected her bruise. 'Where is he?' Len asked in a low, menacing voice. Charly looked like a startled fawn as it dawned on her that her father hadn't just popped round for a cup of tea. Len marched past her into the lounge where Joel was sitting with his leg up on the leather pouf, watching his widescreen TV. Len didn't wait for him to speak or push himself up in his chair, he just grabbed the young man by the throat and punched him straight in the face.

'Feel nice, does it, you piece of shit?' Len punched Joel again. 'Hit my fucking daughter and think that's OK?' And again he punched him in the face.

Charly ran across the room; Len could feel her pulling at his back. 'Dad, don't ... please, no!' she screamed. 'He didn't do anything.'

'Walked into the fridge, did she?' Len spat in Joel's face before punching him again. 'They fucking wreck those fridges, don't they?' He drove his fist into Joel's already bloodied face.

'Dad!' Charly screamed, thumping Len on the back. Len stumbled backwards, looking at the mess he'd created. Joel tried to get to his feet, but couldn't; he was gurgling something incomprehensible.

'If you've got any sense you'll come home now,' Len said between breaths.

'After this? Are you mental?' she screamed.

Len looked at Charly; what was she doing? This lad had money – so what? As Len stared at his daughter he missed the fact that Joel was mustering up every ounce of energy he had. He launched himself at Len, rugby tackling him to the floor, snapping the coffee table in two, with Len's back taking the brunt of the fall. The last thing Len remembered was the impact of the blow knocking him clean out.

*

Charly was in casualty for the second time that day. Her father had been out for the count and had swallowed his tongue. Amazingly some first aid training that Charly had done at school – which at the time had seemed like a thorough waste of hers and everyone else's morning – had probably saved his life. Joel had stayed at home, which was definitely for the best, and Charly had accompanied her dad in the ambulance to St Mary's. He had come round on the way there, but they were keeping him in overnight for observation. The police had come to take a statement but Len had remained tight-lipped, and refused to give any account of what had happened to him, much to Charly's relief.

Charly knew that if the papers got wind of this scandal there would be a bank of paparazzi at the front door so, after she had said her terse goodbye to her father and headed for the door, she decided to see if there was a side exit she might be able to sidle out of. She called a cab company and asked to be picked up at the Academy on Oxford Road. It was a little bit of a walk but she knew where it was and she couldn't risk waiting for a taxi by the hospital.

Charly spied an emergency exit but it was well and truly shut with a break-glass bolt over it for added security – she kept on walking. She eventually found a fire escape on the third floor that was propped ajar, letting air into the stuffy corridor. Charly looked around before pushing it open and finding herself having to shin down an escape ladder. She jumped the last few feet to the ground and dusted herself down while checking that the coast was clear. She walked along the side of the building and out into the street that led from the hospital to the main area of Manchester University. It was a busy night and she was soon being carried along by a throng of students. She didn't reach the venue where the taxi was waiting: she saw a cab with its yellow light on approaching. Charly flagged it down and jumped in. Now she had to go home and face Joel. He should have come to hospital with them, such was the severity of the injuries he'd received at the hands of Charly's father. But he had refused, insisting on cleaning his face up himself and staying in the apartment. Charly felt sick to her stomach. She couldn't imagine the reception she was going to receive when she got home, but she knew one thing: it wasn't going to be good.

*

Charly was exhausted by the time she reached her apartment block. Thankfully there was no sign of any long lens cameras as she paid the taxi driver and walked as inconspicuously as possible through the main entrance. She was dreading seeing what Joel looked like. In the hospital she had tried to call him but he wasn't answering his phone. She had sent him a number of texts but he hadn't responded to any of them. Charly's mind raced. For all she knew, Joel could be lying in a pool of blood on the floor after the injuries he'd sustained courtesy of Len. Or he could just be waiting and seething. Charly stepped out of the lift, her legs weak. She put the key in the lock and as she pushed the door open and shouted hello into the open plan apartment, she saw Joel, sitting in a chair, his face swollen and bruised but cleaner than last time she had seen him, with his injured foot raised. Joel stared at his girlfriend.

'I'm so sorry about everything,' Charly said, beginning to sob. Up until now she had felt totally composed but as her shoulders began to shake she realised that she had been in shock.

'Not as sorry as me,' Joel said flatly. She looked at him and his eyes burned through her. Charly walked over and reached out to hold him. 'Don't even fucking think about it. I want you out of here.'

'What?' Charly was stunned.

'You don't want me to get out of this chair and give you the pasting I think you deserve.' Charly looked at Joel, terrified.

'What pasting?'

'Get your stuff and get out. I don't need this shit. From you or your trampy cunt of a father.'

'Don't talk about my dad like that.'

Joel bolted forward in his seat. 'Out. Now!'

Charly ran from the apartment in the clothes she stood up in. She didn't even wait for the lift, she was so terrified. She ran down every stair to the ground floor, not noticing that she was gasping for air as she ran out into the street. What was she going to do now? Where was she going to go? Charly looked desperately up and down the street before remembering there was one place she would be safe.

*

Markie was having a weird week. His mother adding herself to the unofficial payroll was odd enough but last night he had managed to have the worst night's sleep of his life and it made him feel as

if he was driving through Bradington in some hallu-
cinogenic dream. Tracy was starting her first day
today and Mac had volunteered to take her out.
Markie couldn't quite work out why, now, suddenly
Tracy wanted to go into gainful employment. She'd
been happy to sit on her backside for the last three
decades claiming state benefit, incapacity benefit,
child benefit; you name it, she claimed it. It was a
wonder she'd never managed to wangle herself a
war pension, Markie thought wryly. He knew there
was some reason that she wanted to come and work
for him, but while Markie was figuring out what this
was, he was going to adhere to the old adage and
keep his friends close and his enemies closer. And
anyway, he knew instinctively that his mum was
going to be good at her new job.

Markie pulled into the car park at the front of his
office building and his mum and Mac came out of
the door together, Tracy laughing like a drain.
Markie looked on bemused; he wouldn't have
thought for a minute that his mum would have
managed to drag herself into the office before ten –
and it was quarter to nine.

'I'm just going to take your mum up the Hardacre.'

'Ey, cheeky,' Tracy said, slapping Mac on the
arm.

Markie took a deep breath; the last thing he wanted was some hideous mental image of his mother and Mac courtesy of his mum's innuendo.

'The Hardacre estate, you saucy mare!' Mac said, laughing. Markie didn't know what was worse, his mother's cackling or Mac encouraging her.

'Right, what's the plan then?' Markie asked, hoping they'd both put a sock in their *Carry On* routine and get on with whatever they were meant to be doing.

'Got a few ladies to visit. Going to give your mum a dry run.'

Tracy snorted a dirty laugh again.

'Fuck me, Finbar Saunders,' Markie said, shaking his head.

'Who?' Tracy asked.

'Never mind. Let me know how you get on, won't you. What are we owed up there?'

Mac looked at the printout he was carrying. 'About six grand. Lots of little lump sums. You know, the usual Christmas sob story brigade: "Oh, the hamper company's gone bust and I can't afford to buy little Johnny a quad bike and a Nintendo now."'

'Don't worry, son, I'll have them coughing up in no time,' Tracy said.

'You two should try your Chubby Brown routine; they'll soon be running for their purses just to get shot of you.'

'Shut your face, Markie, you're not too old for a slap,' Tracy said, suddenly losing her sense of humour.

'Charmed.' Markie walked off, leaving the pair to it.

So that was what his mum was after, he thought as he walked away. Poor old Elvis was obviously heading for the scrap heap and she had Mac in her sights. Well, if there was ever anyone who was a match for his mother it was Mac Jones. What an unholy pairing. Markie was going to sit back and watch this one unfold: *Corrie* was getting a bit dull at the minute and Markie liked a good soap.

*

Len was standing outside St Mary's waiting for Jimmy to pick him up. He had tried unsuccessfully to get hold of Charly, but he strongly suspected his daughter wasn't speaking to him and wouldn't for a while. He went back over what had happened yesterday. Joel Baldy had needed a good kicking and Len was the man to give it to him. Thinking he could lay a finger on his daughter. These footballers, they thought they could do what they pleased and bugger the consequences. Well, not where Len was concerned. He was worried though; he'd managed to keep himself in check for such a long time that his recent behaviour had stunned him somewhat. Not because of how he'd acted so much as the fact that he'd enjoyed it. He'd enjoyed throwing a punch at the officious steward at the match, and he'd really enjoyed laying into Joel. The feeling that came over him had been almost serene.

He knew that he needed to get back to work and submerge himself in his routine; that way he'd be able to calm down and feel on an even keel again. The way he felt at the moment, he was king of the world one minute and at rock bottom the next, worrying about what Charly must think of him.

Jimmy swung the heap of junk that he was passing off as a car into the pick-up area where Len was waiting. In the back was a miserable-looking woman. Len couldn't put an age on her – she could have been twenty, she could have been forty. Her hair was scraped back from her head so tightly that she looked surprised, and her stonewashed denim padded jacket with cartoon-print lining didn't look like it had ever seen the inside of a washer. Jimmy threw the passenger door open. 'What the bloody hell have you been up to?' he asked as Len edged into the seat.

'Long story; just get me to my bed.'

'This is Gemma,' Jimmy said proudly.

'Pleased to meet you, love.'

'And you. We've made a bed up at our house for you. Thought seeing as you were coming round that you might as well stay,' Gemma said flatly. Len quickly decided that she was one of those people who just always looked miserable. She could probably win the lottery and her face would still hang like a slapped arse.

'Well, that's kind of you, but you didn't have to.'

'You might have no choice – don't know if the car'll get as far as Bolingbroke. Ours is this side of Bradington, isn't it?'

'Why, what's up with the car?'

'Ringer,' Jimmy said, straining to change gear. The engine sounded like a plane taking off but they were only doing twenty miles an hour.

'What've you bought a ringer for?' Len said.

'That's what I said,' Gemma said wearily.

A 'ringer' was a car where the front and the back belonged to different vehicles and were welded together. AA approved it wasn't.

'It cost two hundred quid and it's good gear when it gets above forty.'

'Oh, well then …' Len said sarcastically.

'Tell him what happened to the last one,' Gemma said.

'Why don't you tell him, seeing as you're obviously so keen to,' Jimmy huffed, like a man who felt he was being ganged up on.

'Back came away from the front. He's sitting there like a lemon at the top of Brown Hill and the back's taken off and goes flying down the hill towards town. Good job the police put the traffic calming things in the road cos of the joyriders, or it could have killed someone.'

'Don't be so bloody dramatic,' Jimmy said, exasperated.

'Who's being dramatic?' Gemma asked. She had a point, Len thought; she couldn't inject drama into that monotone drone if she tried.

'Can we just go home in peace?' Jimmy asked.

'Are you going to say what you said you were going to say to your dad?' Gemma asked. Jimmy exhaled heavily, but she was undeterred. 'I want you to say it before you have a drink this afternoon; no one wants to hear something that's meant to be all heartfelt when it's coming from someone pissed.'

'Jesus, woman, alright!' Jimmy shouted.

'I'm just saying,' Gemma finished, sitting back in her seat. Her constant passionless nagging was enough to drive anyone to distraction and watching it do exactly that to Jimmy was quite entertaining for Len.

'What've you got to say, then?' Len asked.

Jimmy looked like he was about to explode. 'Alright! Dad, I'm sorry for nicking the stuff. There, I've said it. I am. It makes me feel like a twat when I think about it.'

Len looked at his son. This was a big thing for him to say, he knew that. 'Right,' he said slowly.

'Right? Is that it?'

'No, it's not bloody it, is it? You pawned my gran's wedding ring and our Charly's hologram pendant that I got her for her eighteenth. What sort of lad does that?'

'I'm trying to apologise!' Jimmy shouted as he turned onto the motorway.

'I know, but there's some things I want to know. Who did you sell them to?'

'Pawn shop in town.'

'Are they still there?'

'No, I went back for them and they'd gone.' Jimmy looked like he was on the verge of tears.

'Fucking hell, Jimmy, why the jewellery? Of everything you have to take, you take the jewellery.'

'Because I'm a twat, aren't I, obviously.'

Len shook his head. He had wanted to kill him about this over the years, but there was something about Jimmy finally being honest that made Len think maybe it was time to put this behind them. 'Well, you've admitted it, and if I can't get the stuff back then that's better than nothing.'

Jimmy pulled the rust-bucket over to the side of the road, and once parked he looked at his dad. 'I really am sorry, Dad, aren't I, Gem?'

'Yeah, he is. Talks about it all the time. I said I wouldn't mind but he could've given a false address and got credit from Elizabeth Duke, pretended he was going to pay for the stuff over a hundred weeks. Got some new gear and sold it, or just borrowed some from somewhere. There's always a way. He shouldn't have robbed off his own dad.'

Jimmy turned round and threw Gemma a look suggesting that she button it. She pulled a face back at him as if to say, *What? I'm right, aren't I?*

'Well, it means a lot that you've owned up,' Len said gratefully.

Jimmy nodded and turned the key in the ignition

to restart the car. The engine wouldn't even turn over. 'Shit, it's dead!' Jimmy said, exasperated.

'Well, I'm not pushing it again,' Gemma said, folding her arms and sitting back in her seat.

chapter six

Charly had stayed the night at a newfound friend's.
His advice had been invaluable and now she was
setting things in motion to ensure that if it really
was over with Joel then she was covered. She wasn't
going to be turfed out onto the street after everything she had put into her relationship with Joel.
So this morning she was going back to the flat and
she was going to reason with Joel to take her back.
She genuinely loved him, but Charly wasn't stupid.
She knew when something wasn't working, and if it
meant switching into self-preservation mode then
so be it.

She let herself into the apartment. Joel was
sitting in the same position that she had left him
in, but today he was comatose – he reeked of
booze, and there was a bottle of brandy at his side.
The TV was displaying the DVD screensaver.

Charly walked over and pressed eject on the DVD player. It was some dodgy porno entitled *Dangerass*. Charly threw the DVD on the floor and looked at Joel in disgust. While she'd been crying her heart out, he'd been sitting here wanking and getting as pissed as was humanly possible. Lovely, she thought. At this moment in time Charly despised him. Not that she was going to let him know and anyway, she knew that if he changed his mind and showed that he wanted to be with her she could quickly be convinced to put all of this behind them.

She walked over to the chair where he was slumped, his chin rough with stubble. 'Joel,' she whispered. He opened his eyes momentarily. Charly was dressed in a bottom-skimming skirt, six-inch heels and a tight low-cut top, and had liberally applied her favourite scent which she knew drove Joel wild. She leaned forward so that he could see her cleavage. This was the last thing she wanted to be doing at this precise moment in time, with the knowledge that Joel had been making do with *Dangerass* the previous evening, but needs must, she thought.

He studied her for a moment as if he was trying to work out if he was dreaming or if she was really standing in front of him. 'I told you to get out,' he said groggily, with little conviction.

Charly leaned forward and stroked his head gently. 'But you didn't mean it, baby, did you?'

He sat up in his chair as if he was trying to decide what to do next. Charly leaned forward and kissed him deeply, sliding herself onto Joel so that she was straddling him. She took his hand and pushed it under her skirt and between her legs. She felt Joel stir – there was no way he was going to ask her to get off him, she could tell. She definitely had his attention.

'No knickers,' he said, raising a lascivious eyebrow.

'I know; I'm a naughty girl, aren't I? Just how you like me.'

*

At the top of the Bolingbroke estate stood a lone row of shops. The last time she had been here, years ago, the cornershop had been boarded up and the name Mr Shop Right had been doctored by graffiti to read *Mr Shit Right*. Now it still had grilles covering the front but the graffiti was kept to a minimum and was of the usual *Leoni loves Liam*

101% type. She had always wondered, as she'd stood at different bus stops throughout the country over the years, why kids who wouldn't know a percentage if it came up and sat on them insisted on adding them to the end of their graffitied declarations of love.

Bolingbroke didn't look so bad. The council had obviously used some of their much-talked-about grant money for something other than six-foot-high pottery phalluses. (Bradington Council had commissioned a radical Edinburgh-based artist to create a sculpture to sit outside the town hall. She claimed it was a modern-day totem pole, celebrating the uniting of cultures. The man and woman in the street, when interviewed by the local news, disagreed. One man summed up the general feeling perfectly: 'Well, they've spent two hundred grand on a giant knob, haven't they?') Bolingbroke looked clean now, the grass was trimmed and there were even a couple of Victorian lamps and a large wrought iron sign saying *Bolingbroke* at the bottom of the main road into the estate.

She had hoped that when she finally did return to the place she'd sweep in, looking stunning, and knock everyone for six. But she'd just popped in for a drink at the Beacon, and she didn't recognise anyone, which was just as well because she didn't feel particularly stunning. The last decade had put paid to any notions of a midlife being conducted as Michelle Pfeiffer's twin. Her face was puffier than she would have liked it to be. Her slender figure had grown lumpy and shapeless. She still had pretty eyes but she felt that they were buried somewhere in her face rather than being the first thing people noticed about her and she was conscious that her hair colour had stopped looking baby blonde years ago and was now a permanent brittle peroxide with harsh roots. She didn't have a choice though. She didn't have the luxury of buying Nice 'n Easy; she was on a strict budget and she wasn't about to waste it on hair dye. She used the stash of peroxide she'd nicked from the hairdressers where she'd had her last job, over a year ago, to make do. When that was finished she promised herself she'd grow it out, although she was scared to see what colour her own hair actually was.

She walked along the road and came to the top of her old street. She'd never assumed that it would be easy, that she'd just walk back in, shout 'Hi honey, I'm home' and pop the kettle on. But she hadn't bargained on the feeling that gripped her now. She was paralysed with fear. Not the fear of what she would encounter but the fear of change. What if nothing was as she remembered it? She knew that certain things had changed in her family's life; that was obvious and inevitable. But what if things had changed so irrevocably that there was no room for her at all? She faltered at the top of the road and turned on her heel. She couldn't go back yet; she needed to have a serious think if she was doing the right thing. This was the second time in a month that she'd stood at the top of her old road and not had the courage to confront her old life, but it was a lot to confront and she needed to be ready to face up to her mistakes.

*

Tracy left Mac in the car and approached the first door on her rounds. Mac had tried to verse her in what to say but she didn't really need the speech. She knew what to do. Get the money that they were owed. She was quite looking forward to putting her acid tongue to commercial use. A woman answered the door holding a baby. She was in her thirties, scruffy and overweight, and none too pleased to have some woman standing at her door who seemed to be there in an official capacity.

'I've told you lot to fuck off.'

'Charmed, darling, but you've not told *me* to fuck off yet or you'd know about it.'

'You from Social Services?'

'You'll be wishing I was from Social Services when I tell you why I'm here and what I need you to do for me.'

'You what?'

'You heard. Now, you owe my business associates four hundred and fifty eight pounds and seventy two pence.'

'Fuck off, I owe two hundred pounds.'

'Well, if you weren't thick as fuck you'd know what compound interest is but as you obviously are I'll spare you the details. You've missed your last two payments.' Tracy stepped menacingly towards the woman.

'Where's the fella who usually comes round?'

'Don't worry about that, darling; you're stuck with me now till your debt's paid off in full.'

'And what you going to do if I can't pay?'

Tracy put her hand out and touched the baby's head. The woman pulled him away. 'I saw a baby last week badly scalded; tragic really, scarred for life. Turn your back for two minutes and these things can happen, can't they?'

'You're fucking deranged!' the woman shouted.

'That's right, I am. So you'd better get your shit together and make sure that this time next week you've got your weekly instalment ready. Alright?'

The woman looked genuinely terrified. She nodded and shut the door on Tracy.

'How did you get on?' Mac asked, as Tracy got back in the car.

'Told her I was going to boil her baby – seemed to work a treat.'

Mac laughed. 'No, what did you really say?'

Tracy looked at him and raised an eyebrow.

Mac let out a slow whistle. 'Fucking hell, Tracy, remind me never to cross you.'

'I was only bloody joking, wasn't I? She doesn't need to know that though, does she? Now, where to next?' She could get quite into this.

*

Jimmy couldn't push the car on his own and Len hadn't been able to help – he was still suffering from the injuries he sustained the previous evening. Gemma was obviously sick to the back teeth of having to push Jimmy's welded together contraption so they'd had to call a taxi to get them back to the house. Len was now propped up in a corner of the shabby living room drinking a pint of cider and watching the racing while Gemma made beans on toast for everyone. Jimmy had gone down to the off licence to buy some more drink for the afternoon and Len reached for his phone to check for the hundredth time today if Charly had bothered calling him – she hadn't. There was a knock at the door. Gemma shouted through to Len to answer it. He pushed himself up from the chair and headed for the door. When he opened it, the last person in the world he expected to see was standing there: Tracy Crompton. Tracy looked as if she was about to launch into a speech, as if she was canvassing for some political party. Although Len knew well that the only parties Tracy went near had to involve tons of drugs and booze. When she saw that it was Len who had answered the door, she reeled backwards.

'What you doing here?' Len asked.

'Might ask you the same,' Tracy said, trying to compose herself.

'Our Jimmy lives here. I'm just here for the night.' Len was trying to get Tracy to look him in the eye, but it didn't seem to be working.

'Right, well, it's not you I'm after. I'll call back another time.'

'Wait, Tracy. The other night, I wanted to talk to you but you weren't having any of it.'

'No I wasn't,' she said, lifting her head and meeting his eye for the first time.

'I just wanted to clear the air between us.'

'Well, it's too late for all that really, isn't it?' Tracy seemed to be gaining back some of her bravado.

'Yeah, maybe you're right. When our Charly was with your Scott I often thought about coming round but decided not to.'

'Well, you made the right decision. Anyway, I've not got time to stand here idly chatting with you. If Gemma Bartle's in, give her this card and tell her I'll be back next week for fifteen quid.' Tracy looked over her shoulder as if checking to make sure that someone was still there. Len followed her gaze but couldn't see anyone.

Len looked confused but when he looked at the card she had just handed him it became clear that Tracy – for whatever reason – was working for Markie and that Gemma had been daft enough to borrow money from them. Len knew all about Markie's money-lending business. He and Mac were effectively loan sharks, but their rates weren't quite as extortionate as others in the business and their terms were slightly fairer – in that you could hope to keep your head in the vicinity of your shoulders for a little longer than most loan sharks allowed if you failed to keep up repayments.

'Can we just be civil with one another? It's years since we knocked about together.'

Tracy looked at him with burning hatred. 'Knocked about together, is that what you're calling it now?'

'Went out. Were an item. Courted. Whatever,' Len said, looking at Tracy, hoping for some clue as to where all this animosity was coming from.

'Have you forgotten what you did?' Tracy was shaking with anger.

Len stepped back; he obviously had. He and Tracy had been kids when they got together and they used to fight like cat and dog, get blind drunk, have sex, then fight again. 'We did a lot to upset one another – that's what kids do.'

'Well, why don't you piss off back inside and have a long hard think about how you used to be and see if anything comes back to you.' Tracy looked like she was about to burst into tears. It might be nearly thirty-five years since they courted, Len realised, but Tracy was obviously still prone to dramatic histrionics.

'Tracy, wind your fucking neck in, will you?'

Len said, getting ready to shut the door. He'd heard enough. He was waiting for a barrage of abuse back but got nothing; she just turned on her heel and walked away from the house, head bowed. Len looked after her, stunned. He might just be the only person in the world who'd ever had the last word in an exchange with Tracy Crompton.

*

'You alright?' Mac's voice was concerned. Tracy nodded, knowing she obviously didn't look alright. She was shaking and if she looked as sick as she felt she was probably as white as a ghost.

'Fine. Just saw a blast from the past, that's all. Wasn't expecting it.'

Mac nodded. 'So, did you get any money from the woman?'

Tracy looked at Mac; she'd almost forgotten what she'd called at Gemma's for. 'Oh no. Next week. Another fear-of-God job. They'll pay up, don't worry,' she lied.

'Good,' Mac said, looking at Tracy's profile as he put the car in gear. 'This blast from the past …'

'Very old news.'

'Has he ever laid a hand on you?'

'What makes you ask that?' Tracy asked with mock surprise.

'You look terrified.'

'I'm fine.' Tracy was adamant.

'Well, if you ever get any trouble from anyone let me know and I'll sort it. Don't have to tell Markie; it can be our little secret.'

'Thanks Mac, I might take you up on that one day,' Tracy said, gazing out of the window over to the house where she had just come face to face with Len Metcalfe.

*

Charly was sitting in the lounge in her dressing gown as Joel, stark naked, poured himself a bowl of cereal and hobbled over to where Charly was and slumped onto the settee.

'Are you my friend?' Charly asked tentatively.

Joel cocked his head to one side, eyes narrowing. He held Charly's gaze for what seemed like an eternity before slumping back in the chair and shrugging. 'S'pose,' he said.

Charly breathed a sigh of relief. 'I'm sorry about my dad.'

'So am I.' Joel nodded. 'I never want to see him again.'

'I know, course you don't.' Charly wanted to say a lot to Joel about this whole messy situation. She wanted to point out that her dad had only been defending her, that Len's anger might have been out of control but his intentions were purely honourable: he knew his daughter had been hit by her boyfriend and he was sticking up for her.

'I won't be responsible for my actions.'

Charly had grown up with threats and danger never far away on the Bolingbroke estate. Her family were renowned as the hard cases on the estate, not just her dad, but her extended family. Charly's mother Shirley's side of the family seemed to stretch across the length and breadth of the estate and she had cousins she didn't even know were relations until they popped up and informed her of the fact; something that happened regularly throughout her teens.

Her mother's side of the family acted like a protective clan. But once Shirley had disappeared they seemed to close ranks, becoming distant and making Charly, Jimmy and Len feel as if they were somehow responsible for her disappearance. They were also a family of troublemakers, stirring up discord at every opportunity, which meant that Charly knew what it felt like to be permanently on her guard. As a result, Charly was well aware of when she needed to think on her feet and now was definitely the time with Joel. She didn't think things were going to get any better. Whatever her feelings for Joel were, deep down her instincts for self-preservation were stronger.

'I know, babe, I know,' she said, getting up and walking over to Joel. She gently touched his head. He pulled away, wincing. 'Want me to get you some ice for your bruises?'

'Yeah, alright,' he said sulkily. Charly got up and went over to the freezer. She was going to be nurse-maid to Joel until he was better. She wanted Joel to propose to her and for them to live happily ever after but at the moment she couldn't see a time when they'd manage a day without falling out. She wanted desperately for them to be compatible. She couldn't understand why he seemed to hate her so much. But there was a part of Charly that knew what she really should do. She needed to buy herself some time and put a get-out strategy in place. She didn't want to be left with nothing other than a broken heart. This sort of thing should have come easily to Charly, who'd been brought up the hard way. But it didn't. She didn't want to be one of those women who walked away from a relationship and feathered their own nest in the bargain. She wanted to be with the man she loved. But she knew that she was clutching at straws hoping that he was going to truly love her in return.

chapter seven

Jodie and Leanne were sitting in a cafe in Bradington. Jodie had a week off and was thoroughly enjoying the freedom. She lounged around in bed until past eleven every morning and spent the day reading magazines and generally pampering herself. In her hand was one of the celebrity magazines that both she and her sister had featured in countless times. There was something fascinating about them even now that she knew that most of the stories in them were half-truths or that the people smiling out of the pages were only there because they had something to sell. Jodie slapped the magazine on the table.

'Seen this?' she asked. It was a grainy picture of Charly Metcalfe and Joel Baldy on a beach somewhere getting married. The headline read 'Shotgun Wedding'.

'Oh my God!' Leanne grabbed the magazine.

'I know. They've been knocking seven bells out of one another, haven't they? How's she got him to agree to this?' Jodie was gobsmacked. She'd followed their relationship with interest as when the couple had first met Charly had been living with their brother Scott and had been with her and Leanne on a night out. Jodie couldn't help thinking that this was all either a publicity stunt – although she couldn't think what publicity Charly needed at the moment – or for financial security. A lot of these girls got themselves footballer boyfriends but until they were married their rights only stretched as far as the amount of money they were given to spend on Mulberry handbags each month.

'God knows. She's a rum 'un, isn't she?' Leanne said.

'She bloody is. That could have been me,' Jodie said sardonically.

'Yeah, fat chance. He had your card marked the minute he met you. Anyway, there's no way you'd put up with all the rubbish that these footballers chuck at their girlfriends – one bad word from him and you'd have inserted his footy boots where the sun doesn't shine.'

'True.' Jodie nodded, contemplating a WAG

lifestyle. 'They're all thick as pig shit as well, aren't they, footballers?' Jodie looked at the picture of Joel again. 'Pretty, though.'

Jodie's phone began to ring. She rooted in her bag, past the chewing gum and the make-up and the receipts she kept meaning to do something with and the keys – what were those keys even *for*? They weren't her door keys, probably for the bin shed, and she'd been carrying them round for weeks – and finally found her phone. 'Karina,' she said, looking at Leanne and raising an eyebrow. Karina hadn't been in touch since the Elvis night. She was rarely in touch these days; she kept herself very much to herself.

'Aright, sis.'

'Do I fucking look alright?' Karina slurred.

Jodie didn't appreciate being called up and then abused, especially by her unpredictable sister. 'Well, I don't know, do I? I'm on the other end of the phone.'

Leanne's eyes widened in shock. Jodie stuck two fingers up at the phone and flicked them repeatedly.

'I know what you lot are all up to and you're not having her,' Karina continued her rant.

'Right, what are you on about? You're starting to sound like a mental patient.' Jodie didn't have the energy for this conversation; Karina was obviously high, or drunk, or both.

'You're after Izzy. The Social's been round today, so don't deny it.'

Izzy was Karina's three-year-old daughter. As far as Jodie was aware, Izzy was fine. Karina and Gaz, Izzy's father, had split up in the last six months but from what Jodie could tell this was a good thing. They had been one of those couples who argued all of the time and expected one another to take abuse that they wouldn't dish out to their worst enemy. Now Izzy was spending four days a week with Karina and three with Gaz and she seemed to be enjoying it. Karina was a party animal given half a chance, and had often abused Gaz's access to coke, even setting herself up as a dealer, but she made sure that none of this happened when her daughter was around. The days when Izzy was with Gaz were Karina's kick-back days; the days she was with Karina she made sure they did nice things together. Although Jodie, ever the cynic, suspected that Karina was glad when her four days were up and she could have a bender without feeling guilty. Why else would she be wandering around looking like Skeletor if she was an exemplary mother even when Izzy wasn't with her?

'Listen here, Scarface. I'm not interested in looking after a three-year-old if you must know, so it's not me that's rung the Social. If I had a problem with you and how I thought Izzy was being looked after I'd take it up with you, or I'd at least take it up with Gaz. I'm not about to go bleating to the Social, am I?'

Leanne grabbed the phone from Jodie's hand. 'Karina, is Izzy with you now?' She nodded at the response.

'Right, I'm coming round.'

Jodie shook her head despairingly. Leanne was far too nice. Karina and Jodie used to get on well but now she felt that her sister was totally wrapped up in herself and she couldn't be bothered with her.

'Let her sort her own shit out,' Jodie said as Leanne looked around for a waitress to bring the bill.

'She *can* sort her own shit out. I'm just going to go and get Izzy.'

'Let Gaz get Izzy. Why do we all end up getting so involved in each other's lives?'

Leanne relented. Sitting back down, she pulled her phone out of her bag. 'Gaz, it's Leanne. Can you go pick Izzy up? Karina's having a bad day, I think.'

There was a pause as Gaz spoke, and Leanne nodded. 'No problem.'

'He's in Spain. On some jolly waiting for Swing, of all people, to get there. He reckons that's why Karina's freaking out – she's got Izzy all week this week.'

'She's so bloody selfish!'

'Well, we know where she gets that from.'

Jodie was incensed. 'I'm not selfish!'

'Not you!'

'Oh,' Jodie said, realising who Leanne was referring to. 'Mum.'

'Wonder how she is?'

'Scaring the good people of Blackpool, no doubt.'

Leanne laughed. 'Today's the day.'

'Kent has now left the building,' Jodie said in a jokey American accent. She looked at Leanne and they both laughed.

'Poor Kent,' they said at the same time, then laughed again.

*

If Tracy heard another Elvis song she was going to snap Kent's neck. He'd been wandering around the house 'Love Me Tender'-ing for what seemed like the last decade. At least Tracy had been able to occupy herself with work. *Work*. Even thinking that she, Tracy Crompton, Bolingbroke's queen of the dole queue twenty years running, had a job, made her smile. It didn't feel like work. Work was wearing a hair net and screwing tops on bottles at the shampoo factory for two hundred quid a week like some of the other mugs on the estate did. To hear them go on about it you'd think they'd won the lottery. Just because they got a bag of Herbal Essences bottles with wonky labels every week for a pound didn't make getting out of bed at five o'clock every morning any more appealing for Tracy. No, this was her kind of work. Spending her days with Mac Jones and having a pop at a load of mouthy mares around the estates of Bradington was far more up Tracy's street. And she'd surprised herself. She was good at it. In the last week she'd managed to bring in over three grand in arrears. Mac was pleased. So was Markie, although he hadn't been able to quite bring himself to congratulate his mum just yet. Give him time, Tracy thought. She'd have a bottle of Asti Spumante out of him by the end of the month if it killed her.

Today was Kent's big day, though, and they were

on their way to Blackpool. The coach from Bradington had been an ordeal in itself. Kent had insisted on being in character all day and had Elvised himself up that morning. Tracy had spent the two-hour journey sitting next to GI Elvis, and a fat GI Elvis at that.

The competition was being held in the main hall in one of the grander sea-front hotels near the Pleasure Beach and Kent had to attend the dress rehearsal that afternoon. The coach had dropped them by the Sandcastle leisure centre and, while Kent huffed and puffed and insisted that they go straight to the hotel, Tracy decided that she wanted to have a look at the seafront. She could hear Kent heavy-breathing behind her as he lugged the suitcase, which was so old it looked like a prop from *Tenko*.

'Smell that, eh?' Tracy said, breathing in deeply and looking out towards the pier. 'Sea air.' If she was being truthful she would have acknowledged that it wasn't sea air she could smell but petrol fumes and fish and chips.

'Lovely,' Kent said sharply. 'I'm going to be late; I'm off to check in.' He had spotted their hotel over the road and marched off across the tramlines.

'Eh, watch what you're doing. You'll end up

going the same way as Alan Bradley if you're not careful!' Tracy called out. Kent stuck his middle finger up over his shoulder.

'Moody twat!' Tracy shouted. She was going to leave him to it. Once he was in his dress rehearsal she could go to the other hotel that she was booked into for the afternoon.

*

Charly and Joel were sitting in the private jet that Joel had been loaned by the chairman of Manchester Rovers. Charly would have liked to have taken all of the credit for twisting Joel's arm and getting him to propose and marry her in a few short days but the truth was the order had come from a higher power than her. Charly had prised the truth out of Joel the previous evening when they had been sitting on the balcony of the luxury tree-house they'd been staying in, drinking margaritas. Martin Connors, Joel's boss, had a reputation as a hard-line manager. He would tell his players that there was a constant queue of lads out there waiting to take their place if they put a foot wrong. In the past players had challenged his view and quickly found themselves on the subs bench, or worse, being sold to another club, their reputations tarnished.

Joel had been hauled into Martin's office five days ago. Martin had confronted him with his tabloid images and told him that, in his opinion, the best players were the ones who took their aggression out on the pitch. He also said that he liked his players to settle down. There were to be no more stories of lap-dancing clubs and call girls, no more arguments with his girlfriend. Nothing was to distract Joel from his football. He told Joel that there were a million women in the world who wanted to get into his pants but that was never going to help his game. He needed to calm down and focus. And the best players, Martin said, were the ones who were married.

That evening as Charly had been sitting on the settee watching *EastEnders*, Joel walked into the apartment seeming very distracted. In his hand was a box and he paced the room a number of times as if deciding if what he was about to do was the right thing. Finally he'd come over and sat next to her on the settee. He handed her the box. Charly had opened it. Inside was a five-carat pink diamond ring. Charly looked at Joel in shock.

'Will you marry me?' Joel mumbled.

'Are you serious?' Charly felt as if she was dreaming. She'd thought that it would take her a year of being the best girlfriend in the world for Joel to even contemplate getting married.

'Totally. We fly to Ibiza tomorrow, if you're up for it. I can't play for at least a month anyway, can I?' He nodded at his damaged foot.

'Ibiza, what for?' Charly knew she was sounding stupid, but this didn't make sense to her.

'To get married. On a beach – I know you've always wanted that. Sod the guests. They'd just end up fighting. Just me and you. What do you say?'

It hadn't been the hearts and flowers proposal that Charly had hoped for but she was looking at a massive rock and the emotional security she craved. 'Yes!' she squealed, hugging Joel tight. He hugged her back.

'Nice one,' he had said, as if he'd just arranged to go out for a pint with a friend. 'We're getting picked up from here at ten.'

There were a million and one questions that Charly had wanted to ask him but she knew that there wasn't much point. She had got what she wanted and in record time.

*

Charly reached out and grabbed Joel's hand. 'So then, *husband*, how do you feel?'

'Alright, yeah. You?' Joel looked distracted. He had been like this for the past three days. Charly kept telling herself that he was worried about his foot and that getting married was a big deal for any man and he had a lot to think about but she sensed that his heart wasn't in it. It mattered to her how Joel felt, it really did. For all his faults, she loved him. She hated herself for feeling this way sometimes. She was like one of those silly women on *Trisha* who get knocked around the house and when Trisha says, 'Why do you stay with him?' they always bleat, 'Because I love him.' Well, she did love him, and she wanted him to love her back. But if that wasn't going to be the case then Charly was going to have to settle for second best – security. It wasn't just that, though. Charly couldn't explain it, even to herself; it was complicated. When Joel was being the kind and generous Joel who she had first met he could be the most loving person in the world. It was for these increasingly few and far between moments that Charly found herself hanging in for.

'Yeah, I'm fine. Happy, you know?' she said, looking at her wedding finger as the jet began its descent from the clear blue sky through the murky cloud cover back into Manchester.

*

Kent had left an hour ago, Elvised up to the nines, and Tracy had agreed that she wouldn't see him until after his performance. She promised she would be there to cheer him on, but was wondering now if there was a way of getting out of even that. Tracy's second hotel of the day was the Shangri-La, a place that had come highly recommended but on close inspection needed a good coat of paint and some new bedding. Tracy didn't care. She let herself into the room and opened her bag. Inside was some red and black underwear that she'd got from a stall in Bradington market. You wouldn't want to stand next to a naked flame in it, Tracy thought, but from a distance it was pure filth. Once she was dressed, Tracy checked the time on her mobile and positioned herself on the bed. She lay on her side seductively, pulling at her cleavage to make sure it was on display. Not satisfied with that particular look, she leaned on her front, facing towards the door with her finger under her chin and her thong-clad backside waving in the air. That didn't work for her either. She tried legs akimbo and thought that that was pushing things a little too far. Just as she was trying to manoeuvre herself into the best sexy position she could muster, there was a knock on the door and Tracy nearly fell off the bed with shock.

'Come in,' she said, regaining her composure and resuming the first position.

Mac Jones walked in and took in the sight that lay before him. 'Well, don't you look good enough to shag?' he said.

*

The first that Len knew about his daughter's marriage was when he walked into the local newsagents and saw the picture of Charly and Joel on the front cover of one of the tabloids. He felt as if someone had just delivered him a sucker punch. He didn't know whether to flee the shop, pick up the pile of papers and shred them or just sit and sob. What was that stupid girl doing? He bought the paper – he could feel the gaze of the woman behind the counter boring into him, knowing that he was Charly's father – but he didn't flinch. He didn't want her ringing up a newspaper and making a few quid out of his reaction. He walked out of the shop and down a nearby deserted alleyway where he pored over the article. It didn't tell him much. Charly was sporting a huge ring, the pair had disappeared off to Ibiza and the only guests present were two witnesses who were guests at the hotel where they had stayed. They were now back in England. Len read over the article again, trying to take it all in. *Why hadn't she told him?* He took out his mobile phone and scrolled to Charly's number but something put him off calling her. He decided to ring Jimmy instead.

He launched straight into conversation. 'Our Charly's married that bloody Joel lad without even telling us.'

'Good lass.' Jimmy sounded delighted.

'Good lass? Are you wrong in the head? He's a frigging psychopath.'

'Yeah but think about it, he's a rich psychopath. Any more of his tricks and she can divorce him and claim half, can't she?'

'You'll never change, will you, Jimmy? Always thinking about money,' Len said angrily.

'Don't have a pop at me because I'm trying to look on the bright side.'

'You bloody moron.' Len hung up. He wasn't going to keep talking to Jimmy if he wasn't going to talk any sense. He scrolled back to Charly's name and pressed 'call'. Len could feel his heart thumping in his chest.

'Hello,' Charly said quietly.

'You could have told me.' Len's voice was choked.

'It just happened, Dad, I'm sorry.'

'Is that it? Is that all you've got to say?'

'What else do you want me to say? It's not like you and Joel were bezzie mates, is it?'

Len could feel his blood begin to boil again thinking about how the upstart footballer had treated both him and his daughter. 'All the more reason to let me know when you're thinking of doing something as serious as marrying him.'

'Dad. Why don't I come and meet you and we can talk about it?'

Len felt his shoulders relax. 'Where?'

'I'll just come home.'

Len smiled. The fact that Charly still called his house 'home' made him feel better. 'OK, love,' he said, softening. 'What time shall I expect you?'

'Seven. Bye, Dad.'

'See you, love.' Len folded the paper up and stuffed it down the side of a wall as if hiding the information held within its pages from the world.

He walked back down the alleyway into the busy street and thought about what Jimmy had said.

Maybe his son had a point – there were a lot of good-for-nothings that his daughter could have married. At least this one had some money. But he couldn't stay with this feeling for long, not after he'd witnessed Joel's temper first-hand.

*

Charly answered the door to the pizza delivery man. She paid and thanked him, knowing that he was trying to place who she was. She shut the door before he had time to ask. She took the pizza through to the kitchen and plated it up for Joel, pouring him a glass of milk, and bringing the meal through to the living room where he was playing a video game. Joel wasn't looking in the mood to be disturbed.

'Brought you some tea,' Charly said brightly.

'I don't want any tea. I'm off out.'

'Since when?' Charly asked.

'Since whenever. What's it got to do with you?'

'It's got a lot to do with me. I'm your wife. Your new wife. If you're going out on the town then I'm entitled to know, surely.' Charly had hoped things would change now that they were married; that Joel would include her in his life.

'You're going to your dad's, what do you care?'

'I'm only going to be there for an hour. How long are you going to be?'

'All night. What's it matter?' Joel snapped. He pulled the games console angrily up in the air as if the movement would give him some advantage.

'It matters because I want you to think about me for a change instead of just yourself.'

'For fuck's sake!' Joel shouted angrily, throwing the console at Charly, hitting her square in the face. She reeled back in shock, holding her temple. When she removed her hand to inspect it she saw that it was covered in thick crimson blood.

'What did you do that for?'

'You made me lose with your carping. If I'd known you were going to be like this I wouldn't have married you.'

Something inside Charly snapped. All of the abuse that she'd taken from Joel over the last year, all of the anger at him that she'd bottled up came out in that moment. She grabbed the heavy glass vase from the dining table and swung it at Joel, letting out a raw primal scream. Joel saw it coming and blocked it with his arm. He grabbed Charly by the hair and pulled her to the floor, wrapping his fingers around her throat. 'Get off me!' she shouted through gasps.

'You deranged bitch!' Joel shouted.

Charly kicked out but to no avail; Joel was far stronger than her. She saw his fist coming towards her a moment before she felt the impact. She turned her face to the side and tried to curl into a ball. The fight had left her; she just wanted him to leave her alone. But he punched her again, and again. The last thing she remembered stupidly thinking was that Scott Crompton, her ex-boyfriend, might have found out that she was married and be on his way to confront her about it and ultimately save her. But that wasn't going to happen. Scott wouldn't ever think himself a match for Joel Baldy. Too bad, Charly thought, as Joel's punches rained onto her and she finally blacked out.

*

It had been hard to arrange, but Len had managed to get the night off. He was sitting in his kitchen with two plates of fish and chips waiting for Charly to arrive. Fish and chips was Charly's favourite. When she was a little girl and her mum was around they used to get fish and chips on a Friday night. Jimmy and the twins would always moan and leave half, Shirley would have a chip buttie and wash it down with some cheap brandy, but Len and Charly would sit and eat their fish and chips and enjoy every last bite.

Len sighed. He couldn't believe she had married without telling him. He had played through the scenario over and over in his head. Every time he tried to convince himself that this might all work out for the best in the end he only had to think about lying in hospital as a result of Joel's temper to remember that things with characters like Joel Baldy *never* worked out in the end. He'd seen men like him before; the sort that were deeply angry about something and were never going to get over it. The men that Len had known like this, though, had been safely out of harm's way at Her Majesty's pleasure, not feted as the new face of football. As far as Len was concerned, an ego like Joel's and public adoration were a lethal combination. Len checked his watch. It was quarter past seven: Charly was late.

By half past seven Len was starting to worry. He called Charly's mobile but there was no answer. He looked at the fish and chips sitting on the table and wondered if maybe he should eat his and put Charly's in the oven until she got here. Maybe she was running late and didn't want to answer her phone. But Len knew his daughter and knew that under the circumstances if she was going to be late she would have called. He tried her phone one more time and as it clicked through to voicemail he grabbed his coat and headed for the door.

chapter eight

Tracy walked into the theatre where the Elvis competition was being held and looked around disapprovingly. Bleeding hell, she thought, as she took in the peeling wallpaper and the cabaret-style setting with its shabby lamps and peeling Formica tables. She headed for the bar. Nothing was going to dampen her mood tonight, not even this tat palace. She and Mac had had an afternoon of passion that she wasn't going to forget for a while. As they had checked out of their love den, the sour-faced landlady had asked knowingly, 'Was everything alright for you? Only, one of the guests thought they'd heard someone in pain.'

'Everything was fine, thank you,' Mac had replied. Tracy had watched the exchange with interest; it wasn't like Mac Jones to leave someone else with the last word. True to form, as they were stepping out of the door he said over his shoulder, 'That wasn't pain, it was shagging, love. You might want to try it one day. Loosen yourself up a bit.' Tracy had laughed like a drain as they fell out into the car park under the tight-lipped, disapproving glare of the landlady. Mac had grabbed Tracy's bum as they walked across the car park and pulled her in close for another kiss.

'Not here!' Tracy had said, looking around.

'Give up. He'll be swinging his rhinestone pants somewhere. Not hiding in a car park waiting to catch us two at it,' Mac had said.

Tracy ordered herself a double vodka and coke with a whisky chaser and took a seat. The blue-rinse brigade was out in force, she thought, looking around at the crowd. Barry Manilow's 'Can't Smile Without You' was being piped into the room and a load of the old dears were swaying and singing along out of tune, clapping their hands to the rhythm. Tracy hoped that someone would put her out of her misery before she got to the stage where she deemed this the pinnacle of entertainment.

She'd had a couple of texts from Kent, telling her how he was getting on that afternoon. It seemed that the pressure of all the other superior Elvises around the country was getting to him. His last text had informed her that he was turning his phone off in order to concentrate. Tracy had texted back saying that she'd had an afternoon of sightseeing. She didn't think Kent would have appreciated her detailing the actual sights she saw. Tracy ordered herself another large vodka and, hearing her phone beep, took it out of her bag.

There were two texts from Mac: one saying that he was wearing no knickers which made Tracy laugh and the other which read *Look behind you*. She spun around to see Mac standing at the other end of the bar. He made his way over to her. 'What you doing here?' she asked, checking her watch worriedly. 'You've got to be in Manchester for ten, haven't you?'

Mac smiled. 'I'll put my foot down. Just thought I'd come and say bye.'

Tracy wanted to run away with Mac there and then. What was she doing with a loser like Kent? She'd nearly managed to escape a life of boredom with him before but had ended up allowing him to move back in because she felt sorry for him and, if she was honest with herself, she needed a man around; even if he was a useless one who sang to his birds and dressed as a dead rocker.

'Seen anything of Kent yet?' Mac asked. The way

he was tracing her mouth with his eyes let her know that he wasn't really the slightest bit interested in whether she had seen Kent or not.

'No. He's on halfway through.'

'Time for a quickie, then, before I go.'

Tracy looked at him. 'You cheeky get,' she said, breaking into a smile. But that didn't stop her following Mac to his car as the strains of the first Elvis of the night filled the air.

*

Len was standing outside Charly's apartment having broken every Allegro speed record getting into Manchester that evening. He had tried her phone a number of times but got no answer. He didn't have Joel's number to call him, not that he ever wanted to speak to him again anyway. Len had asked his neighbour Maggie to keep an eye out for Charly. Maggie was such a gossip that the notion that something might be wrong and Len was on a hunt for his semi-famous daughter would have her twitching her curtains and on the phone at the first sign of Charly. He looked up at the building: there was no sign of any life from Charly's flat, and Len had had his finger pressed against the buzzer for the past five minutes. As he was standing wondering desperately what he was going to do next, he saw the button for the concierge and pressed that. The speaker crackled to life.

'Can I help you?'

'It's my daughter. She lives in the top flat …'

'Penthouse,' the concierge interrupted.

Len took a deep breath. 'I don't care if it's a mud hut, I need to see her.'

'Well, I'm sorry, sir,' came the hoity-toity response, 'but I don't need to be spoken to in that manner.'

It took all of Len's strength not to bawl down the intercom at the officious little man. 'Look, my daughter is missing and I think that something bad might have happened to her. Now I know you're not going to let me in alone, but I'd really appreciate it if you would come upstairs with me and see if anything is wrong.' He said this with as much measure in his voice as he could muster.

The door buzzed and Len pushed it. Soon there was a tall, overweight man standing in the hallway – his appearance didn't fit the squeaky timbre of his voice at all.

'Is she Joel Baldy's girlfriend?'

Len was about to say 'wife' but couldn't bring himself to say the word. 'Yes, that's right.'

Len entered the lift with the man and the journey to the top floor seemed to take an age. Len tried to picture his relief at his own foolishness when the man opened the door to find the flat empty and he returned home to find Charly in front of the TV with a totally plausible reason for why she was so late. But he couldn't. A gut feeling kept dragging his mind to darker thoughts of what awaited him at the other side of her apartment door.

The concierge knocked on the door; there was no answer. He tried again. 'Look,' he said finally to Len, 'I can't just go opening the door because you're her dad and she hasn't gone to your house.'

Len knew he was going to have to level with him. 'Look ... I wouldn't ask but he hit her the other week. And he put me in hospital.' The man's jaw nearly hit the floor. Joel Baldy – the palatable face of football – was a woman beater; that was news. He rustled in his pockets and produced his keys, and within seconds the door was open. Len ran into the apartment and glanced around.

He didn't see anything at first and felt something approaching relief. The concierge joined him. Len was about to apologise for causing a fuss when the colour drained from the other man's face and Len followed his gaze to the floor, just by his own feet. A pool of blood had been obscured and soaked up by the dark woollen rug. The blood was coming from a wound in Charly's head. She appeared lifeless. Len knelt down beside her and took her hand; he could feel a pulse. 'Call an ambulance!' he screamed at the concierge. The man was shocked out of his stare and grabbed his phone from his pocket. Len bent forward over his daughter, holding his face close to hers, trying to detect if she was breathing. He felt the shallowest of breaths. As he lay across his daughter, waiting for the ambulance, Len began to cry. The concierge put a hand on his back but Len didn't feel it. The pain he felt inside was too great for him to concentrate on anything else happening around him.

*

Jodie was dreading this evening. She used to love going out in town and getting legless for free, but now it always seemed to come at a price and tonight's price was having to be nice to all the other girls that were signed to Leanne's agency and make sure they were all behaving themselves.

They were starting their night in the bar of the Radisson Edwardian, which was a nice enough place to have cocktails, but she knew that the girls would want to move on quickly to somewhere they were more likely to be seen by the paparazzi. Jodie was wearing gold hot pants and a billowing long-sleeved top. Her legs were flawlessly bronzed and she was trying to remain upright in her gold killer heels. Her hair was perfectly coiffed in a Farrah Fawcett circa 1976 style and her make-up was sunkissed LA goddess. All in all she thought she looked rather good, which was more than could be said for some of the girls. Kim and Helen, two of the latest signings, looked like they'd just come from a bikini shoot. They were both wearing the tiniest tops and knickers and both were plastered in make-up. As they realised that their group was garnering a lot of attention from the men in the room, the girls got closer and held hands. Kim pretended to spill champagne down Helen's front and Shauna made a big show of acting outraged. Jodie looked at the pair in despair, knowing exactly what was coming next. Kim followed the champagne dribble along the outline of Helen's breast with her mouth. A group of men who were sitting behind the women all vied to get the best viewing position. Jodie had seen it all before, glamour girls pretending to be lesbians. It was tedious and it was going to get them thrown out of the bar.

Jodie leaned forward. 'Can you two can it or get a room, please?'

The girls broke apart and looked at Jodie like chastened naughty teenagers. 'Sorry,' they said in unison. Jodie knew that they weren't.

'You're not even lesbians.'

'I just get horny,' Helen said loudly for the benefit of the men listening. Jodie's jaw set. *Give me strength*, she thought.

'Course you do, love. But there's a time and a place and here isn't it. Comprendez?' Jesus, Jodie thought, tonight was going to be a long night.

She finally managed to get the girls to the Sea Bar at ten o'clock. It was a private members bar which was far more accommodating of glamour models with penchants for getting off with one another than a lot of places. At least here she felt that she could relax. Whatever the girls got up to in here would generally stay within the four walls and Jodie could sit and sink a few cocktails with the saner of the girls without having to worry about wanting to hit some of the others. She texted Leanne: *You owe me!* Leanne texted back a smiley face.

Jodie was just in conversation with a quiet model named Jess who had been on Leanne's books for a while when out of the corner of her eye she spotted Joel Baldy lurch to the bar. His eyes were black and he looked demonic. Whatever he'd been enjoying this evening, one thing was for sure – it wasn't just alcohol. Jodie thought about not saying anything to him, but she couldn't help herself. She wanted to know how Charly was and she wanted to know why the newlywed was out on the tiles on his own. She asked Jess to excuse her and made her way over to Joel. Before she managed to get to him he was intercepted by Kim and Helen. Joel was staring blankly at the two faux-lesbians. Jodie tapped the two girls on the shoulder and indicated that they should sit down until she had had a chance to speak to the footballer.

'Mr Baldy. How's tricks?'

'Fine. You?' He didn't seem to be in the mood for chatting.

'No Charly?'

Jodie wouldn't have thought it was possible for Joel's face to look any darker but it clouded over. 'She's at home.'

'Who you out with?'

Joel looked at her as if registering for the first

time that she was there. 'What do you care, Jodie?'

'Charmed.' She glared at him. 'I'm making polite conversation, that's all.'

'Well, I'm over it tonight, if you don't mind. So why don't you let your little pretend lezzie mates come over here and sit on my cock.'

Jodie felt her face form into an involuntary sneer. 'Tell you what, Joel, sort your head out before you speak to anyone else tonight. You're in danger of people thinking you're a right nob-head.' A look of hatred flashed in Joel's eyes and he stepped towards Jodie. She recoiled, sure that he was about to strike her. But he laughed and walked away.

Jodie fled to the other side of the bar. 'Psycho,' she mumbled to herself.

*

Tracy was back through the door of the club, tugging at her skirt, in time for Kent's appearance. She didn't hold out much hope for him. He was good, but the standard of performance at something like this was going to far outweigh anything the tin-pot Elvises of Bradington had to offer. Tracy settled into her chair and her fresh large vodka and waited to see what Kent had in store for everyone. The stage went dark and dry ice billowed from under the glittering backdrop curtains.

Kent strode across the stage as if he owned the place. Tracy sat back and watched, impressed. As the first bars of 'In the Ghetto' began to play, Tracy felt a shiver run down her spine. There was something quite breathtaking about Kent's staging tonight. She couldn't quite believe what she was seeing. When he turned round and began to sing, he *was* Elvis. He had the audience eating out of his hand. As he held the last note and brought his hand down to signal the end of the song, the crowd went wild. Well, as wild as they could. Tracy stood up, clapping, tears filling her eyes. It wasn't guilt – she could block out the fact that she'd just had a quickie with Mac in the car park – she was genuinely moved by Kent's performance.

'Thank you!' the compere said over the cheers. 'Thank you. And I see that our judges are looking very impressed by Kent Graham. Will he be the one to win our five thousand pound prize and an all-expenses-paid trip to Memphis? We'll know later this evening …'

Tracy stood to attention. Five grand? He never mentioned five grand, she thought. Maybe she wouldn't be so quick to kick him into touch after all.

There had been some stiff competition but Tracy couldn't think of anyone who'd been better than Kent tonight. The compere came onto the stage holding the gold envelope that contained the winner's name. There was a huge fanfare that ground to a halt halfway through and another man went shooting across the stage under the compere's disapproving glare. There was an ear-splitting sound of a tape being wound back and then the music began again.

'Ladies and gentlemen, we have witnessed here tonight some of the best performances, I think you'll agree, that Elvis has put on since his death …' He smiled, waiting for the laughter. The joke went down like a lead balloon. The compere coughed and soldiered on. Tracy looked at him. *Nob-head*, she thought. Who didn't know to avoid wisecracks when referring to Elvis at an Elvis impersonators competition? Elvis was sacrosanct to these people.

There was a chance that Kent might actually be on the verge of doing something interesting for once. And more importantly, he could be about to give her the holiday she'd been hankering after, not to mention a bit of spends. Tracy had her eye on a jacket in the catalogue and since her account had been closed after she was declared bankrupt, she couldn't do her usual trick and pay for it at a pound a week for the rest of her life. Tracy had jackets older than most of her kids that still hadn't been paid for outright. Maybe now wasn't the time to tell Kent that he was boring her and that she wanted to be with Mac. Mac would understand. They could just continue having a bit of fun until all this Elvis business was over and then see how the land lay.

*

Len was sitting at Charly's bedside holding her hand. Her face was purple and bruised. Her breathing was shallow but the doctors had informed Len that she was stable and she would need rest. She had briefly opened her eyes and smiled sadly at her dad, but now she was fast asleep again. Len thought back to when Charly had been a little girl. She'd always looked like such a little angel with her baby blonde hair and her blue eyes. He would have killed anyone that had touched a hair on her head back then, but now, he was sitting here knowing that this wasn't the first time Joel Baldy had beaten her, and he hadn't done much about it on either occasion. Len felt the knot of anger tightening. He wanted Joel Baldy to pay for this, but he wasn't some ordinary bloke down the pub. Someone Len could just go and find and have it out with face to face. He was a snivelling footballer and he was surrounded by flunkies.

Len heard a click from behind him and spun round. A young woman had poked her phone through the curtain and taken a picture of Charly. Len jumped to his feet and ran after her. The girl shot down the corridor. Len reached out and grabbed the woman's coat, pulling her back sharply and throwing her to the floor. Two orderlies were hard on Len's heels.

'Where is it?' he barked.

'What you on about, you mong?' the girl spat.

The orderlies grabbed Len and pulled him back. 'She's just taken a picture of my daughter on her phone,' he said, trying to wrestle free from the men.

'I never.'

'Can we see your phone, please.'

'No.' The girl set her jaw in defiance.

'Phone. Now!' the larger of the orderlies demanded.

The girl pulled it from her pocket. 'This is against my human rights!'

The orderly looked at her phone. Len saw him press a few buttons before handing it back to the girl. 'I've deleted it.'

'You can't do that, it's against the law.'

'You can't take pictures of other people in hospital just because you think you can sell it to the paper, darling. That's against the law, too.'

The girl grabbed her phone back angrily before storming off.

'Thank you,' Len said.

The orderly turned his piercing gaze on Len. 'And you can't take the law into your own hands.'

Len clenched his fists, fed up with being at the mercy of other people's decisions. 'My daughter is badly beaten and some little scroat wants to take a picture of her? What would you have done?'

The man hung his head. So he should, Len thought.

The smaller orderly stepped forward. 'We're going to be moving your daughter to a different ward soon and visiting time there is between two and eight.'

'You're sending me home.'

'No. But your daughter is stable and visiting hours have to be adhered to.'

'Fine.' Len nodded. 'Fine.' But it was far from

fine. Len was angrier than he'd ever been. He knew that there was only one thing he wanted to do if he left the hospital and that was to find Joel Baldy and make him pay for what he'd done.

chapter nine

Jodie had had an average night. There was a time, not so long ago, when the idea of free drinks all night in glamorous bars and being idolised by men would have been her idea of heaven. Now Jodie saw it for what it was: vacuous rubbish. She might as well have been in the Beacon – the pub on the Bolingbroke estate where she used to work – than propping up private members bars in Manchester. At least the customers were down to earth there and knew how to have a laugh. Thankfully she was staying in the Manchester Hilton, which was an impressive building – the large glass edifice could be seen on the skyline from any vantage point in the city – and was a nice place to rest her weary half-cut head. The other girls were all staying there too, but Jodie didn't expect that many of them would get their money's worth from the room. It was three o'clock now as she crawled into bed; the others had looked like they still had a good few partying hours left in them.

Jodie felt like an old soul as she lay in her hotel room. She wasn't even twenty-one but she knew that her partying days were well and truly over. With a mum like Tracy the party had started early for Jodie and her siblings. Jodie had been given her first proper drink (not including all the whisky she had been fed on the end of her dummy as a child) at the age of six. She remembered feeling dizzy and Markie shouting at his mum, but Tracy had just laughed and put the inebriated Jodie to bed.

From then on, alcohol and drugs were just *around*. When Jodie reached her teens she hadn't felt the need to go out and get rolling drunk in order to rebel. For a Crompton to rebel she'd have had to come home wearing a twinset and pearls and informed Tracy that she was going to university to do a degree in accountancy. Jodie drifted off to sleep thinking about the coming week's work schedule.

The first thing that Jodie knew about the following morning was that it was beginning very loudly and very early. The hammering at her door had started in her dreams but as she sat up in bed and looked at the clock, which informed her it was

4.37, Jodie realised someone was desperately trying to get her attention and, judging from the urgency of the knock, it wasn't housekeeping wanting to check the mini bar.

'Jodie! Are you in there?'

Jodie grabbed the complimentary dressing gown that was hanging in her wardrobe and walked quickly to the door. She knew that it must be one of the other models – she just couldn't work out which one from the sound of their voice alone. Whoever it was was going to receive a severe tongue-lashing, she thought, as she angrily pulled open the door. Standing in the doorway was Kim. She was crying and running on the spot as if trying to get out of her skin.

'He's dead!' she screamed.

Jodie took in the sight that greeted her. Kim was covered in blood.

'Who's dead? Who?' Jodie grabbed the girl's arm and tried to get her to calm down. Kim didn't answer, she just stood there making desperate gulping noises. Jodie looked across the corridor to the room where Kim had been staying and, dragging the girl with her, made her way over. She pushed the door open and looked across the room; her eyes fell on the blood-soaked male body at the side of the bed, a knife protruding from his torso. Jodie fell backwards against the wall and clutched her hands to her mouth. Kim was right: the man was definitely dead. And he was definitely Joel Baldy.

*

Tracy awoke with a desperate thirst and looked at the radio alarm clock at the side of the bed. Kent rolled over, revealing a pillowcase smeared with boot polish from his Elvis quiff. He was still clutching the trophy that he'd won the night before.

'Time is it?'

'Five. I've got a mouth like Gandhi's flip-flop,' Tracy said, making her way into the bathroom and sticking her head under the tap.

'Did I dream last night?' Kent asked, half asleep.

'No. You won. Memphis here we come,' Tracy said, looking at her hazy reflection through blood-shot eyes.

'I could have sworn blind that kid was going to win.' Kent pushed himself up on his elbows.

'I know, you've said,' Tracy said flatly. Kent had got blind drunk once he had been announced winner of the Elvis contest and had insisted on getting the poor lad who was runner-up in a near-headlock, telling him how good he thought he was. He was full of praise for his hip thrust, he said, but he felt that until the lad had watched the entire back catalogue of Elvis films – which as far as Tracy could work out ran to thousands – he wouldn't be able to truly replicate the King. By 1am Kent was so inebriated that he was thoroughly convinced he was channelling the spirit of Elvis himself. He wrote an illegible note to Tracy and said, straight-faced, in his best Elvis voice, 'Give this to Priscilla; tell her I always loved her.' When Tracy finally deciphered it, she realised it read *Engelbert knows what really happened.*

'Engelbert knows what?' Tracy had asked.

Kent's eyes had darkened and he had looked her straight in the eye with a menacing glare. 'What?' he had snapped.

Tracy had rolled her eyes; it had been like dealing with an elderly Alzheimer's-addled relative. 'Your note says *Engelbert knows what really happened* and I said "Engelbert knows what?"'

'Engelbert knows fuck all,' Kent had hissed.

'Right!' Tracy had announced, getting to her feet and grabbing Kent by the arm. 'We're off home. I can't be arsed listening to this.'

Kent had stared at the floor as she dragged him out

of the club. She hadn't seen him like this often and it was usually a product of drinking whisky, but occasionally Kent would become morose and conspiratorial when drunk. The worst time had been when he'd insisted on ringing the UN and asked to be put through to Kofi Annan because he thought Angelina Jolie's tattoos were a code for terrorists. Tracy hadn't managed to get to the bottom of what he'd been on about and she hadn't really cared; she'd just wanted him to shut up as they'd been at his sister's fiftieth at the time. Thankfully his phone credit had run out before he could make a total show of himself to the poor woman on reception at the United Nations.

Tracy had thrown Kent out into the fresh air where he seemed to come around. 'I won!' he announced. He staggered around in a circle for a moment as if his right foot had somehow inadvertently become glued to the floor and then, throwing his arms out to the side, clutching his Elvis trophy and falling to one knee, he began to sing the opening lines of 'The Wonder of You'.

*

Tracy looked at him. It took all her strength not to put her foot on his chest and push him over. But she knew that in two months' time she would be on the holiday of a lifetime with Kent and that was reason enough to grin and bear it for the time being.

'Get up, you soft arse,' Tracy had said, shaking her head. Kent had done as he was told and wobbled his way back along Blackpool front behind Tracy as she marched ahead with her arms folded across her chest, wishing she'd brought a coat.

Tracy came out of the bathroom and looked at Kent. 'You were talking some shit last night.'

'Can't a man have a whisky in celebration?'

'A man can have a whisky, but I'd prefer it if a man didn't start thinking that he was channelling the dead and passing on messages.'

'What messages?'

'Apparently Engelbert fucking Humperdinck knows all about something.'

'What?'

'That's what I said.'

'Did I say that?'

'Among other things.'

'Bloody hell, I must have been pissed.'

'Trust me, you were.'

Tracy came out of the bathroom and was about to get back into bed when she saw the light from her phone come on in her bag. The phone was on silent. Kent turned around in the bed and threw his head under the pillow. 'I don't know if I'll get back to sleep now,' he said, rustling around. Tracy wasn't listening. She was looking at a message from Mac.

'Hi. Can't meet you next week. Had to go away on business. You'll have to do your collections on your own. Back soon.' Tracy looked at the message. This wasn't like Mac. He'd usually have something cheeky or dirty to say in his text. She pushed the phone back into her bag and wondered for a moment what this could mean but quickly dismissed the thought. Tracy never spent much time wondering about people's motives. She was very male in that respect and she'd tried to drill it into her daughters to do the same, with varying degrees of success. There was nothing she hated more than hearing grown women poring over something some bloke's said and saying, 'What do you think he meant by that?' when invariably the bloke in question won't have meant anything.

Tracy got into bed and Kent shifted around; he was evidently wide awake.

'How d'you fancy giving Elvis a blow job?' Kent asked, charm personified.

'Don't push your luck, sunshine,' Tracy said,

rolling over, her back to Kent, pulling the sheets over her head.

*

Len hadn't slept; he'd had a fraught night. After he had left Charly he'd gone in search of Joel Baldy, but Manchester was a big place and one that he wasn't particularly accustomed to. Since he'd returned home he had lain awake thinking of the events of the last twenty-four hours.

He was now positioned awkwardly on the settee, wishing himself back to sleep. It was nearly 9.30am and he couldn't go back to the hospital feeling like this; he needed some rest first. As he finally began to drift off, there was a bang on the door that made Len leap from the chair, his heart pounding.

Len was contemplating not answering it when there was another almighty hammering. 'Police!' a voice shouted. Len's heart leapt. What now? Had that psychotic son-in-law of his got into the hospital and to his daughter? He immediately opened the door.

'Is Charly alright?'

The police officer standing at the door looked

Len up and down. 'Your daughter's fine. Unlike your-son-in-law.' Len looked at the cop. He wanted nothing more than some terrible fate to befall Joel Baldy but right now Len couldn't quite understand what those words meant and what they had to do with him.

'What's he done now?'

'He's dead.' The police officer let the words hang in the air as he watched Len for a reaction. Len fell back slightly, as if he'd just had the stuffing knocked out of him. 'And we'd like to know where you were last night, Mr Metcalfe.'

'I wasn't anywhere,' Len stammered. 'Well, I was; I was here.'

'Just here? You were with your daughter at the hospital last night, weren't you?'

'Well, I was, but …'

'Your daughter, who'd been badly beaten by her husband …'

'Yes she had, but that doesn't mean that I did anything to him.'

'The concierge of the apartment where Mr and Mrs Baldy lived says that you weren't in a particularly forgiving mood last night.' The words *Mr and Mrs Baldy* hit Len hard. He couldn't bear to think of his daughter as Mrs Baldy. She was Charly, his little girl, not some footballer's chattel to be beaten as he pleased.

'Mr Metcalfe?' the police officer said, looking at Len. Len looked at the man – he'd obviously been speaking but Len hadn't heard what he'd said. 'Where were you at four o'clock this morning?'

Len looked the man dead in the eye. 'I was here,' Len said, but he hadn't been. The thought of finding Joel Baldy had become too much for him and he had been in Manchester driving around, wondering where he could find the lout who'd battered his daughter.

'And can anyone else vouch for that?' the officer asked. Len knew that the hole he was digging was only going to get deeper. He shook his head.

'Your car was spotted on CCTV in Manchester city centre at 3am.'

'I woke up here, in my own bed.'

'What does that prove, Len? Nothing. So you're not denying you were in Manchester at three?'

'I never said that.'

'You don't need to.'

'How was he murdered?'

'I never mentioned murder, Mr Metcalfe.' *Hadn't he?* Len thought. *What had he said? Dead? Killed?* He couldn't remember.

'Len Metcalfe, I am arresting you on the murder of Joel Baldy ...' Len felt the room swim in front of him as the officer stepped forward and placed the cuffs on his wrists. There was no way he was getting out of this lightly.

The front door opened, and Len looked up, expecting Jimmy. There was no one else who'd just walk right in, other than Charly. The police officer turned around and looked at the woman standing in the doorway holding some milk and a loaf of bread.

'What the bloody hell are you doing with him?' she asked, outraged.

Len didn't know what to say, but he looked at the woman in front of him and hoped that what he was seeing was real, that she was here, for some inexplicable reason, to throw him a lifeline. 'Joel's been murdered.'

The woman gasped. 'No!' Then she gathered herself. 'Well, he's not got owt to do with it.'

'Last night at four,' Len said.

'Well, he can't be in two places at once and he was in bed upstairs next to me, snoring his head off.'

'You never said you had company, Len.'

'Well ...' Len began but the woman interrupted. 'I'm not bloody company,' she said, throwing the bread on the table and putting her hand purposefully on her hip. 'I'm his sodding wife.'

*

Jodie was sitting in her apartment staring out of the window.

'Eat,' Leanne said, plonking a sandwich in front of her sister.

'I'm not hungry.'

'I don't care whether you're hungry or not, you need to eat.'

Jodie pulled the sandwich towards her and looked at the salami. It turned her stomach. 'I think I'll stick to veg for a while.'

'Right, I'll do you beans on toast, and you're eating it whether you like it or not,' Leanne said, pulling at the cupboard doors to see what food Jodie had in.

Jodie had been back from the police station for a few hours but she couldn't sleep. She couldn't stop thinking about how she had last seen Joel Baldy. The police had questioned her about whether she had heard or seen anything suspicious, which she hadn't. Leanne's boyfriend Tony had picked Jodie up from the police station. It had been early enough for the news not to have broken and for the place to be free of photographers but Leanne had preempted what was coming. Jodie's phone had been ringing off the hook for the past hour and she knew that she was at the centre of a national news storm. But she didn't have anything to tell anyone. Neither did Kim, as far as she could gather. They had both just been in the wrong place at the wrong time. But what about Joel? Who would do that to him? It was common knowledge that he'd turned into a bit of an arsehole as his career had taken off but Jodie couldn't think of a reason why anyone would want him dead.

And then there was the matter of Charly. She was still officially on Leanne's books but more importantly, as much as they hadn't seen eye to eye in the past, she had been Scott's girlfriend and he had thought the world of her. Leanne wanted to see her to make sure she was being properly looked after. Jodie had her reservations. Leanne had called around and found out that Charly was in hospital; she couldn't find out why she was there and didn't even know if she knew about Joel yet. In the end Jodie had told Leanne that she thought it was best if she let the dust settle before contacting Charly. It was all very well offering her support but Jodie didn't want Charly jumping to any ill-informed conclusions about why Jodie had been there when they found her husband's body.

'Have you heard anything from Kim yet?' Jodie asked. She hadn't seen the girl since they had been put into separate police cars early that morning.

'I've left her a message; she's probably still being questioned. I've told her to call me straight away. I know what that one's like – she'll be all over the papers pulling one of those wronged faces and spilling her guts if I don't get to her and tell her that it's only a short-term money-making scheme and then she'll forever be known as the girl who was with Joel Baldy when he was murdered.'

'Yeah, but that's what she'll be known as anyway.'

'True, but it's better for her, and me, if she plays it low key. And anyway, she needs to play this down as much as possible. I wouldn't want to get into the ring with Charly Metcalfe, would you?'

Jodie wasn't scared of Charly but she knew what Leanne meant. She was a Metcalfe and if someone crossed her she'd have her revenge, even if it took her the rest of her life to get it. Thinking this, something occurred to Jodie.

'D'you think she did it?'

'From her hospital bed?'

'We don't know, do we? She finds out Joel's sneaking back to some page three girl's room and she goes schizo. Not beyond the realms of possibility.'

'True, but she'd have knifed Kim before she knifed Joel, wouldn't she?' Leanne reasoned, pouring the beans from the saucepan onto the toast.

Jodie thought about this for a moment. Leanne was probably right. But the reality was that neither of them knew the truth and probably wouldn't until the rest of the country found out.

chapter ten

'Alright, Len, you can pick your jaw up off the floor,' Shirley said. She'd been there for nearly two hours. The police had taken her statement and she'd kept to her story of having been in the house last night. Something that she knew was probably hard for Len to swallow as she hadn't been near the house for ten years.

'Why?' he said.

'Why what?' Shirley asked. But she knew why.

'Why everything. Why this? Why'd you leave? Where did you go? Why've you come back now? Who've you been with? What about your kids?' With each question Shirley could see Len getting angrier and as much as it annoyed her to have to face these questions, she knew that he had every right to ask them.

'I've been back a few times but I've bottled it

whenever I've got near the house.' This was her fourth attempt to knock on her old front door and she would have probably bottled it again if she hadn't watched the police arrive and heard what they'd said.

'Not surprising.'

She ignored the jibe.

'And this –' She waved her arms, indicating her being there under the circumstances they both found themselves in '– well, this is because I saw the coppers pull up outside and followed them to the door. I heard what they were arresting you for and I thought that it was rubbish. There's no way you'd have murdered that lad.'

'How do you know?' Len asked angrily.

'Well, did you?' Shirley shot back.

'No.'

'Well then. So I nipped to the shop and bought some stuff to look like I was just coming back in and I hoped to God that the door wasn't on a Yale lock because I don't have a key.'

'You do.'

'What?'

'I never changed the lock.'

Shirley looked sadly at Len. She had hated him when she'd left. But she'd hated everything: she knew now, she'd known for years, that it hadn't been Len's fault for how she felt, it had been hers. And then she had convinced herself that he would turn the kids against her and that they wouldn't want to know her until staying away had just become part of who she was. She had her stock response that she'd honed over the years: she was Shirley, from Bradington. Yes, she had two kids, but they were with their dad. She saw them when she could. But she didn't and she'd never tried to. Now, standing here in her old house, feeling her old life all around her, she realised what she had done; she'd left Len a broken man.

'I'm sorry,' Shirley said.

'What for? Because I didn't change the lock?'

'No. Because ... everything.'

'Well, it's not just me you need to apologise to.'

Shirley nodded. She didn't need to say anything; she knew that she had years of apologising to do to Charly and Jimmy. Shirley suddenly felt exposed; she could feel Len was looking at her. She wanted to hide her head in the polo-neck jumper she was wearing.

'What you after?' Len asked finally.

'I'm not after anything,' Shirley said. She was genuinely affronted.

'Pull the other one, Shirl ...' Len began to get angry.

'I just wanted to see you.'

'Yeah … and?'

'And nothing. I wanted to get to know my family again.'

'We're not a bloody drop-in centre.'

'I never said you were.'

'You don't need to. I know how you work, don't I?'

'You never knew how I worked, that was the problem.' Shirley didn't mean it, she just needed to retaliate.

'So you running off and not showing your face for ten years, that's my fault, is it?'

'I never said that. I just didn't think you understood me.'

'Oh boo bloody hoo, Shirl.' Len jumped to his feet. Shirley hadn't expected everlasting gratitude but he could at least lay off for a few minutes – she had after all just prevented him from being arrested for murder.

'Len, do you want me to go again? Because I don't want to, but I will.'

Len looked at her, scrutinising her from top to bottom. 'No,' he said sadly, shaking his head. 'But I want to know why you're back.'

Shirley was about to explain things to him.

'And I don't want any cock and bull stories from

you either, I want the truth. Understand?' Shirley nodded her head. But she wasn't ready to face her past herself at the moment, so she gave him a brief watered-down version of events.

*

Charly couldn't work out where she was. It took her a few minutes of feeling completely trapped in her own body and not being able to make any sense of her surroundings before she worked out she was in a private room in a hospital and the person who had put her there was her husband.

She pushed herself up in the bed and felt as if every muscle in her body was asking her not to do that again. She daren't look in the mirror; she had no idea how her features were currently arranged, but things didn't feel too good. The door opened and a nurse came into the room. She seemed shocked to see Charly awake.

'Oh, morning. How are you feeling?' she asked distractedly.

'I've been better. Do I look awful?' Charly put her hand to her face and could feel that her cheek was distorted and swollen.

'I've seen you in photos looking better,' the nurse

said diplomatically. 'I don't think we'll be keeping you in much longer, though.' She looked at Charly sympathetically. Charly wanted to cry. She didn't need this woman's sympathy. She didn't want to be just another victim of domestic violence who came through the doors of the hospital to be fixed up and sent home to receive another pasting. But that's what she was, unless she did something about it. Yet right now she couldn't think of anything worse. She just wanted to go home to Joel, listen to his apology, believe him this time, and crawl into bed. Charly wanted desperately to be the one in a million who could change her husband. They must be out there somewhere, those women who'd succeeded, otherwise why would so many women try? Where was Joel, anyway? Shouldn't he be here at her bedside, racked with guilt and promising her the earth in return for her forgiveness and silence?

The nurse made some notes on the clipboard at the end of the bed. When she had finished she looked at Charly. 'There's a police officer here to see you. She's been waiting a while.'

Charly's heart sank. There was no way she was pressing charges; it would be all over the papers and Joel would never forgive her if she did that. The nurse smiled sadly at Charly and left the room.

Charly had had enough of her sympathy. She could send in the police; she wasn't saying anything until she'd spoken to Joel. There was a knock on the door and the policewoman came into the room. 'Mrs Baldy …' she said somberly, in a voice that Charly was certain only coppers could muster. She was just about to say that she had nothing to say to her but the officer continued. 'Your husband Joel is dead.' She paused for a moment as if that was all that was required for the enormity of such news to sink in. 'He was found in the early hours of this morning in a hotel in Manchester city centre.'

Charly felt her body shake with angry convulsions but she wasn't crying, she couldn't cry. The nurse re-entered the room just in time to see her begin to shudder and ran over to Charly's bedside, checking her pulse and looking desperately at the policewoman. She took a needle and administered a sedative to Charly's arm. Charly felt the shuddering come to an abrupt halt and she fell back against her pillow. She looked at the nurse as if trying to work out what she had just done, then she looked back at the policewoman and said simply, 'But he can't be dead. I saw him last night.'

*

Len's day hadn't got any better, or any less surreal. Shirley's appearance would have been something in its own right on any other day of the year, but today it was just another bizarre occurrence in a day packed full of them.

After Shirley and Len had had their preliminary talks he had gone to bed for a few hours. He needed to see Charly, but knew he would have to have his wits about him. He didn't think that anyone would tell his daughter about Joel until she was well enough to leave hospital, so he assumed he had a few hours' grace. How was she going to cope with this? Charly was going to fall apart, he knew that much, and seeing her feel so deeply for a piece of scum like Joel was going to hurt Len. He was trying to push his own feelings towards his deceased son-in-law to one side. They shouldn't matter, but they did. Len was glad he was dead. His type usually cruised through life hurting people, not caring about how their actions affected others and then, in the end, died a natural death, oblivious to their ruinous ways. Well, not this time. Joel Baldy had got exactly what he deserved and Len, for one, was glad. He was going to have to put a mask on his feelings, he decided, as hard as it was. He was going to have to pretend to Charly that he was deeply sorry about Joel's death.

As for Shirley and her story, he really didn't know what to believe. She had told him that she had been living in Tooting in London with some bloke called Mike Newall. Len didn't know him even though he was from Bradington. She said that she'd stayed away because she just felt like a total failure and knew that he could do a better job on his own. A little bit of Len wanted desperately to believe her flattery. Yes, he was a good dad, and yes, she was a failure. But something at the back of his mind wasn't quite buying it. Shirley hadn't been perfect but she'd been a good enough mum. Why would she leave it all behind?

Len had asked her to give him the day to himself. Shirley had decided to go round to her cousin's, which Len knew was going to cause ructions as they hadn't seen her for years. But he had left her feeling that she was big enough and ugly enough to take care of herself. Her family seemed to have their own code when it came to behaviour; you only had to look at the way that Shirley had acted to realise that. They could all fight one another to the death, end up in prison, keep houses that looked like skips with windows, but run away and not tell them where you were going? That was tantamount to family death and that was what Shirley had done. Len had been convinced for years that one of them must know where she was, but it had become increasingly apparent to him – or so it seemed at least – that none of her family knew where she was. He had even grilled the twins but they didn't know where their aunt was. They were the only ones out of that clan who knew where their loyalties lay. Len had taken them in when the rest of their family had turned their backs on them. They'd made concerned noises but no one other than Len was willing to take them in and see that they weren't taken into care by Social Services.

Len had a quick wash, shaved and dressed and then headed downstairs. He knew he had to go to the hospital. Pulling back the curtains in the front room, Len was confronted with at least six photographers snapping his picture. He quickly pulled the curtains shut. His blood ran cold. He didn't need to ask what they were doing there. He knew that Joel's death would be big news; he just hadn't thought that he'd be implicated and subjected to any press attention.

Len didn't have a clue what to do. He couldn't sit there all afternoon watching whatever he'd

forgotten to Sky +. There was something about a
murder and having a good portion of the nation's
press camped on your doorstep that made an otherwise appealing luxury leave a bad taste in your
mouth. He wasn't about to ring the police either. It
wasn't something he would have ever entertained,
especially today. But he needed to brave it out. He
was going to have to brave it out. He had to get to
the hospital.

With his coat on and a cap that said 'Bradington's
Bouncing Back' on it – which he'd found at the back
of the wardrobe and had no idea where it had come
from – Len deftly exited his side door with his key
in hand. He quickly locked the door and walked
head down through the awaiting press as a barrage
of questions were fired at him.

'Did you have anything to do with the suspected
murder of Joel Baldy?'

'Did your daughter know that you wanted Joel
Baldy dead?'

'Have the police charged you with anything, Mr
Metcalfe?'

'Len, over here. You're a violent man, Len, bet
you enjoyed it, didn't you?'

Len powered through the crowd. He wasn't
about to react to accusations like this. But as Len

walked along the street something that should have been startlingly obvious to him struck him: he'd lent Shirley the car. What was he thinking? Aside from the fact that she could be in Aberdeen by now living under an assumed name and he'd never see his Allegro again, he was now walking along the street being tailed by the paparazzi. The thought of standing at the bus stop waiting for the 640 to arrive was more than he could bear. He looked up and down the street like a rabbit in the headlights, and a rabbit wearing a stupid cap at that. Len thought about those pictures he'd often seen that the tabloids managed to snap of probably fairly ordinary-looking men, but that made them look like the monsters that their crime should indicate they were, and he had visions of himself joining those ranks and being hung, drawn and quartered by the red-top-reading population before he'd had a chance to defend himself. He knew he needed to keep quiet at the moment. If a passing journalist asked him the right probing question he was at risk of saying exactly what he thought and how he felt. Len was glad Joel was dead. He couldn't think of a nicer lad for it to happen to.

Suddenly a car swung around the corner and

powered towards him. The passenger door flew open and Jimmy shouted, 'Get in.' Len had never been so glad to see his son.

'Switch your bloody phone on,' Jimmy said tersely as he pressed his foot hard on the accelerator and screeched away from the crowd of press. Len felt in his pocket and brought his phone out, looking at it feebly.

'Sorry. It was on silent.'

'Jesus, Dad. If there was one day to use your bloody mobile, today's it. Isn't it?'

Len wasn't great with technology but he knew that Jimmy was absolutely right.

'What the bloody hell's gone on?' Jimmy asked.

Len took a deep breath; this morning was going to take some explaining.

*

Tracy wasn't in the mood for Elvis today. She'd had just about enough of him for one lifetime. When Kent went to press play on his twenty-five-year-old Walkman, Tracy grabbed his wrist. 'No more Elvis.'

'You what?' Kent exclaimed as if his ears were deceiving him.

'You heard. It's doing my fucking nut in.'

Kent let his hand drop and Tracy ejected the tape. She rummaged in her bag and handed him a tape. Kent reluctantly put it into his Walkman and pressed play. 'Sweet Caroline' began to play. 'Thank the Lord for Neil Diamond,' she said.

Kent pulled his ear plugs out. 'Neil Diamond's not just got you a free ticket to Memphis, has he?' Kent snapped. Tracy looked at Kent. What was this? Dissention in the ranks? she wondered. Kent never said anything that could lead to an argument. Tracy usually had to scrabble around for tidbits of things that Kent had allegedly said or done in order to have a go at him. Yet here he was genuinely standing up for himself.

'No, maybe he hasn't but at least he can sing,' Tracy said, knowing that this was a classic example of her swearing that black was white. If Kent had any sense he would laugh at this preposterous assertion that Elvis couldn't sing, but he obviously wasn't in the mood.

'That's it,' Kent said angrily.

Tracy looked at him, gobsmacked. 'What?'

'You heard me. You've no respect. That's it. Once we're off this bus, me and you ...' He pulled his hand across his throat in a cutting motion.

'Finito.' Kent looked straight ahead, gripping the back of the headrest angrily.

'You can't be serious.' Tracy began to laugh. Kent turned his head, his body resolutely facing forward; giving the manoeuvre an eerie *The Exorcist* look.

'Deadly,' he said, eyes flinty.

Tracy was taken aback. She'd never seen Kent like this and if she was honest, there was a part of her that quite liked it. One of her biggest bugbears with Kent – and there were many – was that he was far too soft. Well, this wasn't him being soft, this was him finally sticking up for something he believed in. She now had a choice: argue with him, which would undoubtedly see her getting off at the next stop and thumbing a lift back, wishing she'd kept her trap shut, or not argue with him, which would be new and refreshing pastures for Tracy. She chose the latter.

'Fine, stroppy knickers, have it your way,' she said, handing Kent back his Elvis tape to play. Tracy looked out of the corner of her eye to see if Kent was happy to have won the battle, but he was just staring straight ahead, simmering. Tracy took a deep breath. What she was about to say was going to be extremely hard and not something she even considered to be part of her vocabulary, but her free holiday was riding on this. 'Sorry,' she said, almost inaudible. The air shifted in the coach.

'Good,' Kent said, obviously thrilled with his small victory.

*

A few moments later the coach pulled into the services. Tracy needed to stretch her legs and have a cigarette. Kent wandered off to the shop with a swagger about him that Tracy hadn't witnessed before. She couldn't say that she had a new grudging respect for him; that would be going too far. And she knew that if he pulled the answering-back trick once too often she'd fight fire with fire and they'd end up having the sort of rows she used to have with her ex, Paul. But for that moment Tracy was just glad that Kent had, for once, stuck up for himself.

Kent came out of the garage armed with newspapers, walking purposefully towards Tracy. 'You're not going to believe it.' Tracy looked down at the headlines: Joel Baldy Murdered.

'Fuck me,' Tracy said slowly as the information sunk in. She quickly scanned the print. All that Tracy could think was that Scott, her son, might be somehow incriminated. But there was no mention of him. She knew that Scott wasn't capable of harming a fly but as Charly's ex he would without doubt be questioned over this. But it was Jodie's name that leapt out at her, not Scott's. 'What the bloody hell was she doing there?' Tracy wondered out loud.

'That's what I was thinking.'

'And why didn't she call me and tell me? You get some juicy gossip like this and you keep it to yourself?'

Kent looked at Tracy; she knew as soon as the words were out of her mouth that she'd overstepped the mark.

'You'd have thought that she'd have called me to put my mind at ease that she was alright.' Kent shook his head at Tracy's obvious backtracking. 'What?' Tracy asked innocently, turning her attentions back to the paper. She read on. 'Bloody hell! Len was arrested.'

'Len?'

'Charly's useless fat lump waste-of-space dad. Runs the club.'

'That Len?' Kent asked, getting caught up in the gossip.

Tracy cackled with glee. 'Be a right shame to see that fat twat behind bars again.'

'What's he ever done to you?'

Tracy looked at Kent. She was about to tell him exactly what she thought of Len but didn't. She didn't want to share things with Kent. There was no little story or any dark information from her past that she ever felt like divulging to him. It was a shame really. At the beginning she'd wanted to tell him everything but now she couldn't even be bothered to tell him anything any more. Not like Mac: Tracy could sit and chat to Mac all day long. 'Nothing,' she said finally. 'He's just hurt my Scotty in the past, that's all,' Tracy added, glancing at Kent to see if she'd got away with her white lie. He didn't flinch. Good, she thought. It seemed she had.

*

Charly was sitting in her hospital room with her bags packed, her dad and Jimmy by her side. She had declined a lift from Jimmy, knowing that most paparazzi could run faster than his rust-bucket. She was waiting for Terry, her driver, to pick her up. She felt numb. She had listened to her voice-mail messages from Joel over and over. Not that any of them said anything loving or out of the ordinary – it was enough that it was his voice; a voice that she'd never hear again. Charly couldn't believe it.

'Want a cup of tea, love?' Len asked. It was probably the fifth time he had asked her if she wanted a cup of tea.

'No, Dad, I'm fine,' she said. Len wasn't comfortable; he could hardly sit still in his chair. Charly watched him for a moment.

'What's up with you?'

'Me? Nothing, why?' Len asked.

'Where were you last night?' Charly asked, realising there were a few things that were going to need answering close to home.

Len looked at Jimmy and then back at his daughter, slowly taking the time to answer. 'I was at home.' Charly looked at him, sensing there was more to come. Len looked at Jimmy again, who didn't seem to be providing much support. 'And then I was arrested and taken in for questioning.'

Charly gasped. She didn't want to think that her dad had anything to do with Joel's murder but if the police were questioning him, and given the circumstances, what else could she think? 'And what did they say?' Charly asked, avoiding the obvious burning question that she really wanted to ask. Her dad had every reason to want to kill Joel and Charly knew that somewhere in him he still had the temper but she didn't want to think about this as a possibility. She couldn't.

'I know me and Joel didn't exactly see eye to eye, Charly, but I didn't do it,' Len said. Charly looked away from him. She didn't want to be having this conversation.

'So they just questioned you for a bit and let you go?' Charly asked.

Jimmy opened his mouth to say something. 'Yes,' Len said, cutting him off. Charly looked at the pair, knowing that they were keeping something from her.

'What? Tell me,' Charly said just as there was a knock at the door and Terry entered.

'You alright, sweetheart?' he asked. Just seeing someone who had a direct link to Joel made Charly crumble. 'Come here,' Terry said, helping Charly to her feet and giving her a hug.

'We'll get you back to the house. Least there's big gates there,' Terry soothed. Charly was grateful. The last place she ever wanted to be was the apartment where things had been at their worst with her and Joel.

'Thanks.'

Charly got to her feet and Terry picked up her bags as Len and Jimmy took her arms. She looked at her dad. 'What were you about to say?'

'Nothing.' Len smiled sadly at his daughter. 'It'll keep.'

*

Everywhere Charly looked there were reminders of Joel. Football trophies he'd won as a kid, pictures, clothes. Everything held a memory or made her think of something that she needed to do now that he was gone. She was sitting staring at a picture of Joel with his dad, thinking that she really should ring his father but that she didn't even know his number (Joel's dad had, emigrated to Benalmedena two years ago and Charly had only ever spoken to him on the phone). Jimmy entered the room and stood behind Charly. When he had been standing there for over a minute without speaking, Charly said, 'What's the bad smell impression for?'

'Char, there's something I need to tell you.' Jimmy hung his head.

Charly looked at her brother. He seemed nervous. There was no need to be. Whatever he had to say would just go in somewhere and mix with all the other feelings of numbness and loss she was experiencing at the moment. 'Go on then, what else?'

Jimmy looked at her. 'Mum's back,' he said quickly, as if throwing up the words.

'No, she's not,' Charly said bluntly; she wasn't ready to take this in. There was no way Shirley was back. God only knew if she was even alive.

'She is. She gave Dad his alibi.'

Charly took in this information as well as she could. Her mother, who she would have killed to see any other day of her life but today, was back? And she'd given Len an alibi, meaning that he'd obviously needed one. Charly shook her head as if this would somehow make the raw facts of the day go away.

'Sorry, Charly.'

'Where is she now?'

'Dad said she went round to Maureen's.'

Charly began to giggle. She couldn't help herself. Maureen, her mother's cousin, hadn't had a nice word to say about Shirley since she'd left, but knowing her mother's lot they would be sitting there thick as thieves by now.

'What's funny?' Jimmy said, genuinely perplexed.

Charly continued to laugh. Nothing was funny,

she thought, but she couldn't help it, she felt as if the giggles were beyond her control. Charly felt calm as she laughed. The fact that her mother had disappeared out of her life for over a decade and had suddenly reappeared didn't seem to matter for that brief moment as she sat laughing. Jimmy was standing, his face contorted into a smile as if hoping to contract this infectious laughter. But Charly suddenly stopped dead and looked at her brother. 'What the fuck is she doing back, Jimmy?' she demanded, suddenly feeling the weight of everything that had happened today. 'Where's she been? Why does she think she can just waltz back in and everything will be alright? Why?'

Jimmy crouched next to his sister and grabbed her wrists. Charly looked at him and then at his hands, wondering if she had looked like she was about to do something dangerous. 'Forget her, she's not worth it. You need to sort stuff out with you now. Fuck Shirley Metcalfe. Or whatever she's calling herself these days. She's nothing to us.'

Charly looked blankly at her brother as if he'd gone mad. They'd both waited years hoping that one day Shirley would come back. Charly blinked slowly as heavy tears began to roll down her face. 'Course she is. She's our mum.'

*

Tracy looked up to see her son Scott standing in the doorway, his eyes bloodshot. 'Bloody hell, son, you look like shit!' she exclaimed. She had just poured herself a well-deserved vodka. The clock, after all, had just struck midday.

'I feel like shit,' Scott mumbled as he sloped into the house.

'Vodka?'

Scott looked at the tumbler his mother was proffering and shook his head. 'No, couldn't stomach it.'

'What's up with you, then?' Tracy asked, sparking up a cigarette. She had a fair idea what was wrong with him but didn't want to make any assumptions. She knew her son too well, though; he was a soft arse and all this stuff about his ex and her murdered boyfriend would have knocked him for six.

'The police have had me in. They thought I'd done it. I might not have wanted us to split up but I'm not about to knife the nob-head, am I?'

Tracy thought carefully about what to say next and then decided to just say the first thing that had come into her head anyway. 'Bet you're glad though, aren't you?'

Scott looked at her in horror. 'No, I'm not! I don't want to see anyone dead, ta very much, Mum.'

'Sorry, me and my big mouth.'

'Yeah, you and your big mouth. Button it, if you've nothing nice to say.'

'So, you been at the cop shop?' Tracy decided to change tack.

'Yep. They think they know it all, that lot. They haven't got a clue. He's a bloody footballer – for all they know some deranged dick-head City fan could have hunted him down and yet they're looking at me because I used to go out with Charly. And it's all over the papers.'

'I know, I read them yesterday.'

'Why didn't you call me?' Scott asked pathetically.

'Ey, stroppy knickers, I did call you. Your voice-mail was telling me that I couldn't leave a message and that I had to call back later.'

'Oh. Sorry,' Scott said quietly.

'I should hope so. I'm on your side, Scott, not anyone else's.' Tracy took a large swig of her vodka. 'So then, what did they say to you? You have an alibi?'

'Course I do. I was out at the Admiral all night. Pissed out of my head with the lads from work.

They had a lock-in. Which means that the landlord is never going to speak to me again because he's up for serving alcohol without a licence, but a lot of people, as pissed as they were, say that I was singing "Shaddap You Face" on the karaoke when the police think that he was murdered.'

'Saved by Joe Dolce.'

'Am I laughing, Mum? I could've been royally fucked. What if I'd just gone home and gone to bed? They could have made out that I'd done it.'

'There's such a thing as forensics these days, you know. Haven't you ever watched *CSI*? They might have tried to pin it on you, but whichever clown did this will get found out soon enough.' Tracy loved *CSI*. She could happily sit making her way through every episode Sky had to offer while simultaneously making her way through a bottle of vodka. Kent didn't understand *CSI*. He said it was way above his head. Tracy had pointed out to him that *Teletubbies* was way above his head.

Scott sat down at the kitchen table. 'I feel really sorry for Charly,' he said, tracing the grain of the table with his index finger.

Tracy couldn't believe what she was hearing. *Where*, she wondered sometimes, *did she get him from?* 'What do you feel sorry for that little slapper for? She's been swanning around the place, lapping it up since she chucked you. And now what? Boo hoo, poor Charly because things have turned out shit for her?'

'What is your problem with her?' Scott demanded.

Tracy had always had a problem with Charly. She didn't like the girl but she wasn't about to roll over and admit that it was just plain old dislike that made her react the way she did to Charly Metcalfe – to any Metcalfe for that matter. 'She treated you like shit.'

'No.' Scott shook his head. 'That's not it. There's more to it. You were down on her from the day I brought her round here, giving it all that about the Metcalfes as if they were the scum of the earth and we were somehow royalty.'

'That's not true. I knew her kind. I knew she'd hurt you.'

'Well, thanks very much, Mystic Meg, but you didn't know anything of the sort.'

'She did though, didn't she? They're all the same, that lot.'

'Is it Len? Is it cos you and him once went out with each other?'

'It's nothing to do with him and I won't have that fat bastard's name mentioned in this house again.'

Scott relented. 'Fine. All I'll say is that I don't hold any grudges against Charly, and neither should you.'

'I'll hold a grudge with who I want, when I want,' Tracy said truculently.

Scott got to his feet. 'Course you will, Mum. Why am I thinking otherwise?' He walked towards the front door.

'You need toughening up, lad. Take a leaf out of our Markie's book ...' Tracy shouted after him. 'Then you wouldn't get mugged around so much.' Scott had closed the door behind him before Tracy had managed to expel the full extent of her rant.

chapter eleven

Swing was sitting outside a cafe that was offering all-you-can-eat English breakfasts for five euros. It was a tatty place but they did a good cup of tea and the owner, Mike, a tattooed, balding ex-con, just wanted a quiet life and as such made the best breakfast in Benalmedena and kept himself to himself.

Swing took a handkerchief from his pocket with his initials JR embroidered on one corner – his real name was John Russell – and mopped his brow. The fact that his initials were JR but at times he felt more like Sue Ellen wasn't lost on him. Since the debacle at the wedding the year before where, as Markie's best man, he let slip after too much booze and a couple of Es that he'd slept with the bride, Swing had become persona non grata within the Markie and Mac empire. He and Markie had made an uneasy truce and Markie had made it clear that he could come back and earn but that he didn't want any dealings with him; he had to work through Mac. Mac was alright, Swing thought, but he was getting on a bit and his incessant stories about the old days, blokes he'd never heard of who were still serving twenty in Strangeways because they were being loyal to some nob-head who'd long since died, could grate.

Swing wiped the handkerchief across the top of his bald head and pocketed it again. 'Everything alright?' Mike asked, clearing Swing's plate.

'Lovely,' Swing said, patting his non-existent stomach. Swing was a gym man. That was one of the reasons that a trip to the Costas wasn't something that particularly floated his boat. He spent as much time in Fizeek, Bradington's number one steroid gym, as he could. He felt like training kept him sane. He wasn't into steroids, not any more. He'd seen too many people messed up on them. But here in the apartment where they were staying, the thing that they tried to pass off as a gym was like one of those all-in-one affairs from the Argos catalogue. Swing could have lifted the entire thing above his head if he wanted to.

He quite fancied the idea of opening his own place out here, but that took time and money. He had plenty of time; it was money he was short of. He hated the fact that he was still at the beck and call of Markie even though he wouldn't even look him in the eye these days. They'd grown up together, been mates throughout school. But one stupid mistake – and it *was* a stupid mistake in Swing's opinion; Markie's ex Mandy had been nothing to write home about – and he was cast aside, forever to do what Mac wanted him to do. And Swing was finding that what Mac wanted him to do was increasingly more extreme. He felt that Mac was becoming ruled by his ego. But Swing wasn't about to tell him that; he needed the work too much. Take this weekend, for instance. Swing had been sent on a wild goose chase. He'd had to come over here on a false passport, in Mac's name, and now he was sitting here like a lemon, waiting for Mac to turn up, to receive further instructions, like some half-baked Bond villain. Where was Mac? he wondered. His plane was due in at eleven; he should be here by now. Swing wondered how many passports Mac had and why he felt the need to have so many; it was hardly like he was Ronnie Biggs.

Swing watched a taxi draw up at the side of the road. He pulled his aviator shades down and watched Mac get out of the car. He had a small weekend bag with him; he didn't look like he was intending to stay long, but you never knew what Mac was planning from one minute to the next.

Mac walked towards him. Swing almost laughed. Today he reminded him of the Man from Delmonte – all George Peppard hair and chinos. Mac shook his hand and sat down, ordering a beer from Mike.

'Thought you'd be drinking G & Ts,' Swing said, taking a swipe at Mac's attire.

'What?'

'Nothing.'

'I've had a hard week. I don't need any smartarsery from you.'

Swing didn't respond.

'Right. There's another passport in there. I need you home on it this aft. I've got some sorting out I need you to do then you're back here as fast as your little legs can carry you. And make sure no one sees you, yeah?'

Swing nodded. That was all Swing ever seemed to do when Mac was around, nod. Nod like Mac's own personal nodding dog.

chapter twelve

It was Monday morning and the press had gone into overdrive speculating on what had happened to Joel Baldy in his final minutes. Jodie was fraught. She couldn't believe she'd somehow been dragged into all of this. She'd had to switch her phone off and Leanne was fielding calls from as far afield as China and New York as the press tried to do what the police seemed to be unable to: find the person who had killed Joel Baldy. The police had issued a few statements saying that they were confident that they were getting close to the killer and that they had a number of leads, but Jodie knew first-hand that this was just flannel. They didn't have a clue. If they did they wouldn't keep contacting her and asking her to go over every minute detail of the night.

Jodie jumped out of her car and ran into Leanne's

office. A couple of photographers were waiting and snapped her as she went. She hadn't washed her hair as she was due at a photo shoot in Liverpool later that day. No doubt one of the papers would use the shot and pretend that this was her the morning after the night before, in question.

Jodie fell into Leanne's office. Tony was sitting on the desk. 'Morning. What you doing here?' she asked Tony. He didn't come to the office very often.

'Security guard, aren't I?'

'Have they been trying to get in?' Jodie asked, a feeling of dread crawling over her. She didn't want to be turned into the next national freak show by the press.

'We've had every paper bidding on your story when all of this is over. Can you believe it? You can't speak to anyone yet as that's prejudicial, but after this is all sorted everyone wants to interview you,' Leanne said.

Jodie looked at her sister. Had she had a bang on the head? 'Well, everyone can fuck off, can't they? You think I'm going to go blabbing my mouth to the papers?'

'No, of course I don't. All I'm saying is that at the end of this the papers will make up what they want to anyway. We just need to manage how you come out of it and maybe doing one exclusive to get your side across is the best thing to do.'

'I thought you'd know better than anyone that doing an exclusive is madness. Then you just become someone who had a price and you know something, Leanne? I haven't got a price when it comes to seeing people stabbed through the chest. I'd rather just carry on getting my tits out for my hard-earned cash, thanks very much.'

'Alright, Jode, I'm just giving you your options.'

'My options are to put up and shut up, right?'

Jodie caught Leanne giving Tony a quick glance. 'You know what I mean, don't you, Tone?'

Tony nodded. 'She's right, Leanne, start flogging stories and it's a slippery slope. They'll be rummaging in her bins before she knows it.'

'I know, I'm sorry, I'm just trying to tell you as your manager ...' Leanne said, her sentence tailing off, indicating that her heart wasn't in this hard-arse manager front. Jodie smiled. Leanne was a big softy and did a great job representing her and the other girls, but sometimes she felt that she had to act how other managers acted and it didn't suit her.

'The ball-breaker routine doesn't wash with me, sis,' Jodie said. Considering there was a good five years between the two girls and Jodie was the younger, she had always been bossier and more confident than Leanne. 'So, what's the plan now? Shut up, get on with my work and wait till the phone stops ringing off the hook?'

'Pretty much. What time you in Liverpool?'

'Two,' Jodie said, looking at her watch.

'Tony'll take you.'

'Get lost, I can find my way down the M62.'

'Yes, and so can the paparazzi. Tony, tell her.'

Jodie pretended to huff sulkily but she quite liked the fact that she had her big sister looking out for her.

*

'You seen Mac?' Tracy asked. It was Monday and she hadn't heard anything since his text saying that he'd be back 'soon'.

'He's away,' Markie said matter-of-factly as he leafed through his post.

'That much I'd gathered. He's meant to be my mentor. Like they get on *X Factor*.'

Markie gave his mother an incredulous look. 'What?'

'You know, he's meant to be looking after me on the job.'

'He's had this planned for months. Didn't he say?'

'No, he didn't,' Tracy said, trying to sound as if she was enquiring after a colleague rather than ranting as to why she had been seemingly spurned by a lover. She had tried his phone a number of times but it had gone to answer machine. She was sure that she and Mac had a connection and she wasn't usually wrong about these things. She wasn't usually made a mug of, either, and she wasn't about to start now.

'It's three years since his wife died. He always goes to Palma – they had an apartment there. It's where he scattered her ashes.'

Tracy's eyes narrowed. 'He never said.'

'Well, if you'd checked in with Tammy like you're meant to every week you'd know what our diaries are.'

Tracy looked around at Tammy, who was sitting on reception oblivious to the conversation. 'That bin-head? I come straight to you when I need to know where you are.'

Markie rolled his eyes. 'Jesus, Mum. What's the chip for? She's alright, Tammy, and she runs this place no bother, so it might be an idea to be nicer to her.'

'Nice? I'm fucking lovely!' Tracy said without a hint of irony.

Markie laughed. 'Course you are, Mum, sorry. Just forgot myself for a moment.'

Tracy eyeballed her son. *Sarky twat*, she thought, but decided not to air her opinion right now. 'So Mac, when he pisses off to Palma, does he get in contact?'

'I'm leaving him to it. I know what needs doing when he's away. And let's face it, he sorted me out for two years when I was inside, so it's not like I don't owe him one.'

'Right, so muggins here'll just soldier on doing her own thing without Mac.'

'Bloody hell, Mum, he's only in Majorca. He's not joined the Foreign Legion. He'll be back.'

'Really?' Tracy said angrily, wondering if he'd been thinking of his wife's memory the other afternoon in Blackpool. Somehow she got the distinct feeling that he hadn't been.

'So what d'you make of us all being back in the papers?' Tracy said, itching to talk about Joel Baldy.

'Hardly "us", is it? I've checked in with our Jode and I've got Tony round there making sure that she doesn't get too much shit from the photographers. It'll die down. These things always do.'

'Bloody hell,' Tracy said, not quite believing that Markie didn't have more of an opinion on this story.

'Look. The lad's dead. He was a nob, but I'm not sure he deserved it and I know our Jodie could do without being dragged in and out for questioning. OK?' Markie said, making it clear that he didn't want to discuss this further.

'I think Len did it,' Tracy said contentiously.

Markie raised an eyebrow. 'Len?'

'Metcalfe.'

'And what makes you think that?'

'Because he's a fat little turd.' Tracy couldn't help herself. This was exactly what she thought of Len Metcalfe and she wasn't about to bite her tongue now.

Markie sighed. 'Eloquent and reasoned as ever, Tracy.'

'What d'you want me to say? "I think he's a lovely bloke"? You don't know the reputation he used to have around here.'

'I've heard a few things.'

'You have, have you? What like?'

'The usual shit that people talk round here when they've nothing better to do.'

'Well, anything you've heard about him is probably bob-on. Don't let him fool you with his

Mr Pillar of the Community routine. Once an arsehole always an arsehole.'

'What've you got on today then?' Markie nodded at the stacked file of papers that Tracy had under her arm. He obviously wasn't interested in his mum's feelings about Len Metcalfe.

'Some mouthy cows up our way. I'm quite looking forward to it. Had one the other day trying to offer me some sovereigns that she'd nicked from the warehouse where she works picking and packing.'

'What did you say?'

'I told her they weren't legal tender any more, that I'd be back this week and I didn't want her trying to pay me in gold coffee beans either.'

Markie smiled.

'What you smiling at?' Tracy asked.

'Nothing,' Markie said.

'I'm good at this, aren't I?' Tracy said.

'Don't fish for compliments, Mum. It's not becoming.'

*

Markie was walking along the Bradington canal; he needed some air. He had to hand it to his mother; she seemed to have found her vocation in life. She was an asset to the business but some of her views were beginning to rankle. Until now he'd only ever had to see his mum when he chose fit. And a couple of times a year was enough to dilute Tracy's brand of honesty to something approaching palatable. Now, it was like having some deranged pundit in his face every day with her constant barrage of opinions. He'd had to draw the line when she had started on about Len Metcalfe. He didn't think for a second that he'd had anything to do with Joel's murder, but mud like that could stick and Markie felt that his mother needed to rein her opinions in.

Another thing he hadn't needed was his mother drilling down on him this morning with her sharp-as-a-tack eyes. Markie really did hope that Mac was in Palma but he couldn't be sure. He had received a voicemail from him the previous day saying that he'd had to go away; he had a lot of thinking to do. It was the anniversary of Mac's wife's death, that was for sure, but Markie couldn't one hundred per cent attest to the fact that this was why Mac was away. Markie had decided that he wasn't going to ask any questions for the time being. He had returned Mac's call, but it had gone straight to voicemail, giving no clue as to whether Mac was out of the country or not. He'd left a message saying, 'Mac, it's Markie.

Hope everything's OK. If it's not, call me, won't you? Anyway, meantime if anyone asks I'm saying you're at the old place in Palma, yeah? See you, mate.' He could be an odd sentimental old bugger sometimes, Mac. Markie just hoped that that was all there was to it. And even if it wasn't he was going to have to deal with it. He couldn't very well pick the phone up and report him as a missing person.

The business itself was running fine; Markie couldn't complain. It was just a constant nagging stress but it would be the same whatever Markie was doing and he'd take stress over boredom any day of the week – two years in Strangeways had seen to that. For a time he'd felt that he and Mac were doing everything on their own, but now he felt as if there was a team back around him: Tony, Leanne's boyfriend, was now firmly back in his employ, and Swing, Markie's old best mate who had slept with his ex and been ostracised by Markie, had recently returned cap in hand. Markie had told him he didn't want to have anything to do with him but if Mac wanted to work with him then fine. Swing had kept an extremely low profile since. Markie knew he was doing some door duties for Mac and the occasional knocking of heads when required but other than that he wasn't interested in what Swing did as long as he stayed out of his way. And then there was Tracy. His mother was so far doing a sterling job and seemed to be in the office bright-eyed and bushy-tailed at half eight every morning. Markie had never thought he'd see the day; Tracy had never been a reliable mother so he was finding it hard to come to terms with the fact that she was turning out to be a reliable employee.

So until recently Markie had had a good feeling about everything, but today he had a sense of foreboding and he knew to trust his instincts; they had always served him well. The trouble was he could place where it was coming from, he just couldn't place quite what it was. It could be Mac, it could be his mum's increasing involvement in his affairs, or it could be any one of a number of things playing on his mind and vying for his attention. Markie decided that he needed more than a walk along the canal to clear his head, but time off was a luxury he couldn't afford at the moment. Especially not with Mac going AWOL.

*

Tracy's first port of call in Bolingbroke was near Canterbury Avenue, where the Metcalfes lived. It was no coincidence that her rounds had brought her here. She had been following the media furore with interest since Joel's death the other night and was glad to see that speculation of her family's involvement was kept to a minimum even though everyone, including her, wanted to know exactly what Jodie had seen. The main focus had been on Len Metcalfe: everyone seemed to think that any father in his right mind would want Baldy dead if the speculation was true and he had been beating Charly.

Tracy was enjoying Len's fifteen minutes of infamy. If only there was a way for her to prove that he'd had something to do with the murder, but that was never going to happen. Her detective skills didn't stretch to much and she didn't think the local constabulary would welcome the intervention on this high-profile case from Tracy Crompton, the first person over forty to hold an ASBO in Bradington. She wouldn't have minded but she didn't think she even deserved the ASBO; it had been Kent's idea to have a party. People had got wind of it from far and wide and when Tracy found some woman rummaging through her jewellery box at three in the morning, she didn't think she could be totally held responsible for dragging her into the street and taking to her with a bin lid.

Standing at the top of Canterbury Avenue, Tracy could see Len's house and a couple of cars parked across the road that Tracy assumed – having been papped herself on account of her daughter Leanne's previous infamy – belonged to photographers. She walked towards the house with her files under her arm. As she passed the parked cars there was no sign of Len but a journalist jumped out of the car when he recognised her. A photographer leapt out of the passenger seat and took her picture. Tracy was delighted to be wearing a suit. Any other pictures that had been printed in the press had always made her look as if someone had just dragged her out of bed and straight through a hedge.

'What do you think of all this then, Tracy?' the journalist asked. Must be from a tabloid, she thought, using her name and pretending to be all matey.

'No comment,' Tracy said. She'd always wanted to say that. She'd always wanted to say a lot of things but usually her mouth ran away with her and she ended up saying something abusive.

'All dressed up and nowhere to go?' the journalist asked. Tracy wasn't about to rise to it. She knew that these hacks could say far nastier things than that to provoke a response. Leanne had once told her about a time she had been called a slut by a journalist just so that the photographer could get a picture of her looking angry. Tracy wouldn't have been responsible for where she'd have shoved the camera if she'd been there.

'I have, actually. I'm working, if you don't mind.'

'Heard anything from Len Metcalfe?'

Tracy thought for a paranoid moment that this woman might know that there was a past connection between her and Len. Then she realised that she was just trying to get any quote she could. 'Why would I?' Tracy asked simply.

'Your lad used to go out with Charly.'

'Doesn't mean Len's crying on the blower to me every time he's arrested for suspected murder.' Tracy glared at the journalist. 'Anyway, if you don't mind, some of us have got a decent day's work to do.'

The woman laughed and got back in the car. Tracy waltzed on down the road as if she owned the place and, judging by the amount of outstanding debt owed to Markie and Mac, it appeared for the time being she did.

Tracy's thoughts were still with the journalist when she saw a woman walking towards her. She wouldn't have recognised her at first if it hadn't been for the walk. She'd always had a walk that suggested she thought she should be strutting down a catwalk in Paris rather than slumming it in Bolingbroke, but the once shapely figure was now bloated and pear-shaped. Tracy couldn't believe her eyes: it was Shirley Metcalfe.

Shirley obviously saw Tracy and was about to duck out of her way but then realised she couldn't get out of the meeting and had to brazen it out. Tracy slowed as they neared one another and the two women finally came face to face.

'Well, well,' Shirley said, 'look what the cat's dragged in.'

'Well, well,' said Tracy in response, 'look what's eaten everything the cat's dragged in.'

'Don't get mouthy, Tracy; you know it just gets you into trouble,' Shirley said, trying to stare Tracy out.

'I won't bother taking advice from someone who fucks off and leaves their family to rot, thanks very much,' Tracy said, enjoying a rare moment occupying the moral high ground.

'And you're Mother of the Year?'

'Never said I was, but I'm here, aren't I?' She looked down on Shirley, having the advantage of a good three inches on the woman.

'Bet your Charly's worth a penny or two now that husband of hers is dead.'

'What you suggesting?'

'I'm suggesting nowt. Just saying, funny time for you to turn back up.'

Shirley didn't miss a beat. 'You still selling stories on your Leanne? I read about that. Nice touch.'

Tracy wasn't in the mood for lectures on how to conduct herself from someone like Shirley Metcalfe. 'I think you'd better watch your mouth round these parts. There's a lot of people who won't like the fact you're back.'

'Really? Who?' Shirley asked.

'My lot, for a start.'

Shirley laughed. 'Your *lot*? The Cromptons?' She didn't have to say anything else; Tracy knew what she was thinking. Her scummy lot had been a force to be reckoned with for years; not any more.

'Ask anyone on this estate and they'll tell you, things have changed. Our Markie runs the show, so if you're thinking of sticking around, which I'm sure you're not – first sign of a better offer and you'll be off – then you'd be well advised to be a bit nicer to me.'

Shirley made to walk off. Tracy couldn't help herself; she couldn't just have the last word, she had to have the last paragraph. 'You seen Charly yet?' Shirley slowed but didn't turn around. 'You haven't, have you? Well, she's had a week of it, hasn't she?'

'What's that supposed to mean?' Shirley stopped.

'She's been telling everyone you're dead for years: husband in the morgue and a mother back from the dead all in the space of a weekend. That's something to get your head around.'

Shirley walked away, picking up speed as she went. Tracy smiled to herself. One nil to me, she thought, as she watched the larger-than-life girth of Shirley Metcalfe sashay off down the street, a little less confidently than it had approached.

*

Shirley walked along the side of her old house and sat on the rickety garden bench that had been there since she and Len had moved in. She looked down at her hands. They were shaking. Tracy bloody Crompton, she thought. Of all the people to see; she hated that woman. Tracy had been a year above Shirley at school and had made her life a misery. She hadn't liked Shirley because she was pretty (which had never made sense to Shirley as Tracy had been a knockout when she was younger). But

Tracy was just one of those mouthy girls who couldn't help herself.

It hadn't helped that when she and Len originally got together he still held a torch for Tracy. And Tracy wasn't shy about announcing the fact to the entire estate. She never got to the bottom of what had happened there, she hadn't really wanted to find out if she was honest, but they had had a rocky, intense relationship, she knew that much. And as much as she tried with Len over the years, Shirley had never felt that she could match up to Tracy. In the end she'd got on with cooking the tea and washing the pots and had stopped trying to create any magnetism between her and her husband. She had loved Len but she was never quite sure how much he loved her back.

When Leanne, Tracy's daughter, had briefly become the centre of tabloid attention over a year ago, Shirley couldn't believe it. She was living miles away from Bradington but could get a sneaky look at what was going on on the estate. Tracy had made great tabloid fodder with her 'fuck you' attitude and her interesting approach to parenting. And then when it transpired that she had been feeding stories to the papers about her own daughter, the moral majority were up in arms. Shirley had pored over every paper at the time; anything for signs that maybe Tracy and Len had somehow got back together. So it had come as a surprise to see Charly's name mentioned in connection with the Cromptons rather than Len's. She had been dating Scott Crompton and had traded him in for a better model in the shape of Joel Baldy.

Shirley had been so homesick reading these articles, reminding her of her old life and making her think about what she had now – which wasn't much – and what she had left behind. She didn't have an answer for why she hadn't come home earlier. She had wanted to, but every time she thought about it the reality of having to face up to her abandonment of her own family kept her away.

She looked around the garden. Nothing had changed here. There was still a potting shed, something Len had erected in a bid to be the next Alan Titchmarsh, but that had only ever been used to store junk. There were flowerless flower beds and a little paved area that was neat and tidy; Len had always been almost fetishistic about weeds. She thought about the summers that she had spent in this garden.

There was something about the past, Shirley thought, that always made her remember it on a sunny summer's day, just as the light is fading and all seems well with the world. What she had to remember was that this garden had felt like a prison for many years. This was where she hung the washing out, where the kids played as they weren't allowed to go out on the street (there was a halfway house two doors down for young offenders that were being reintroduced into the community but weren't exactly there with the socialisation as far as she and Len had been concerned). Her life had seemed like one long round of watching *This Morning*, cleaning and sleepless nights. She had even turned to drink for a spell but that just made her like everyone else around here as far as she could see: pissed, maudlin and wanting to make the kids dance to 'Under Pressure' when they'd never even heard of it. The drunken mother routine wasn't a look she liked in other people and she despised it in herself. She'd had ambition once. It had been aimless, but it had been there – plain ambition. She had wanted to see the world, go on holidays with her family, get out of Bolingbroke once in a while. But that had all faded as she became this invisible woman who occupied 29a Canterbury Avenue.

Len had never listened. No matter how often she told him that she was fed up or lonely he just thought that she was being sensitive and expecting too much from life. Len was a realist. He'd been in prison and had come out with the attitude that anything was better than that. 'My glass is half full,' he'd once said to Shirley.

'What of, piss?' she'd replied, leading to one of their arguments that in turn led to days of silences.

Sitting on the bench now, she couldn't quite work out what she had come back for. It certainly wasn't this house, or a ready-made family life, as her children had grown up and moved on. But for some hard-to-define reason, she was glad to be back. And the one person she wanted to see more than anyone was Charly. She just wasn't sure that her daughter would feel the same way. She'd soon find out though: she was going to get the address from Len and get a taxi to Charly's place. And she was going to pay the fare with the little bit of money that she'd brought with her; the only money that Shirley had to her name.

*

Charly was sitting in the wingback swivel chair that Joel had insisted on letting his interior designer buy because the man had informed him it was cool.

Charly had pointed out at the time that it might be 'cool' but it was about as comfortable as sitting on a spike. Now that Joel wasn't here, she didn't want to get out of the pointless designer chair. It was another fading connection to him that she was desperate to cling to.

The family liaison officer who had been assigned to Charly was sitting opposite her. Her name was Carol and Charly couldn't help feeling sorry for her that this was her job; constantly surrounded by other people's grief.

'Would you like a cup of tea?' Charly asked.

Carol smiled gently. 'That's the tenth cup of tea you've offered me today.'

Charly looked at the floor. 'Sorry.'

'Don't apologise. It's hard to know what to say to anyone, isn't it?'

Charly nodded. She felt as if she had been taken out of the world of polite conversation and was now forever to be the person who was defined by the shocking events of the past week. Managing to ask someone repeatedly if they fancied a cup of tea felt like progress.

Carol had been explaining to Charly what she could expect to happen now. Charly hadn't been able to bring herself to identify the body so Joel's father had flown back from Spain and had confirmed that it was Joel. Charly had met with him briefly but there was something detached about the man that made Charly feel uncomfortable. She had wanted to fall into his arms and cry about Joel, to ask him for every bit of information he had about his son, as if by talking about him she was somehow keeping Joel's spirit alive. But he had seemed closed off and quiet. Charly thought for a moment that maybe he thought of her as a gold-digger – someone who'd just wanted his son for his money – but that would have been rich coming from a man who decorated his bar in pictures of Joel to attract British tourists and had only recently tapped Joel up for a fifty thousand pound 'loan' which Joel had told Charly he would never see again. Or maybe he just didn't want to share his loss with someone he hardly knew. Either way Charly felt that he didn't particularly want to talk to her and that he was more concerned with the practical arrangements.

Carol explained that an inquest would be set up into the cause of death. Once the cause of death and where the police investigation was currently up to was recorded, the inquest would be adjourned whilst the criminal investigation could continue. The words felt syrupy and remote to Charly. All that she could think of was Joel and why someone would want to murder him.

'When will the funeral be?' Charly asked. The idea of leaving the house at the moment was a daunting prospect, never mind leaving it to attend the funeral, but she knew it was something she had to do.

'It may be a long time before the body is released for burial,' Carol said, reaching out her hand and touching Charly's.

Charly looked at her. 'What?' She couldn't be serious, could she? 'How long? We can't all sit around waiting for weeks, can we? Is this what happens?'

'I'm sorry, Charly, I really am.'

Charly stood up suddenly. 'Who did this to him? Why?'

'We'll do everything we can to find out.'

'Who would be so evil?' She began to sob. She hadn't cried for the first few days but now she felt like it was all she did.

Carol let her cry. Charly felt foolish showing such emotion in front of this woman but there wasn't anyone else to cry to. 'They think it's my dad, don't they?' she asked, wiping her nose.

'I'm not involved in the police investigation.'

'I didn't just mean the police, I meant the entire country.' Charly had caught a glimpse of a tabloid yesterday and hadn't realised how much attention Joel's murder had grabbed. She felt sick when she saw the picture of her dad on the front page.

'Your father's been released. I think it would do you some good to see him.'

Charly shook her head. She wasn't ready to see him at the moment. She felt too confused by everything that was going on.

There was a gentle knock at the door and Terry came in. 'Someone here to see you, Charly, and she's not taking no for an answer.' Charly looked confused. Standing out in the garden she could see someone straining their neck trying to look into the house. Charly felt her stomach lurch. The figure was older and chubbier, but there was no mistaking who it was: her mum Shirley. Charly put her hand to her mouth. 'Oh my God,' she said, almost to herself.

'Everything OK?' Carol asked, looking round.

'Shall I tell her to go away? She barged through the paps without a care in the world.'

'No, let her in.' She felt sick.

Charly had imagined countless scenarios where she and her mother would be reunited over the years. But as angry or relieved as she'd always pictured herself to be at such a meeting, she could never have imagined that the next time she saw her mother would be under such fraught circumstances.

Shirley walked into the room and looked at Charly. Charly stayed in her seat. Carol stood up, sensing that now was definitely a good time to leave. Terry looked at Charly. 'If you need me, love, I'll be outside,' he said. Terry left and Carol followed, leaving Charly in a room with her mother for the first time in over a decade.

'I didn't know if I'd find this place, but it was quite straightforward,' Shirley said, jamming her hands in her coat pockets.

Charly looked her mother up and down; she'd changed. She looked beaten down somehow.

'That it?' Charly asked. There was no heat in her voice; she didn't have the energy. 'Is that your opening gambit?'

'There's so much to say that I don't know *what* to say, if I'm honest.'

'What about the weather? Shall we have a little chat about that?'

Shirley moved towards her daughter, but Charly pulled her legs into her chest to ensure that she was sitting in an impenetrable ball. 'I'm sorry,' Shirley said, sitting down and inspecting the palms of her hands.

'Really? Pick your moments, don't you, *Mum*?' Charly said, using the word to spear Shirley.

'What does that mean?'

'Mum? That's a word I wouldn't be slinging around in relation to you. What's the Shirley Metcalfe definition of the word? *Someone who fucks off when the going gets tough*?' Charly knew she was being a bitch but she didn't care. She wanted to lash out at someone and there wasn't a better person on this planet deserving of her anger as far as she was concerned. If Shirley had turned up prior to this weekend, Charly knew that she would have been far easier on her. That she would have been grateful, even after all this time, for her mum to have come home in order to see her family. But now she just wanted to know what her mum wanted and why she had done precisely what she pleased for the past ten years.

Shirley looked at Charly. 'Things haven't been easy for me. I know you're not interested in hearing it, but they haven't. And I've wanted to come back loads of times but I've never had the bottle until now. I didn't intend for it to be the weekend that the world's press are camped on yours and your dad's doorstep – it's just the way that things have turned out.'

'And were you with him when you told the police you were?'

Shirley paused for what Charly thought was too long before nodding. 'Yes.'

'You weren't, were you? You're lying.'

'I was; we were talking.'

'At half four in the morning?' Charly wasn't stupid. She might not have seen Shirley for ten years but she knew when she was lying.

'It's been a long time.'

'You don't have to tell me that,' Charly shot back.

'We had a lot to talk about. Your dad didn't kill Joel.' Shirley looked squarely at her daughter. 'Although he would have been well within his rights to.'

'What?' Charly asked, astonished. 'Within his rights?'

'The lad was beating you, according to your dad. What were you doing in hospital?'

Charly couldn't believe her mother's audacity. 'I loved him!' she screamed. 'He wasn't a bad person; we just rubbed each other up the wrong way, that's all. Not that it's any of your bloody business.'

'Looks like he'd done more than rub you up the

wrong way. Look at your face. You're bruised. And, if what your dad says is true, you're lucky to have come out of it at all.'

'Well, he would say that, wouldn't he, Dad? He didn't like him,' Charly said, blindly defending Joel. 'Anyway, why are we sitting here slagging off someone who can't even defend himself? Let's get back to you, eh Mum? Tell me what you've been doing for the last ten years.'

'I went to London, lived in Tooting.' Shirley paused as if she was about to say something but then pulled back. 'I fell on hard times.'

'The violin routine,' Charly said wearily. 'And at no point did you think to ring, see how I was, see how Jimmy was. See how the twins were, even. Mind you, why you'd give a shit about them when you couldn't even be arsed with your own kids is a mystery. You just did your own thing down there and waited till now to reappear, is that it?'

'It's not like that,' Shirley persisted. 'I wanted to see you, I wanted to contact you.' She opened her mouth to say something else, but quickly fell silent as if she'd thought better of it again. This time Charly noticed.

'What?'

'Nothing.'

'You were going to say something. Spit it out.'

'I didn't think your dad wanted me. I wasn't thinking straight.'

'Understatement of the century. So it's Dad's fault now, is it?'

'I never said that.'

'Do you have any idea what he went through when you left? Do you have any notion in that dyed blonde head of yours what it was like for him?'

'Of course I do. It had been my life for long enough, hadn't it?'

'I mean you leaving, not the day-to-day getting on with life with kids. What was so bad about us, Mum?' Charly asked. Her voice cracked. She didn't want it to, she hadn't wanted to show her mum any emotion, but there was little chance of that today.

'Nothing was so bad about you. I loved you all. I still love you all.'

'Why, then?'

Shirley shook her head. 'I haven't got a decent answer.'

Charly glared at her mother for a minute. It was hard to find the words to respond to such an admission. 'When I was fourteen I was leathered at school by some girl called Jenny Williams. Battered me up and down the playground for being "too pretty", which was nice of her. And I knew I could go to my dad or our Jimmy and get it sorted out, but dads and brothers don't sort things like that out, mums do. And you weren't there. I cried myself to sleep about that for days and it wasn't even because I was bothered about her battering me, it was because you weren't there to stick up for me.' Shirley hung her head. 'Do you know what people used to say about you at school?' Shirley didn't look up. 'They used to say that you were a prostitute and you'd run off with your pimp. Something else for them to laugh at me about.'

'I'm so sorry.'

'So you've said, but you don't know what it was like.' Charly looked at her mum. She wanted to hate her so much but there was a part of her that was glad she was there, even if she was using her as a battering ram. 'And now all this has happened and you turn up ...' Charly could feel the tears building up again; she tried to fight them, to swallow them back, but she couldn't. She began to cry. Shirley got up from the sofa and went over to the chair in which Charly was sitting. As she cried she felt her mum's hand on her knee. Then she felt her pull her forward to hug her, gently stroking her hair. Charly kept on sobbing and stopped talking. She needed this, someone to hold her and listen to her cry. As she was sitting there she realised that, despite everything, her mum was the only person in the world that she wanted with her right now.

chapter thirteen

Jodie hadn't dared to switch her phone on for the past four days. Journalists had somehow got hold of her number and had blocked up her voicemail with requests for comments on what she'd witnessed.

She was in the middle of a photo shoot on a blustery hilltop in the Yorkshire Dales. Jodie was feeling less like Cathy and more like a drowned rat. The photographer had promised her that the weather would make the pictures look windswept and moody, but the last thing that Jodie wanted to do – this week of all weeks – was stand around in a decidedly unsexy place having to look sexy. As she stood pressed against a rock, her head thrown back and her gossamer top ripped provocatively to the nipple, she could see two women heading up the limestone steps to where she was teetering. Jodie grabbed a towel; they'd been assured privacy for the hour that they needed to get the right shot but these women were heading towards her and the photographer, bold as brass. One thing was for sure, they didn't look like ramblers who were stamping their feet about their right to the use of public footpaths at all times.

'Jodie, can we have a word?' the first woman asked.

Jodie looked at her photographer. *What was going on?* 'Depends.'

'We're from the *Globe* and …'

Jodie looked at the pair. She had to tread carefully. The *Globe* newspaper had given her her first break and was still a large contributing factor to her income. But she was damned if they were sneaking up on her like this. She smelled a rat. Her photographer had gone quiet. If he had known nothing about this he'd be telling them to take themselves back to where they came from as quickly as possible, but he was inspecting the lens on his camera as if this somehow negated all that was going on around him.

'Did you tell them we were going to be here?' Jodie demanded. He looked guiltily at her and shrugged. Although he was freelance, he too got a lot of work through the *Globe*; he was probably only doing what he thought was necessary to ensure future work. It didn't stop Jodie wanting to kill him though. 'Right,' she said, pulling her jeans on and quickly slipping into the jumper and coat that she'd been fantasising about as she stood there sodden. 'End of shoot. I'm not making any comment. If you want to talk to me then you need to go through my agency.'

'Leanne told us you were here.'

Jodie faltered, but only for a split second. 'Pull the other one.' She knew that Leanne would never do that without informing her first. No, it was definitely the photographer. She tramped away from the three, making her way down the five hundred or so steps that led to the bottom of the sheer cliff face and towards the car park. Jodie wasn't happy. The photographer, who had hastily packed his kit up, was hot on her heels, as were the journalists.

One of them was a step behind Jodie all the way down. 'Can you tell us just a little bit about what it was like to see Joel dead in the hotel room?'

Jodie didn't answer. She didn't want to think about it: it had been horrific.

'How do you feel about the fact that Charly probably stands to make a lot of money from this?

Weren't you and her good friends? Rumour has it that on the night she and Joel met you were there and that he spurned you for her.'

Jodie wanted to wheel around and shout at the woman to get her facts straight, but she knew that this was exactly what she wanted: a quote of any kind so that they could splash it across the front of the paper that they'd got an exclusive with her. Jodie faced forward and kept trudging down the steps, wishing to God the photo shoot had been in a studio.

'What do you think to your brother's arrest?' the woman asked. Jodie stopped momentarily but didn't look around; she was putting all of her energies into not faltering on the steps, which were proving tricky to negotiate, and she wasn't about to give the woman the satisfaction of rising to the bait. *Poor Scott*, she thought. She had known it was probably only a matter of time before – as Charly's ex – he was hauled in for questioning. When Jodie didn't answer the journalist continued, 'The police seem to think that Markie had some kind of relationship with Charly. Know anything about that?'

Markie? Jodie thought, alarmed. They must have the wrong name. She certainly didn't know anything about it. Not that she was about to tell these women anything.

'He's been in overnight. The police don't keep you in for nothing, do they?'

They do where I come from, Jodie thought. But again, she didn't say anything. Her mind was racing. Why had Markie been arrested? She was really struggling to keep her mouth shut and they were still about twenty minutes away from the car.

Jodie put her head down and pressed on. It might be the longest twenty minutes of her life, but there was no way these women were getting a word out of her.

*

Len was cleaning the optics and the lines for the beer. One good thing about working at the club was that all non-members had to be signed in and as people around here were a loyal bunch, no one was signing in anyone they didn't know. Too many journalists had tried their hand at getting in over the past few days and all of them received short shrift. Even the ones that did get through the door were swiftly escorted off the premises by Ron the security guard once their cover was blown. But that didn't mean that he wasn't on his guard: every time the door opened he looked up and panicked, thinking that he was about to face another grilling that he could do without.

The door at the far end of the room opened and Len looked up, hoping to see Marge or one of the other women who worked in the club but instead saw a small figure wearing a cap pulled down over their eyes. He couldn't work out if it was a man or a woman from where he was standing. Len finished replacing the bottle of gin he was dusting and watched the stranger walk towards him.

'Dad,' she said, stepping up to the bar.

'Charly! I've tried calling. I was going to come to the house, but my lawyer said I'd …'

'Your lawyer?' Charly interrupted him angrily. 'Your *lawyer*? Is that what we've come down to? My husband gets knifed to death and you don't come and see me because your *lawyer* says you can't?'

Len stepped from round the bar and went to hug his daughter. She stepped back from him and said sternly, 'Don't.' Len backed away.

'I didn't do anything, Charly.'

She couldn't look at him. 'Where were you on Friday night?'

'I was with your mum.'

'Tell the police what you want, Dad,' Charly said, pulling her cap off and placing it on the bar. She looked drawn. 'But tell me the truth. If Mum had just turned up out of the blue in the middle of the night, you wouldn't even have heard her knocking on the door.'

'I never said she turned up in the middle of the night.'

'So go on,' Charly said angrily, 'guide me through it. After you left me at the hospital you came home and put your feet up.' Charly looked at her dad. He didn't need goading on this subject.

'Did I buggery. I went looking for that bloody Joel. The state of you. No man should ever treat a woman the way he treated you. He could have killed you.'

'So you killed him, is that right?' Charly's eyes sparked with hatred. As close as he and his daughter had always been, right now he felt like he was speaking with a stranger.

'No, I did not,' Len said angrily. Then added, 'Someone should've, but I didn't.' Charly looked at her father in horror as he continued. 'What? It's the truth, isn't it? What sort of father would I be to find my daughter beaten up like that and think that the lad that did it deserved a second chance?

Or fifth chance, or however many chances he was on.'

'The papers say that your car was spotted in Manchester at 3am.'

'I didn't kill him, Charly,' Len said again.

Charly suddenly flew at her dad. He caught her arms before she could do anything. She struggled to get free but he pulled at her wrists, trying to get her to stop struggling and make her calm down. 'I don't believe you!' she shouted.

'There's not a lot I can do about that.'

'You wanted him dead. I hate you!' Len looked around to make sure that no one else was party to this family rift.

'Don't say that, love. You're angry.'

'And you're a murderer,' Charly said, taking the opportunity of Len's shocked reaction to pull her wrists free. She ran out of the room crying.

Len looked on after her for a second, hoping that all of this was just shock and she would come round and realise that he was nothing of the sort. He hurried to the main entrance of the club, just in time to see Charly jump into the back of a smart black car, as a few photographers took her picture. Seeing a startled Len at the door they turned their attentions away from the blacked-out windows of the vehicle. Len quickly slammed the door and headed back inside.

*

Markie slid his shades on and slumped into the driver's seat of his Range Rover. A lone photographer was at the passenger window taking shots of him as he drove away from the police station. Markie didn't have the energy to get out and insert the camera somewhere painful as he would have liked to. He needed to get to the office and change cars. The previous day had been interminable. The police had arrested him at 6am. Markie could never understand why they couldn't wait until a sociable hour; it wasn't like he was going anywhere. He had then spent the next day and night being held for questioning. It wasn't like on the TV, where a suspect was held and constantly questioned until they went mad and cracked under the pressure, demanding to sign anything if the police would just give them a few moments' sleep. It was the opposite. Red tape saw to that. So Markie had been at the hands of officers who had to make sure all of the correct forms were filled out, that they weren't making any cock-ups in their line of questioning that could, in future, lead to the case being thrown out of court and that Markie got the right amount of breaks due to him. Markie would have preferred one of the old IRA internment-type grillings; at least they gathered some momentum.

The police had got nowhere with him. Markie knew exactly what to say. And what he kept saying over and over again was that on the night of Joel Baldy's murder he hadn't been anywhere near the footballer or the hotel he was staying in, or his sister Jodie for that matter.

Then the police produced what they considered to be damning evidence to suggest that Markie might have a motive for Joel's murder. Markie had looked at the file, Joel's loan file, with several missed payments, and been truly gobsmacked. He genuinely hadn't realised that what the police were suggesting had been anything to do with him. Mac looked after all of that. And he'd gone away for the week claiming to need to attend to business in the north-east. The last thing Markie had wanted to do was drop Mac in it and admit that he knew nothing about what he was being shown. But that would have shown a weakness and a lack of control over his own affairs. He felt that he had offered them enough to get himself off the hook but not implicate Mac for the moment. The police had informed him that they wished to question Mac. But Mac had flown out of the country on Friday afternoon, according to their records, meaning he wasn't a suspect in the case.

The only thing was, Markie was fairly sure that Mac had been in the country until Saturday. Not that he was about to tell the police.

Markie pulled up in front of his mum's house. It was lunchtime and she was working in the Bolingbroke area all week so chances were she'd nipped home for lunch. He walked to the front door and let himself in.

'Don't bloody knock then,' Tracy said, clutching her chest to indicate that Markie's arrival had surprised her. When she saw that it was Markie she asked angrily, 'Where the bloody hell have you been?'

'In the nick.'

'What?'

'You heard.'

'What about your one phone call. Could've let me know.'

'"How are you son?" I'm fine, Mum, bit sleep deprived but thanks for asking.'

'Don't give me that. Mac's rolling around in his ex-missus's ashes, you'd gone AWOL, what do you want me to say? I'm left holding the fort and it's hardly like I know what I'm doing – I even had to speak to that Tammy. And anyway, I only started working for you to help you out.'

Markie sneered. 'You only started working for us because you knew you could get paid to be on a power trip. Busman's holiday for you, that, isn't it?'

His mother glared at him. 'What they haul you in for, anyway?'

'What do you think? They thought I'd killed him, didn't they?'

'You? Joel Baldy? Why would you do that?'

'Well, they've got a few reasons up their sleeves, haven't they, Tracy?' Markie glared at his mother. She cut her look away from him. He wasn't going to put words in her mouth. He wanted her to come clean and say what they both knew. Markie stood in deafening silence, staring at his mother. The silence was broken as Kent entered the room.

'Markie Mark and the Funky Bunch!' Kent exclaimed.

Markie ignored Kent and looked at his mother. 'Am I meant to be in the fucking mood for him now as well?' Kent slunk past Markie and Tracy. Tracy allowed her eyes to momentarily meet her son's. She was giving nothing away – he could have strangled her. *Why couldn't she just come clean for once in her life?* he thought.

'You want a drink?' Tracy asked, trying to diffuse the situation.

Markie didn't respond; he couldn't be bothered. He turned on his heel and slammed out of the house. He wasn't in the mood for his mum; there was someone else he needed to see.

*

Terry pulled the car into the driveway. 'She might be sleeping. If it were me that's what I'd do. Sleep through it all and hope when I woke up that it was just some terrible nightmare.'

'Thanks for the lift,' Markie said gratefully, patting Terry on the shoulder. He had parked his own car near an old building that he once owned and had arranged for Terry to pick him up so that he wasn't followed.

Markie walked into the lounge and looked around. He'd never been to the sprawling Hale Barns residence before. 'Hello,' he shouted through into the dining room. There was no answer. Markie pushed the door open to the large oak hallway and shouted again. 'Hello!'

Charly came out of a room dressed in pyjamas and a dressing gown. She looked tiny to him. He walked towards her and pulled her close briefly. 'How are you?'

She waited a moment as if the question was taking its time to register. 'Shit,' she said finally. 'And you?'

'I've been better. Spent the last God knows how long being questioned.'

'Oh no, Markie, why?' Charly asked, putting her hand to her mouth.

'They know about us.'

Charly squirmed uneasily.

'How?'

'How do the cops know anything? I don't know, they just do.'

'Shit,' Charly said, almost to herself.

'But that's the least of your worries, isn't it?'

Charly nodded numbly.

'We need to get something straight, Charly. I was this close –' He held up his thumb and index finger and joined them, indicating no distance at all '– from giving him the hiding he deserved.' Charly looked at him with wounded horror. Seeing her reaction, Markie made himself clear. 'No, it wasn't me. But that doesn't mean to say I'm not glad he's dead.'

'You can't say that!' she shouted. 'I love him.' Markie walked towards her and she lashed out with her fists. He pulled her to him, embracing her as she struggled. 'I loved him,' she wailed, as if the fact that Joel was now forever to be a thing of the past had just dawned on her.

'And he was a right bastard to you.' Markie was knackered and as much as he wanted to protect Charly's feelings, and realised she was going through a really rough time, he knew she needed to wake up sooner or later to the narrow escape she'd had. 'I'm not saying you'll be thankful that any of this happened; I wouldn't wish this on anyone. But I think you'll realise that he was a nasty bastard and you weren't the only person he was a nasty bastard to.'

'That's what Dad said.'

'Did he?'

'I was horrible to him. I accused him of doing it,' she said.

'Do you think he had anything to do with it? I don't, for the record.'

'I don't know what to think.'

'I think you need to start thinking about yourself and bollocks to everyone and everything else.'

'That's a lot easier said than done,' Charly said morosely.

They both fell into silence for a moment. 'Does your mum know about any of this?' Charly asked finally.

'Mum?' Markie said, confused for a moment. Gone were the days when he ran to Tracy to cry about the fact that he'd been arrested. Suddenly the penny dropped. She didn't mean about the arrest, she meant about Charly and Markie.

'No. And she's not going to, if I have my way.' Markie was adamant. But he wasn't sure if his way was going to come into it. This whole situation was beginning to feel decidedly out of his control. Mac wasn't returning his calls and the police seemed to think that Markie had a good enough reason to want Joel dead. It would only be a matter of time before they built a case against him if they didn't get a more suitable suspect.

'I think she has a right to know,' Charly said, taking a tissue from a box in the middle of the coffee table and blowing her nose.

Markie's eyes narrowed. There was no way he needed a hysterical Charly shooting her mouth off to his mother. He was fine with the way things were; he didn't need Tracy in on this as well. She'd find out when he was ready to tell her and not before. He'd spent long enough having to listen to his mum's lies and bullshit without having to roll over and tell her everything he knew just because Charly was on edge. 'She hasn't got any rights in this. She's just my bloody mother, that's all, end of.'

Charly fell into an armchair. 'Don't shout at me,' she said pathetically, dissolving into tears again. Markie looked at her. He didn't want to come across as a nasty piece of work in all of this, but his rope was beginning to unravel. He decided to chance the subject and get things onto a more practical keel. 'Have you called a solicitor to look at what you're entitled to? You've got the stuff that Joel signed, haven't you?'

'I'm scared.'

'What of?'

'I put all the money stuff in order so quickly, they might think it's part of a set-up. That I did it and wanted something to happen to Joel ... They've asked me loads of questions.' Charly was finding it difficult to finish a sentence without crying.

'But you've told them nothing?' Markie ran his fingers through his hair and turned his back on Charly, needing a moment to think.

'There's nothing to tell, is there?' she asked desperately.

This was true as far as Markie knew with regard to Charly. He had advised her to get her financial arrangements in order, but because Joel was so volatile and unpredictable, not because she wanted him dead. Now Charly was entitled to a lot of money from Joel – on paper at least – but she was probably in for the roughest ride of her life from both the law and the press if she pursued it. This situation had black widow written all over it.

'Right,' Markie said, trying to decide as he spoke if the things he was suggesting constituted wise advice or if he was just talking in order to say something – anything – to make Charly feel better. 'Leave it for a couple of days. Then I'll get my legal guy to give you a call.'

Charly nodded.

'Have you got enough money?'

'I've got money stashed all round the house. Joel was like some old man; money under mattresses, in plant pots, everywhere really.'

Markie walked over and kissed her on the forehead. 'Well, get it all out of the plant pot – or wherever else you're hiding it – and make sure you know exactly what you've got. Don't let anyone else see it.' Charly didn't seem to be taking in what he was saying. 'Yeah?' Markie asked sternly.

'Yes,' Charly said immediately, as if she had been jolted from a daydream.

Markie left the house and pulled his phone out to call Terry. He needed to get home and get some sleep. Only then would he get some perspective on the week's events and be able to work out what he needed to do next.

chapter fourteen

It was nearly a month since Joel Baldy's death and the police were no nearer to finding the murderer. The CCTV footage showed nothing incriminating. There wasn't a single person with a motive to kill Joel who had showed up on the hotel's security tapes from that night. This wasn't wholly unusual, according to the papers, who had been following this story with morbid fascination. If it had been a lower-end hotel there would have been CCTV all over the place, but due to the salubrious reputation of the place, the security cameras were at a minimum and were mostly trained on the reception area and the valet car park beneath the building. Likewise, the staff who had been working on the night in question didn't have much to offer the police. There had been the obvious sightings of Joel Baldy falling through the door on his way to the glamour model's room in which he was found murdered, but this sort of thing was fairly normal and the reception staff had just raised a knowing eyebrow when they saw someone famous follow someone else famous to their room. Whoever it was could have got to the room by simply asking another guest if they could let them through the carded security doors. One guest, a young woman visiting Manchester for the night, had come forward and said that such a thing had happened to her on the night in question, but she had been so inebriated that she couldn't give any sort of description other than to say that it'd been a man. The computer log showed that the time she swiped her card coincided with around about the time Joel was attacked, but without a description the police were no nearer to knowing who had attacked Joel.

The press themselves had been holding their own kangaroo court and had decided that there were a number of people who had every reason to want Joel Baldy dead. Scott Crompton was high on their list. As Charly's cuckolded ex-boyfriend he had every reason to be jealous of the young footballer, but neither they nor the police had anything that linked Scott to the murder. Len Metcalfe too was being routinely hounded at his place of work and his home. His private life was now a topic of debate across kitchen tables up and down the country. This loner of a man whose wife left him and his kids years ago and who, it seemed, had conveniently popped up at the time that Len needed an alibi. Len was keeping a dignified silence. Gone was the angry Len who only a short time ago had been in the press for hitting football stewards and abusing photographers. In his place was a calmer man, one who spoke politely to the waiting paparazzi, insisting on his innocence and pleading with them on an almost daily basis to leave his family alone and afford them some peace.

There had been a few mentions of Markie Crompton but as he wasn't directly connected to Joel in any salacious way that the press could work out yet, speculation surrounding him had been short-lived. And then there was Charly. The press hadn't come out and directly accused her of being linked to the murder; but the Great British Public had. Websites and forums were jammed full of speculation about her involvement in Joel's death. There was a lot of sympathy for Charly, but there was an equal measure of cynicism; people who thought that she'd been in it for the money and was now just biding her time, playing the grieving widow until such a time when she could claim what money was due to her.

Tracy didn't know what to think. And she didn't particularly care. She'd thought at first that Len was going to be charged with the murder and she could sit back and gloat as he was sentenced to life imprisonment. But that wife of his was still floating around and sticking to her alibi. The one thing that concerned her – *concerned* probably wasn't the right word, *bugged* was more accurate – was that Mac hadn't called. She had left a number of messages for him and had received nothing in return. Tracy wasn't soft enough to start thinking that something might have happened to him and that a search party needed sending out; she knew when someone was avoiding her. And spending a dirty afternoon with someone in a hotel only to disappear off the face of the planet, last seen heading for a Spanish island was, in Tracy's opinion, a good example of someone who was avoiding her. Tracy was convinced that Markie was hiding things from her. She didn't think that his business partner could vanish for a whole month and Markie not hit the roof and demand that someone find him. But he hadn't. Tracy wasn't quite so stupid as to think that she and Mac had had something beautiful together;

not quite yet. But she had fancied him rotten and she didn't like being ditched. *She* did the ditching in her relationships.

Tracy was in the Leversmith district of Bradington, wondering if Michelle Bennett of 43 Thorncroft Crescent was going to be true to her word and pay up this week. Tracy had had very few altercations in the first weeks of her new role as Collections Manager. A few women had refused to pay her, told her to come back or tried to get their husbands to deal with her, but Tracy had a very persuasive knack, it seemed. She had thought in the first week that it might be beginner's luck but a few months into it she knew it wasn't, it was something she was genuinely good at. Michelle answered the door. She had the money ready in her hand.

'Thanks, love, same time next week?' Tracy said.

'Yes, course,' Michelle said, smiling nervously.

Now that Tracy had established her rounds, people just expected her and paid up. And if she did encounter someone who was unwilling to play the game and cough up the money then she'd enjoy telling them that this wasn't an option. There wasn't a downside to this job, or so it seemed to Tracy.

Hearing her mobile phone ringing, Tracy pulled her handbag up to her ear before delving in to answer it. Private Number. Tracy didn't usually answer numbers she didn't recognise but since Mac had gone she'd changed her policy. 'Hello.'

'Trace, it's me. Call me from a payphone.' It was Mac.

You bastard, she thought. Ringing up like this, totally out of the blue. 'On what number?'

'The one in the car.'

'What car?' Tracy asked. But the line had gone dead. Tracy walked over to the car that Markie had lent her and opened the glove compartment. Nothing. She looked in the boot, under the mats, in the arm rest, even under the pedals, until she finally flipped down the sunshield on the passenger side and found a neatly folded piece of paper. She pulled it out and read it. Sure enough, there was a mobile phone number. Tracy looked around to see if anyone was watching her. She quickly drove to the nearest call box and jumped out. She was fully expecting it to be vandalised but it was working. She rummaged around in her pocket and found a pound. Mac was going to have to call her back. She was damned if she was standing there firing her hard-earned cash into a payphone to talk to someone on a mobile – those things ate money. Tracy pulled the receiver to her mouth. 'Jesus!' she shrieked. 'Who pisses on a public phone?' She spat on the receiver and wiped it with her sleeve. She punched in the number she had memorised and waited for it to ring.

'Hello?' Mac said.

'Where the hell have you been?' Tracy demanded.

'Been over in Palma.'

'That much I know. Bit of an extended holiday though, isn't it? A month!'

'I thought the police might come looking for me.'

'What for?'

'What d'you think?'

'Bloody hell. Joel Baldy. What the hell would they come looking for you for?'

'He owed us money, didn't he?'

'Did he?'

'There was a file in the office. They got a warrant to search the offices; your Markie said. Once I heard that I thought it best to lie low.'

'Yeah, they did, but they didn't find anything.' Tracy didn't want to say too much. She wanted Mac to tell her what he was driving at. 'What's in the file?'

'They found nothing?'

'Don't think they knew what they were looking for. Anyway Mac, like I said, what's in the file?'

'When Baldy first came to Rovers we bankrolled some of his gambling. It's fairly normal stuff. These lads come to the big city, green as grass; we know they're going to make a mint once their contracts are signed and they need some cash to look the part in the meantime. A lot of the time they're so young their parents hold the purse strings till they're twenty-one. So while they could be out living the high life they're holed up in their flat waiting for Domino's to drop off the pizza their mum's ordered. We supply bridging finance. Footballers usually pay up straight away; scared to death of any aggro. But Joel Baldy wasn't a case in point. I'd been on his back for a while. He owed us twenty-five grand. I wouldn't mind but twenty-five grand was change to a little shit like him.'

Tracy was listening intently, her mind whirring.

'I don't trust the coppers, they'll be after me,' Mac continued. 'If they've had your Markie in, then they'll have me in, I guarantee it.'

'Why don't you come home and stop being paranoid. Face the music.'

'I am home.'

This was news to Tracy. 'Well, if you're home

they'll know because your passport will have come up, won't it?'

'No. I can't explain now. But it won't.'

Tracy wasn't sure that Mac was the innocent man he was making himself out to be.

'Trace, I need a favour.'

Here we go, Tracy thought, raising an eyebrow. She wasn't a big fan of giving out favours; she was far better at receiving than giving.

'Can I come to your house tonight, when Kent's out? I'll explain everything then.'

'Get there for ten,' Tracy said quickly. With Kent out and a desperate Mac who she hadn't seen for a month, Tracy knew if nothing else she'd be in for a good time.

*

The knock at the door came at ten o'clock sharp. Tracy answered it. She wasn't Mac's number one fan at the moment but there was one thing he was good for and it was that one thing that was the reason she had agreed to see him; not because she wanted to help him. Tracy was wearing her dressing gown and nothing underneath it. This wasn't her usual tea-stained dressing gown though;

this was a new fake silk one that she'd bought from her special knicker shop in the market. The way she slinked to the door, she half reminded herself of Joan Collins in *Dynasty*. Mac was standing at the door looking wild-eyed; she opened it and he stepped in. At first it was as if all of Tracy's efforts had gone to waste. But once the door was shut Mac moved towards her. He looked around nervously. 'Don't worry, the coast's clear,' Tracy assured him as he ran his fingers over her, desperate to touch her after a month apart.

Their lovemaking was hard and fast and as it came to a shuddering abrupt end for both of them, Tracy slumped back on the kitchen table trying to catch her breath.

'Still a dirty get, I see,' she said appreciatively.

'Well, I've not spent the last month at finishing school, if that's what you were wondering.'

Tracy smiled at him as she pulled her dressing gown from the floor and wrapped it around herself. But now that he had finished what she wanted him for, she was back to loathing him again.

'What have you spent the last month doing?' Tracy should have stopped there, but restraint wasn't her strong point. 'Other than moping round after your ex.'

'What's that meant to mean?'

Tracy put her hands up in a placatory manner. 'What our Markie said, not me.'

'Well, your Markie needs to keep it buttoned where that's concerned. It's none of his business.'

'You could have called. I thought we were getting on.'

'We were,' Mac said shortly.

Tracy lit a cigarette and inhaled deeply. 'Right, let's try again. Forget I said anything. What have you spent the last month doing?'

'Seeing a few people,' Mac said without meeting her eye.

'What people?' she asked. He wasn't getting off that lightly. Mac's gaze fell on Tracy.

'I need a favour,' Mac said, buttoning his fly and tucking his shirt back in.

'You said on the phone.'

'You said that the police hadn't taken the file. Can you get me it?'

Tracy sized Mac up for a moment. 'I suppose so. Why can't you go in and get it?'

'I need to stay out of the office. Once you've got that file I don't mind going in but if I go in myself and get it I think they'll have me for perverting the course of justice.'

'But it's alright for me to pervert the course of justice?'

Mac laughed. Tracy knew he was thinking that it was rich, her beginning to care now about staying on the right side of the law. His reaction only served to make her dislike him even more.

'You can go in and pick a file up and walk out with it. Doesn't mean you're doing anything bad, does it?'

Tracy wasn't altogether buying this, not that she was about to tell Mac. 'I suppose. Alright, which file is it?'

Mac described what Tracy was looking for.

'OK, I'll get it first thing.'

'Great,' Mac said, checking his pocket for his phone and preparing to leave.

'Where you going?' Tracy asked.

'Got stuff to do. I'll see you tomorrow, yeah? Once you've got the file for me.'

'What you going to do with it once you've got it?'

'Shred it. What else?'

'Why don't I just save you the bother and shred it for you?'

Mac looked at Tracy momentarily. 'No, Trace,' he said, 'I'd like to do it myself.'

'Fair enough,' Tracy replied affably. But as Mac turned to the door Tracy's eyes narrowed; Mac had just done himself absolutely no favours. He might as well have come straight out with it and said that he didn't trust her.

'You need to tell our Markie what you're up to. He's got shit he needs to straighten out,' Tracy said, as if she was conducting business as usual.

'Yeah,' Mac mumbled in agreement. He walked out of the door looking preoccupied; he didn't even kiss Tracy goodbye. She watched him go, wondering what was going on in his head, what his next move would be, but knowing one thing: she would beat him to it.

*

It was midnight and Tracy had let herself into the office. She found the file that Mac needed and leafed through it. There was a record of exactly how much Joel Baldy had borrowed, how much he owed, and a list of cryptic notes about his lack of payment that weren't too hard to decipher. The last notation said, 'Next time he pays up or we go to level three.' Tracy didn't think a person had to be Einstein to work out that level three wasn't a rap on the knuckles. She pulled the rest of the paperwork out of the file and leafed through it. There were a number of famous names among this little lot and Tracy flicked through them with interest.

Once she had made sure that there was nothing else in the office that might alert the police to any wrongdoings of Mac's, she walked over to the door. Next to the door was the photocopier. Tracy fired it into life and stood back to inspect it. It would probably take her all night to work out how to make this thing do what it was meant to, but she didn't care. She was going to make two copies of every-thing in this file and then she was going to post one to the police. Nobody took Tracy Crompton for a mug, especially not some half-arsed extortionist like Mac Jones.

*

There was a knock at the door. Tracy was sitting in front of the TV in her dressing gown watching a cookery programme, wondering exactly who it was who took the advice of these chefs and parboiled then roasted a load of spuds to make the perfect chip. The Wing on the estate did the perfect chip in her opinion; her definition being that it was a chip and she hadn't had to cook it. She wasn't getting up to answer the door. Let Kent get it, she thought. She'd had a hard day's door-knocking herself; she wasn't about to start answering them in her spare time. The knock came again, this time louder and harder. 'Kent!' Tracy shouted. There was no response so she climbed out of her chair. 'If you want something doing, kill Kent and then do it your bleeding self,' she mumbled. But before she had chance to get to the door, Kent had beaten her to it. She walked into the hall and two police officers were standing at the door.

'We'd like to speak to Tracy Crompton.'

'Why, what's she done?' Kent asked suspiciously.

The copper at the front, who seemed like the one who did all the talking, looked at Kent as if his days were numbered. 'That's something we'll be discussing with her, isn't it?'

Tracy pulled her dressing gown tightly around her. Her mind was racing. She hadn't done anything really illegal for a while. She'd helped Karina shift some hooky gear on eBay but there was no way they could link her to that. And it was years since she'd been allowed to have a catalogue account so it couldn't be that either.

'It's alright, Kent, I'll talk to them.' This couldn't be anything to do with Mac, could it? she thought, but quickly dismissed this as paranoia. Nothing in what she had sent anonymously to the police implicated her in any way, she was sure.

Kent stepped back, letting Tracy go to the door.

'Could we come in, please?'

'I'd rather you didn't,' Tracy said cockily.

'Of course you would, and I'd prefer not to have to take you in for questioning, but sometimes these things happen, don't they?' the copper said, matching Tracy's pluck. The younger police officer behind him smiled to himself.

'You can come in if Laughing Boy there wipes the smirk off his face,' Tracy snapped.

'Now, Mrs Crompton. Let's have less of the abuse towards a police officer.'

Tracy stood back and allowed the coppers into the house. She quickly looked outside to see if anyone on the street was watching – she'd be a laughing stock if people thought she had just rolled over and let the police in her house. But then, she had to remind herself, she'd never really cared much what her neighbours thought about her, even when it came to cooperating with the police.

Tracy sat down at the kitchen table. The police

officers followed suit. 'What d'you want?' Tracy asked wearily.

'Cup of tea'd be lovely, thanks, I'm spitting feathers.'

'That's a shame,' Tracy said, not making any move to get out of her chair. 'Like I said, what do you want?'

Kent was hovering around in the background.

'No tea?' The officer doing all of the talking turned to his subordinate. 'That's not very nice, is it?'

'No, it's not.' The pipsqueak shook his head.

Tracy eyeballed the pair.

'We came here to talk to you about a very delicate situation but it looks like we're just going to have to come right out with it.'

Tracy was maintaining an icy composure but there was something about the way the copper was enjoying what he was saying that made her think she might have been better off putting the kettle on and breaking out the Garibaldis. The copper pulled a picture out of his jacket and threw it on the table. It was a CCTV image and it wasn't the clearest she'd ever seen but there was no mistaking who was pictured. It was Tracy with Mac at the hotel in Blackpool. He had his arm around her and was kissing her. Tracy looked at it with horror.

'This is one of the last sightings of Mac Jones. The landlady of the Shangri-La in Blackpool gave a statement saying that between 2.35pm and 4.49pm on the day in question you and Mr Jones were there together.' Tracy wanted to jump up and cover Kent's ears. 'Seemed like you had a very nice time, too,' the policeman added for good measure.

'And how would you know that?' Tracy asked, wondering how on earth she was going to get Kent to believe that this was all a huge misunderstanding.

'We have a statement from the owner of the Shangri-La stating that when asked if everything was alright as she had heard some noises that she thought to be someone in pain, you and Mr Jones took the landlady's innocent question as a slight and replied.' He read the statement out in a slow monotonous drawl '–"That wasn't pain, it was shagging, love. You might want to try it one day. Loosen yourself up a bit."' He folded the statement up and looked at Tracy. She wanted to thump him.

Kent walked out of the room. 'Kent!' Tracy shouted, jumping to her feet. Kent didn't turn around; he marched straight ahead and out of the front door. He slammed it behind him with such ferocity that the boarded-up top part of the door that Tracy had been meaning to have fixed for over a year fell out onto the floor. She ran back to where the police officers were sitting. 'Happy now?' she demanded.

'Well, Tracy, if you *will* go playing away with someone who's now wanted for questioning, these things will bite you on the arse.'

'Wise words,' the pipsqueak agreed.

'Alright, Confucius, I don't need a bloody lecture. I don't know where he is. He's my bloody business partner, he's my son's business partner and he's done one, leaving us in the shit.'

'But you were conducting an affair?'

'What's that got to do with the price of fish?'

'Everything. Answer the question, please.'

'What went on with me and Mac is nobody's business.'

'We've got pictures saying it is.'

Tracy looked at him. She wasn't going to win this argument. And there was something about the fact that it was being conducted with her in her dressing gown that made her feel she was at a distinct disadvantage.

'You've just wrecked things between me and my other half so what else do you want from me? I don't know where Mac is.'

'Have you heard from him since that day?'

Tracy didn't falter for a moment; one thing she had on her side was that she was a natural born liar. 'Not a word.'

'After this picture was taken, where did you go?'

'I went off to see Kent win an Elvis competition.' A knowing look passed between the two police officers. 'And you can knock the funny looks on the head. This isn't some moral crime you're here for, is it? Where I get my kicks is nothing to do with the Bradington constabulary. After the Elvis competition me and Kent went back to our hotel and then got the coach home the next day. Call the Ponderosa if you don't believe me,' she said, referring to the hotel she and Kent had stayed at.

'We do because we already have. Thanks, Tracy, but nice to know where to come when I've forgotten how to do my job.'

'Anyway, what you after Mac for?'

'It's come to our attention that Joel Baldy owed your boyfriend quite a bit of money. You knew that though, didn't you, Tracy? What with you working for him and Markie now.'

'No, I didn't. I deal with any women on the books who've fallen behind on their payments.

Pretty-boy footballers aren't my bag, officer. All extremely legitimate though, the business. But then again, you know that, don't you, otherwise you'd no doubt be blagging my head about that an' all.' Tracy wanted this pair of halfwits out her house. She had to get hold of Kent. He was a soft arse, but he hadn't deserved to find out that Tracy was having an affair in such a cruel and unexpected way.

'No need to be defensive about the business, Tracy. I'm sure it's all above board. But just so you know what to say to Mac Jones if he does get in touch. He needs to answer a lot of questions and he's not helping himself by staying away. He's making himself look like he's very definitely got something to hide.' The policeman got to his feet and his sidekick copied him. 'Be sure to call us if you hear anything, won't you?'

'I'll be straight on the blower,' Tracy said sarcastically.

'Good, because you're the nearest thing he's got to an alibi at the moment.'

'Get lost. I've just told you, I was with Kent that night.'

'Well, according to Mac's passport he was in Majorca the same day, flew out that morning. But as these pictures prove, things aren't always what they seem, are they?' Tracy looked at him with steely conviction but underneath she was quaking. *What had she let herself in for here?* It looked as if Mac knew far more than he'd been telling her if he'd planned to make it look like he was out of the country on that day. Tracy didn't have a clue what was going on.

As the officers left, Tracy pulled her mobile phone out of her dressing-gown pocket and called Kent. There was no answer. She ran upstairs and pulled on a pair of tracksuit bottoms and a jumper and shoved her hair into a ponytail. Stepping out into the cold night air, she closed the door behind her. Seeing the board on the floor she picked it up and placed it back in the hole it had fallen from. She looked at it; it'd do. No one in their right mind would break into the Cromptons' house anyway, Tracy thought, knowing that although everything else might be falling in around her, her hard credentials were still firmly intact.

*

Markie was sitting at the bar of the Glasshouse sipping a neat bourbon and wondering when Mac was going to make an appearance. He had had enough of all this bullshit. Mac needed to come back and face whatever music he needed to face like a man. Markie had been hauled in yet again and informed that not only did he have a personal gripe with Joel through his loyalty to Charly but he had a professional one too. The police knew about the loans that his business gave to new footballers and Markie had spent hours convincing the interviewing officer that he had nothing to do with that side of the business.

Markie didn't think for a second that Mac was responsible for murdering Joel Baldy; Mac was a lot of things but an amateur he wasn't and killing someone so high profile was amateurish. But he could do with showing his face and sorting out this mess himself so that they could all get on with their lives. Anyway, Markie wondered, what good was a dead Joel Baldy to Mac? He owed them money, something they were never going to see now that he wasn't around to pay it. Markie had managed to make sure that Mac's side of the business was covered in his absence. It wasn't something that either of them talked about but since Markie had spent a few years inside, they had both ensured that their businesses – although better when they were both around – didn't suffer if either one of them suddenly wasn't there. Leanne's boyfriend Tony had filled in as far as running the club doors was concerned. And Karina's ex-boyfriend Gaz had stepped in to oversee Mac's collections that weren't being handled by Tracy. Swing, that idiot, who Markie still couldn't bring himself to speak to, had stepped into the breach to up his collections when he had returned from a week's holiday to find Mac AWOL.

The stool next to where Markie was sitting angrily scraped away from him. He looked across to see who was making such a point of sitting down: it was Kent. Markie was so unused to seeing his mother's boyfriend in this setting that he didn't say anything for a moment. Kent looked at him. 'Markie,' he said as if he was here for *Men's Business*.

'Kent. To what do I owe this pleasure?' Markie was genuinely interested; he couldn't imagine what had brought Kent down here.

'Where's Mac?' Kent asked angrily, his eyes narrow.

'Your guess is as good as mine. Haven't seen him for weeks,' Markie said truthfully.

'He's been having an affair with your mother, but

I suppose you'd know all about that,' Kent spat bitterly. Markie's eyes widened. It had been on the cards but Markie hadn't thought that anything was really going on. He shook his head.

'I don't think he is.' Markie wanted to protect Kent, the poor sap. 'He's still not over his wife passing away. I think someone's winding you up.'

'Coppers just came round our house with some pictures of them in a hotel in Blackpool. All over each other they were. Day that Baldy kid was murdered. Same day I'm singing my heart out and your mother's there, cheering me on, bold as brass. She came and watched me that night like nothing had happened.'

'Can I get you a drink?' Markie asked. He wanted to calm Kent down. He didn't need him going over the edge in the club; he knew he could be volatile where Tracy was concerned. But Markie's mind was reeling – his mum and Mac? They'd been friendly enough but he'd thought it was just two old people flirting. The thought of them actually being *at it* turned his stomach.

'A large one of anything you've got.'

Markie waved the bartender over. Out of the corner of his eye he saw a familiar figure. It was his mother, marching towards him.

'Nice of you to make the effort,' Markie said, looking at her shoddy attire. She wouldn't have been allowed through the door if it hadn't been for the fact that she was his mother.

Tracy glared at him and pulled at Kent's arm. 'Kent, come home, I'll explain.'

'How did you know I'd be here?'

'I knew you'd come and find our Markie. What's that got to do with it? Come on, let's get off and have a talk.'

Kent turned to Tracy. Markie wanted the ground to open up and swallow him. There was something utterly tragic about seeing a man so usually buoyed up by life being serious because he knew that he had been made a fool of yet again by his other half. 'I know you, Tracy. And I know that if you hadn't done anything you'd be screaming blue murder at the fact that anyone suggested you had. You're as guilty as sin.'

'No, I'm bloody not. I work with him.' Tracy turned to Markie. 'Don't I? Tell him.'

Kent turned to Markie. 'And does she book into hotels and canoodle with everyone she works with?'

Markie held his hands in the air. 'This is a conversation you two need to have. Alone.' He got off his stool and walked away, leaving his mum and

Kent to it. He couldn't spend a moment longer watching poor old Kent fall apart.

*

It was 4am, Kent's bags were packed and Tracy had done more pleading in one evening than she'd ever done in her life and she was now officially over it. Kent had made himself clear; he was leaving and she most definitely wasn't going to Memphis with him. She was gutted. Well, if that was the way he was playing it then fine, but she was going to tell him exactly what she thought of him.

'You can stop clip-clopping round on your high horse now, I've heard enough,' Tracy said wearily, dragging on a cigarette.

'I'm going.'

'So you keep saying. Well, if you're going and you're going to be such an arsehole about it, you might as well know that yes, I was shagging Mac Jones and yes, he was a better shag than you.' She pointed at a neglected plant on the window sill and continued, 'In fact that plant's probably a better shag than you.'

Kent looked at her, hurt burning in his eyes.

'You're only out for yourself, aren't you? Always have been, always will be.'

Tracy stared back at him. She felt totally numb, as if she'd shut down. She knew she was being cruel but didn't care. She'd nothing to lose now; Kent was going and she was going to be on her own. She might as well stick the boot in. 'Am I?'

'You tell me.'

'I've had enough of you and your *me*, *me*, *me* attitude. Elvis this, Elvis that ...'

'That's rich. You do what pleases you, whenever it pleases you. Paul last year – you wanted him back 'til you found out he had no money.' Kent was referring to Tracy briefly getting back with the father of her kids when she believed he'd come in to some money. As soon as she found out he hadn't she shipped Paul out and Kent back in. 'Mac this year. I'm nothing to you, am I? Just some voice you fancied on the radio a few years ago and thought you'd try your luck with.'

'Don't remind me,' Tracy mumbled.

'What?'

'Nothing.' She sighed. She couldn't be bothered with this any more. 'If you're going, get gone.'

'I am going, aren't I? You don't deserve anyone who cares about you,' Kent said, pulling his bags to the door. Tracy sat down and pulled out another cigarette, lighting it as Kent struggled to get his stuff into the car. He didn't say goodbye. He simply shut the door behind him.

Tracy sat at the kitchen table drawing on the fresh cigarette. She would have liked to have cried; she quite enjoyed feeling sorry for herself. But she couldn't even muster any self-pitying tears. She was just pissed off. Pissed off with herself for having been found out, pissed off with Kent for having left before she'd had a chance to jet to Memphis with him, but most of all she was pissed off with Mac. All of her feelings towards him had soured. She now just saw him for what he was; a weak man who couldn't face the music and someone who had buggered off leaving everyone else to muddle through. Tracy didn't like being taken for a mug and that was exactly what Mac had done. Here she was, manless and holidayless.

She'd met Mac with the file that he'd requested and he'd once again gone to ground. He hadn't been interested in her at all; all he wanted was to get the contents of the file from her and be on his way. Tracy had noted all of this with malevolent interest. He didn't have a hope in hell of staying hidden once this information came to light, she knew that for sure; the police would catch up with him sooner or later. Tracy hoped that he got just what he deserved. And she was going to do everything in her power to make sure he did.

chapter fifteen

Charly was lying in the bath staring at the oak-beamed ceiling. She was numb. A month had passed and she felt that nothing had changed. She woke every morning and realised that her life was now public property, her every movement was pored over and scrutinised in the papers, and she was a widow in her early twenties. She was receiving advice from everyone from Manchester Rovers' financial specialists to the bin man, but none of it made sense to her and anyway, she didn't really care about what anyone else thought. She needed someone to grab her and shake her back to life but she didn't really feel she had anything to live for. She missed Joel terribly, but even that seemed to Charly to be something she wasn't allowed to do. Everything the papers said about him was true. He had beaten her. He had been cold and distant. He had taken his wealth and fame for granted. But she had loved him and that was hard to explain to anyone. He had chipped away at her confidence but there had been so many things that Joel had said to her that Charly believed he was right about. She could be argumentative, she hadn't known how to judge his moods and when to leave him alone and she had wound him up. He had an important and stressful job and she really could have taken that into account. Charly didn't see that her thoughts were those of someone who had been in an abusive relationship, she just thought that Joel had been right and she had been wrong. She only wished she could have him back to tell him how she felt.

Charly pulled herself out of the water and towelled herself dry. She had always been petite but her size six clothes were now falling off her skinny frame and as she pulled the towel over her ribcage she could feel every bone. It wasn't even that she wasn't eating. Every time anyone came to the house they force-fed her; she was just burning everything off with the nervous energy that also kept her awake most nights. Shirley was due around later that day. Charly had decided to start calling her mum Shirley, just for her own sanity. She hadn't acted like a mum in Charly's opinion so she didn't deserve the title – not that she'd said as much to her. She just avoided having to address her as anything and waited until she was looking directly at her to speak. Charly couldn't quite believe that she was still around after a month. She had tried to work out what her mother's motives were, what she was hanging around for, but it had been as if the last decade hadn't happened and she had slipped back into mother mode. Charly had asked that her dad not come to the house. She knew instinctively that Shirley was lying when she said that she had been with Len on the night that Joel had been murdered. And she couldn't push from her mind the thought that her father was responsible for Joel's murder even though no DNA evidence had come back to place him there. She needed the police to find whoever was responsible and for that person to not be her father. Only then could she be sure.

Charly could hear her mobile phone ringing downstairs. She didn't rush to answer it. She slowly pulled some oversized jogging bottoms on and scraped her hair back. By the time she was descending the stairs there was a hammering at the back door. *Who the hell is that?* Anyone who was coming to see her either came in with Terry, who let them in with his key, or had to go through Manchester Rovers' press department. Charly walked slowly down the stairs, not knowing who to expect. When she saw that it was Kim, the glamour model who had been with Joel on the night he died, Charly felt the old Metcalfe bile rising. *How dare she come to her house?* She marched to the door and pulled it open.

'What do you want?'

'I need to speak to you. I need to say sorry. To tell you how bad it's been for me, to tell you how bad I've been feeling.'

By now Charly's feelings of numbness had evaporated and she was filled with anger and hatred. She didn't care; she was grateful to be having any feelings at all. 'Well, you'd better come in then, hadn't you?' Charly said, grabbing the girl by her hair extensions and pulling her into the house. She threw her across the hallway with almost supernatural force. Kim landed awkwardly against the wall. Charly flew at her, thumping her straight in the mouth.

'Get off me! I can explain.'

'Really?' Charly said, thumping her again.

Kim managed to struggle up the wall and, getting to her feet, ran to the other end of the large entrance hall, holding her hands out in appeasement. 'Charly, please. Stop. I just want to say that I'm really sorry.'

'Me too, sorry that you ever clapped your slutty little eyes on my husband.' Charly marched towards her, but was distracted by the noise of the door opening. She turned around to see Terry with Leanne Crompton standing with him. Terry ran over and seeing the state of Kim pulled Charly away from her. Leanne stepped forward.

'I've been calling you, Charly,' she said before turning to Kim and asking her angrily, 'What the bloody hell did I tell you?'

'I needed to see her to make my peace.'

'You don't deserve any peace!' Charly screamed, bolting for Kim again. Terry locked his arms around her and pulled her back.

'Charly, I'm sorry,' Leanne said soothingly. She turned to Terry. 'Will you take Kim outside, I just want to have a word with Charly if that's OK.'

Charly looked at Leanne. She didn't really want to have a word with her. She knew what Leanne thought; that she was a gold-digger who had dropped her brother Scott when a far better offer in the shape of Joel had come along. Kim began to sob as Terry guided her out. 'I don't know what you're crying for!' Charly shouted after her.

Once they were safely outside, Leanne took Charly's hand. 'How are you?'

Charly shrugged. 'Been better, you know how it is.' As she finished the sentence Charly laughed wryly to herself, knowing that nobody could know how it was.

'I can't say I do totally, but I know what it's like to have the whole country talking about you over their cornflakes.' Charly looked at Leanne and half smiled. Of course she did. Charly had been so envious of Leanne when she had been going out with Scott. Leanne seemed to have everything: a glamorous life, money, a child. And then it had all come crashing down and she had come home to Bradington with the country's press hot on her tail. When speculation had become rife that Leanne's daughter Kia was the lovechild of superstar footballer Jay Leighton – an ex-colleague of Joel's – every aspect of Leanne's life had been splashed all over the papers.

Charly looked down at her right hand; her knuckles were red from where she had just hit Kim. 'That'll give them something else to talk about, won't it?'

'Don't worry; I'll get Kim to keep her mouth shut about this.' Leanne paused. 'She's had a hard time ... I know it's not what you want to hear but she has. The police have ruled out any involvement. She's just a stupid star-struck girl but because she was there she keeps being dragged back in and questioned.'

'My heart bleeds,' Charly said, hard-faced.

Leanne looked around as if she was unsure of what to say next. Charly couldn't help her; there wasn't much small talk to be made in view of the enormity of what had happened to Charly in the past month.

'Scott's been asking after you,' Leanne said finally.

'Really?' Charly said. She was genuinely touched. Scott Crompton may not have been the man of Charly's dreams but he had been kind and thoughtful to her throughout their relationship and she would have given anything to have a moment of Scott's kindness right now.

'He wanted to call you but didn't think it was the right thing to do. I can understand why.'

Charly nodded in agreement. 'Would you tell him that he can call me any time? Give him the number you've got, I'd really love to see him.' She knew that if Scott came to see her she could put her feelings about everything that was going on at the moment to one side and just be in the company of someone who had genuinely cared for her. She didn't want anything from him, other than his time. 'OK.' Leanne nodded slowly. Charly could tell that there was something else she wanted to say but that she was choosing her words carefully.

'What?' Charly asked, prompting her.

Leanne looked Charly in the eye. 'Tony works for Markie again.'

'Right,' Charly said, thinking, *And your point is?*

'I know that you and he have been spending quite a bit of time together.'

Charly took a deep breath before answering. She wanted to shout at Leanne that she hadn't been knocking her other brother off as well, if that was what she was suggesting, but she liked Leanne and she didn't need to make an enemy of her. 'I think that's something that maybe you should talk to Markie about,' Charly said diplomatically.

'Right.' Leanne nodded. 'Well, I'd better get off.' She walked towards Charly and gave her a hug. 'If you need anything, give me a shout.'

'Thank you,' Charly said, touched by Leanne's good intentions. She locked the door behind her and walked through the empty sitting room and drawing room of the enormous house, on her way to curl up on the settee and stare into space. She hadn't meant to put the ball so firmly in Markie's court as she had just done, but neither could she be the person to tell Leanne why she and Markie had been spending time together. That was Markie's job, not hers.

*

Tracy marched into the office, ignoring Tammy on reception, and headed straight for Markie.

'What's up with you?' Markie asked. When Tracy was in a bad mood, everyone knew about it.

'Mac Jones is what's up with me.'

'Don't bring your personal life in here – it won't work.'

Tracy eyeballed her son. What did he take her for? Some hysterical filing clerk who'd just split up with her boyfriend? 'I've got some eggs in my bag you can teach me how to suck while you're at it.'

'Well, if it's not personal, what is it?'

'He's weak.'

Markie laughed.

'What you laughing at?' Tracy demanded.

'He's hard as nails, Mac.'

'I'm not on about flattening people; any mug can

do that. I mean he's weak minded. Why else stay away for a month? You wouldn't have; you'd have faced any music coming your way. As it is the police want to question him and were so kind as to turn up on my doorstep throwing photos around of me and him together so that Kent's fucked off and now I'm left on my lonesome, with no sign of a holiday to America and no Mac to explain why he's such a pussy.'

Markie nodded as if this was all making sense now. 'So it *is* personal?'

'Listen, cloth ears, as I've said, it couldn't be further from personal,' Tracy lied. 'He's not helping us, is he?'

Markie rose from his desk and walked over to his mum. 'When I was in the nick for two years and you were sat at home eating Hobnobs and only getting off the settee every two hours to pull your knickers out of the crack of your arse, who do you think was in here sorting everything out?' Markie asked, pressing his face up to his mum's.

'Don't talk to me like that, I'm your mother!' Tracy spat indignantly.

'And a shining example you are, Tracy, but that doesn't deviate from the fact that I owe Mac. Things are alright here; ticking along. They don't need you sticking your two pence worth in just because you've got good at getting money out of a few scrubbers around the place.'

'I could run this place in my sleep.' Tracy wasn't having Markie belittle what she had contributed since she had begun working for him.

'You wouldn't know where to start. Anyway –' Markie shook his head '– what are we on about that for? Let's stick to the point. Mac has stuck by me, so I'll stick by him.'

Markie turned away from Tracy and walked back to his desk, suggesting this discussion was over. Tracy wasn't having it, and anyway, a penny was dropping. 'You've heard from him, haven't you?'

Markie shrugged. 'What if I have?'

'We're in the shit here, and you're harbouring him.'

Markie laughed. 'Harbouring him? Who are you, Cagney or Lacey?' He added almost under his breath, 'The blonde pissed one, whichever one she was.'

'You what?' Tracy said with utter indignation.

'Nothing. Joke,' Markie said dismissively.

'Listen you. You're going the right way about a slap. And you can tell that Mac that he needs to get his arse back here.'

'Can I?'

'Yeah, you can,' Tracy said, slamming out of the office.

'Bye, Tracy,' Tammy said with sugary sweet sarcasm.

'Shut it, perky tits,' Tracy said angrily. She wasn't in the mood for anyone today, especially some over-made-up phone monkey.

Tracy stormed along the street and, seeing her old favourite haunt Yates's was just opening, she popped in, pretending momentarily to herself that she was going to order a coffee but instead ordering a large gin and tonic. What was it with men? she thought. Bunch of weak, soppy-minded individuals. And Markie, her own son, was siding with Mac over her. Pathetic pair. He needed hauling into line, Mac. If he'd been her business partner she'd have told him to get his act together, get back out earning and clear this Joel Baldy mess up. As it was they were all waiting around for the inevitable to happen. He was going to be arrested and if he didn't come up with something good soon as to why he'd disappeared from the radar, he would be charged. There was enough circumstantial evidence accruing to convict him, Tracy thought.

She pulled out her mobile phone. She had stored

the number that Mac had given her to call from the payphone. Hiding her number, Tracy called it. To her surprise Mac answered.

'It's me, Tracy.'

'What you doing ringing me?' Mac sounded anxious.

'Charmed. I'm ringing to tell you I'm going to have a word with the police and tell them what really happened that night, so you can come back.'

'What did *really* happen that night?' Mac asked curiously, obviously wanting to know what Tracy had to say.

'You know as well as I do that after Kent went to bed pissed out of his tiny mind me and you met up in Blackpool. Went for a walk on the sea front. We were there for hours. There was another couple on the beach; maybe they could vouch for us. But then again they'd be almost impossible to trace. You didn't set off until gone five in the morning, did you?'

'That's right, Tracy, I didn't. But why go to the police now?'

'Because,' Tracy said, playing along with the line of questioning, 'now, Mac, I've nothing to lose. Kent's gone. I'm on my own. There's no one left to protect.'

'He's left? I'm sorry.' *Bet you are*, Tracy thought.

'So are you going to come back?' Tracy asked.

'Well, there's not much reason for me to stay away, is there?' Mac said cautiously.

'Make your first stop the cop shop, won't you, then me and you can sort things out after.'

'Nice one,' Mac said, sounding genuinely relieved. 'And Tracy … thanks.'

'Don't mention it.' She ended the call. Tracy pocketed her phone, wishing that for once in her life she could meet just one man who wouldn't turn out to be a complete sap and could see what she was up to and try and at least match her at her own game.

*

Len walked downstairs to the smell of bacon. This had become a regular occurrence since Shirley had returned. He knew that when he entered the kitchen there would be a pot of tea made, bacon, eggs, sausages and toast and a copy of the *Mail* waiting for him. Like everything else since Shirley's return, Len didn't dare question it. But he wanted to desperately; he just couldn't find the words. Len had seen on one of those daytime shows that he was loath to watch, some American woman talking about people ignoring problems that were glaring them in the face because they didn't want to talk about them, or couldn't somehow face them. She had likened it to there being an elephant in the room that everyone knew was there, but no one was mentioning. Len understood the analogy now. But in his case he felt like an entire herd of elephants had set up camp in his house and he and Shirley were just squeezing their way around them.

'Morning. There's some orange in the fridge,' Shirley said chirpily.

Len slid into his seat at the kitchen table. The feelings inside of him were so pent up he felt like a pressure cooker waiting to explode. 'Shirley …' Len said, wishing for something of substance to attach itself to the word in order to form a sentence. She looked at him.

'I … er …' Len stammered.

'You seen that on the front of the paper? Castle in Kent being turned into luxury apartments for asylum seekers.' Shirley shook her head as if the world had gone mad. 'Might apply for asylum myself.'

'We know better than most that what the papers print should be taken with a pinch of salt. They always exaggerate these figures, don't they? I mean, come on; how many asylum seekers do you know?'

'None,' Shirley said, plating up the eggs and bacon.

'There you go.'

'I wouldn't though, would I? What, they going to trail all the way to a shit-tip like Bradington when they can live in a castle in Kent?'

Len wasn't quite sure how he'd managed to get sidetracked into a political discussion first thing in the morning, especially when as far as he was concerned he and Shirley had far more important things to talk about.

'Ever live in Kent?' Len said, coming straight out with it. It wasn't the ideal in to the conversation he'd wanted to have for over ten years, but it was a start.

Shirley turned back to the cooker. 'No.'

'Where did you live?'

'I don't really want to talk about it,' Shirley muttered.

Len paused for a moment, wanting to choose his words carefully, afraid of scaring her away again, but he had to say what was on his mind. 'You've been back a month after a decade away and we're no nearer to discussing where or why you went.'

Shirley didn't answer so Len filled the gap, 'Or what you want now that you're back.'

'I don't "want" anything.'

'I mean want for yourself. For us, if there is an us.' Len knew he was kidding himself. It had been strictly separate rooms since Shirley had returned.

Shirley placed the two plates of food gently on the table. Sliding into her chair she tried to look at Len, but eventually let her eyes rest on the brown sauce bottle in front of her. 'I find this really hard to talk about.'

'You and me both,' Len said, tentatively sliding his hand across the table to touch Shirley's. She let it rest on top.

'When I left I had a breakdown.' Shirley began to shake with nerves. Len leaned back in his chair. 'I don't want you to think that I'm a total nut job.' She was obviously finding it as hard to put things into words as Len was. 'I left here and I went to London. I didn't know anyone there. I know you think that I'd run off with some fella from here, that's what everyone thinks, but I didn't. I ended up in Bethnal Green. I was working in a sandwich shop in the City. I wanted you to come and find me. In my head if you'd put your back into it you could have traced me. That's how I felt at the time. It's so hard to explain. I wasn't thinking that I'd just disappeared and hadn't left you any way of finding me. You don't think like that when you're ill ...'

'Ill?' Len interrupted.

'I know it sounds daft. Let me explain,' Shirley implored. Len nodded.

'I was just functioning like a robot. I missed the kids but kept thinking that they didn't want me and you didn't want me. Then I kept scouring the "missing" pages in the *Big Issue* and the police missing register to see if you were looking for me. When I didn't see my picture there I just thought you didn't care. It's hard to explain to someone who's never felt it what depression is like. But I didn't do any of this to hurt you.' Len listened intently; this was the first he'd known about any depression.

'I was convinced that the kids were far better off with you.' Tears began to roll down Shirley's cheek and she pushed her food away; it seemed she was unable to stomach it. 'Then one day I'd gone in to work and my head was all over the place. You don't think it at the time, though,' she said, looking at Len suddenly as if trying to convey exactly what she was saying. 'You think that everything is ordered and makes perfect sense. Think of the most intense feelings you've had. I don't know, like when you found out that Joel had been hurting Charly.' Len didn't have to think about it. That feeling was still there, raw and undealt with. Unfinished business that would have to stay unfinished. 'Well, that level of anger is there all the time and seems to apply to even the most normal things. Is this making sense?' Len nodded; it was, oddly. 'Well, I was standing in the sandwich shop and some bloke had asked for coronation chicken on ciabatta and I was so angry, but so calm at the same time, I'm looking down at this knife and I'm thinking, *I don't care about your poncey ciabatta and you don't care about me, no one cares about me*. All my thoughts suddenly snowballed and instead of picking up a ciabatta and cutting into that, I pulled the knife across my wrist.'

Len winced, his eyes widening in alarm.

'It was pandemonium after that but I can't really remember; it just seemed to happen in slow motion. I was sectioned. They said they were going to contact you but I made out that you were the reason I was like I was.'

'But I'd have come and got you. I wasn't that bad, was I?'

'No. No, you weren't. But I wasn't thinking straight. I was in there for over a year. I remember thinking that I needed a plan to get out of there. And it seemed that the people who helped with the little tasks like washing up and making beds were the ones who seemed to be seen as getting better. So I started to do everything. This was where I met Mike. One day when I was washing up. He was from Bradington. At the time we thought it was this amazing coincidence, but really it was just something we had in common. Turned out to be the only thing we had in common. I got out and was placed in a halfway house and he was let out soon after. We stayed in touch and then just fell into living together. But in the end it all came to nothing. I told him about the kids and he said he didn't want to be with someone who could just up and leave like I had. He was right, wasn't he? Who would?' Shirley wiped the tears from her face.

Len was floored; this was a lot to take in. In his mind Shirley had left him and the kids and gone off to enjoy the high life somewhere. If he'd known any of this maybe he could have intervened.

'After that I spent a lot of time on my own. I got the odd job here and there and then I ended up involved in one of those pyramid schemes that collapsed and left me broke, but to be honest that was nothing new.' Shirley sighed. 'Such a bloody sob story, eh, Len? Who'd have thought it when we first started knocking around together that you'd end up being the sane one and I'd be the mad one.'

Len smiled sadly. 'You're not mad.'

Shirley laughed genuinely. 'I've got the certificate to prove it.'

'Why didn't you come back sooner?'

'Shame. Didn't know how you'd feel about it. Then when Charly ended up in the papers because she'd landed a famous boyfriend I convinced myself that I couldn't come back because you'd all think I was after something.' Shirley looked sadly at Len. 'I'm not, for the record. I just want the opportunity to make things right.'

Len nodded. He didn't know anything about Shirley's illness and he didn't know where to begin to understand how she had felt but for the first time he felt sympathy for her. She hadn't just high-tailed it off and spent her days cruising the Med. She'd had a worse time that he'd had, by the sounds of things. 'I just wish you'd stayed, or that I could have helped you pick up the pieces.'

'So do I, but it's done now, isn't it? I don't expect you to forgive me, but if you could put the past behind us then I'd like to stay here.' Shirley said this with such trepidation that Len could feel her fear. 'I understand if you don't, though.'

He got to his feet. 'Come here,' he said. Shirley stood up and moved towards him awkwardly. Len folded his arms around his wife and she began to sob. He kissed her on the top of her head and let her cry into his chest. He wasn't sure where they would go from here, but for Len this was the start he had been hoping for since Shirley had walked away from her life.

chapter sixteen

Shirley left the house the following day as if she was walking on air. She knew that this was only the start of the explaining that she had to do, but getting this off her chest after so many years was a relief that she couldn't have imagined. She checked her purse for the present she had for Charly and called Terry to see if he could collect her from Manchester Piccadilly bus station. She had signed on at the Job Centre, something she hated doing – it reminded her of when she hadn't been well and had spent years on benefits. But she had to do it just to have some money to get about and to get by; she didn't want to scrounge off Len. She had asked around for a job and was starting at the fruit market in Bradington the following week. She had worked in Bradington market before, years ago, and was quite looking forward to returning; as she remembered it was hard work but everyone had a good laugh.

It was ten thirty when the bus pulled up outside Piccadilly Gardens. Shirley looked covetously at the large Primark across from the bus station. When she had some money she was going to come into Manchester and treat herself to a new outfit. She couldn't wait. She felt like she'd been trailing around in the same old rags for years. Terry was waiting in a parking bay at the back of the bus station, ready to whisk her off to what was, as far as Shirley was concerned, another world.

'I told you, I'd have come and picked you up,' Terry said, leaning over to open the passenger door of the Navigator for Shirley to climb in. She looked at the car. She'd never stepped foot in something so luxurious.

'I can't have you showing yourself up coming to Bolingbroke, not in this thing,' Shirley joked.

'I've been to worse, let me tell you.' Terry smiled at Shirley in the rear-view mirror.

'I bet this car hasn't. It'd be on bricks before you'd put the handbrake on.'

They drove out of Manchester along a triple carriageway and onto a small stretch of motorway before veering off into the smart leafy village of

Hale. The journey took less than half an hour and Shirley found that once the initial pleasantries were out of the way, she and Terry were able to sit in comfortable silence and she could take in her surroundings.

Terry pulled the car along a steep hill that rose to the even smarter area of Hale Barns. Tucked behind trees was mansion after mansion set in their own manicured grounds. Shirley still found it hard to equate the place she had now visited a number of times with being her daughter's home. She somehow got the feeling that Charly was of a similar mind. She never seemed to know where anything was and she rattled around the rooms like a lost soul. Pulling up in front of the house, Shirley could see that Charly was waiting for her. Shirley was nervous. Len had taken the news well but he was different to her Charly and Jimmy. She had left them in their formative years. She could completely understand if they turned their backs on her after their initial positive response. Until now Shirley had felt that Charly was so wrapped up in what had happened to her that having her mother turn up hadn't properly registered with her. She was concerned that when it finally did, Charly wouldn't want anything to do with her. That was why today she had decided she was going to take Charly somewhere nice – Terry had agreed to drive – and tell her what she had told Len yesterday; the truth about where she had been and what had happened to her.

Charly answered the door. 'I'm not sure I feel like going anywhere,' were the first words out of her mouth. She was obviously worrying about leaving the house. Shirley looked at her daughter. She was skin and bone and she had the faraway stare that Shirley herself remembered having when she was in the depths of her illness.

'Come on, love, let's get some proper clothes on you and wash your hair,' Shirley said, guiding her daughter back into the house. Terry followed them inside. 'We'll be half an hour,' Shirley whispered to Terry, walking Charly towards the stairs. 'There's only one photographer outside from what I can see. We'll give him the slip and have a nice day together. What do you think?'

Charly shrugged, as if even the smallest opinion was beyond her.

*

An hour later and Charly and Shirley were walking around the grounds of Tatton Park. Neither had been here before and both were impressed by the country house and its stunning grounds.

Charly had treated them to lunch and they were now walking through a deserted vale leading down to a small lake. 'I can't believe how quiet it is,' Shirley said. 'It's not even an hour to Bradington from here; seems like a million miles away.'

'Thank God it's quiet. No one around taking pictures with their mobile phone.'

'Who does that?'

'Everyone! I've seen it so many times with Joel in the past. People pretend to be taking a picture of something near you, but you know really that they're taking a picture of you. And seeing as I'm Public Enemy Number One at the moment I reckon my picture's worth a bob or two.' Charly didn't think she was being paranoid. What press she had seen hadn't been painting her in the most favourable of lights.

Before Charly had had a taste of fame, she thought that to be famous was like being a member of an exclusive club. One where everyone wanted to know you and be you and above all, liked you. But as time had gone on she realised that it was lonely being well known. Everyone thought that they knew you but they only really knew what was presented to them in the press. And currently the British public thought that Charly was a gold-digger who had bagged herself a rich footballer and who was now somehow – even though there wasn't a scrap of evidence to substantiate it – implicated in his murder. Charly had never had many friends, but now she felt totally alone. She couldn't confide in her dad, not after accusing him of Joel's murder. They hadn't spoken properly since then. Len passed messages to Charly through Shirley and she passed messages back. They were both pretending that everything was alright but things were far from alright. Until the police could tell Charly exactly who had killed Joel, her accusation against her father would always hang in the air.

There was no one else she could turn to. She couldn't confide in Jimmy because he was the worst listener in the world. Anita and Tanita may have been brought up in the same house as her but they had never felt like her sisters; they were twins and seemed to only need one another to get by. They kept themselves to themselves and hadn't been particularly forthcoming with any offer of emotional support since Joel's death. Then again, what could she expect? Both of them were as daft as a brush and went to pieces every week when someone was voted off *X Factor*: emotional rocks they weren't. The one person that Charly wanted to confide in was standing by her side. But she couldn't, not yet. She couldn't allow herself to think that her mother was going to stay for ever. Shirley could leave again at any moment. She'd done it before. What was to stop her doing it again?

Shirley came to a stop at the lakeside and spread her coat on the floor. Sitting down, she patted it to indicate Charly come and join her. Charly smiled and shuffled alongside her mother. They both looked out over the water in silence. The place was so remote that Charly felt like she had momentarily escaped all of the claustrophobia and intrusion of the last few weeks.

Charly suddenly felt that there was someone behind her. She quickly turned around to discover that it wasn't someone, but some*thing*. A deer had wandered over to drink from the lake and was eyeing Shirley and Charly cautiously. Charly stared at the creature, totally mesmerised. Its huge brown eyes looked at her quizzically. Its gleaming coat and proud antlers made her feel small and insignificant.

'Hello, sweetheart,' Shirley said, smiling at the beast.

'He's beautiful.'

'I think it's a she,' Shirley said.

The deer looked at them for one remaining moment before heading down to the water. Charly felt suddenly overcome. The sight of the deer touched her for some reason that she couldn't place and suddenly she was crying. Something about letting her emotions out at this precise moment, in this precise place, wasn't about Joel, or about the way she was being treated by the press, or the fact that her mother had returned; it was about her. She felt small and lost in the world and needed to find her place again as Charly Metcalfe, whoever she was or might turn out to be.

Charly felt her mother's arm around her and her warm breath in her hair as she curled into a ball in her arms.

'Come on, love, it'll be alright,' Shirley said reassuringly.

'Will it? Can you guarantee it?'

'No one can guarantee anything.'

'They can't, can they? Everyone leaves in the end, don't they? You did.'

'I'm back now.'

'That's big of you,' Charly said, knowing that the comment was hurtful but needing to say it; feeling a hit from being spiteful to someone who had hurt her so much. Shirley looked as if she was about to say something but Charly stopped her. 'Sorry, Mum. That was out of order.' She breathed in sharply, realising that she had just said *mum* without it being a title loaded with sarcasm – so that Shirley knew that she thought her to be unworthy of it.

Shirley didn't say anything, but Charly knew being called mum by her daughter meant a lot to her. Charly wasn't sure if she was ready to give Shirley something that meant a lot to her.

'I told your dad the truth the other day, about what happened when I went away …' Shirley said quietly. Charly's stomach knotted. She had no idea what this story entailed. Over the years she'd imagined so many different variations that she didn't know what to think about her mother's vanishing act. 'I can tell you too if you want to know.' Charly shrugged as if nonplussed. But really she was surprised that her mum couldn't hear her heart trying to thump its way out of her chest.

*

Jodie was sitting in her apartment watching a DVD when the phone rang. Seeing that it was her mum, she answered it with a look of confusion.

'Hi, it's me. I'm outside,' Tracy barked.

'What you doing outside?'

'Can't I come and see my daughter once in a while?'

'Course you can,' Jodie said, matching her mum's indignation. 'But you've never been here before so I'm just wondering why you're starting now.'

'Let me up, you stroppy mare,' Tracy demanded.

'Push the buzzer,' Jodie said, replacing the handset.

A few moments later Tracy wandered into the flat. 'How's tricks?' she asked.

'You know … the usual. Police still wanting to know if I've had a bang on the head and suddenly remembered something, world's press ringing up to see if I'll agree to an exclusive once the murder is solved, just your bog standard few weeks really,' Jodie said wearily.

'That lot on the estate are loving all this. Sod 'em, I say. They wish they were famous, don't they. They're all jealous of us lot.'

Jodie looked at her mum. *Was she for real?* 'If this is fame you can keep it. It's not like I'm accompanying Colin Farrell to the Oscars, is it? I saw someone dead with a knife through his chest.'

'I'm just saying, aren't I? That lot on the estate

love all that. Gives 'em something to think about when they get out of bed in the morning other than their shitty little lives.'

Jodie's eyes narrowed. Her mum used the phrase 'that lot on the estate' to intimate what she was really thinking herself. 'What you mean is that you're quite enjoying the fact we're back in the news again. You like it, don't you?'

Tracy's eyes narrowed. 'If I liked it I'd be milking it like some of these low-life mothers you see in the papers. Not me. Keep myself to myself, don't I?'

'You're a real trooper, Tracy,' Jodie said sarcastically.

'Button it, gobby.'

'You button it.' Jodie was indignant. Her mum had a nerve, coming round to her house and calling the shots.

'Anyway, I'm not here for a row …'

'Makes a change.'

'I'm here to see how you're fixed work-wise.'

'I'm fixed fine work-wise, why?' *Where on God's earth is this going?* Jodie wondered.

'Well, I've been doing my collections and I was thinking I could do them a damn sight quicker if I had my mouthy daughter in tow. I'd split it with you fifty-fifty …' Tracy didn't seem to see that Jodie was standing with her mouth agape, thinking that her mother was truly unbelievable. 'We're not sure when Mac's coming back and I'm not waiting around for him to put in an appearance and then get some stranger in to help me.'

'Are you insane?' Jodie said when Tracy finally paused for breath.

'What you on about?'

'What I really don't need right now is to draw even more attention to myself by joining my mother loan-sharking around the highways and byways of Bradington. And – if you haven't noticed – I've already got a job – some might even go as far as to call it a career – as a model.'

'Bloody hell. Don't get your knickers in a twist. I was only offering you a business opportunity.'

Jodie laughed. 'Listen to you. You've been wandering round tapping up women for a fiver a week for a couple of months and you think you're JR.'

Tracy's eyes narrowed. 'Don't underestimate me, Jodie. I've come here to be nice. If you don't want to do it then fine. Don't throw it in my face.'

'I've never underestimated you, Mum. I know exactly what you're capable of. Anything.' Jodie smiled sweetly.

'You can be an unremitting little bitch when you want to be, can't you?'

Jodie nodded; this was the Tracy she was used to. 'That's more like it, Mum,' she said. Tracy turned on her heel and headed for the door.

'Let's go for a drink soon. Get everyone together,' Jodie shouted after her mum, feeling the slightest twinge of guilt that she had offended her and shouldn't leave things on a sour note. Tracy didn't look back; she simply gave her daughter a one-fingered salute over her right shoulder and marched out of the door.

'Lovely,' Jodie said, totally resigned to the fact that this was all she could ever expect from her mother.

*

Tracy wasn't happy. She was marching down the street like a woman possessed. *That cheeky little cow Jodie*, she thought. *Belittling me like that. Who the hell did she think she was?* The fact was that Tracy might have only been working for Markie a short time but she was good at what she was doing and she knew it: so did he, she could tell. Markie played his cards close to his chest but he had been amazed at how quickly she'd picked things up; she'd seen it in his face when she, week on week, delivered the outstanding money. And it wasn't just the loan collection part; that was easy to Tracy. But things like how the office itself was run, how the clubs operated, how they made money from people by buying their houses from them to release equity and renting them back. She had taken a real interest and it all made sense to her.

The biggest part of running a business like Markie's was looking to be in charge at all times. The fact that Mac had gone to ground hadn't seemed to bother Markie in the slightest. But Tracy knew he must have had a few sleepless nights about it. Markie was a master at striking a balance between being a total professional in everything he did and looking as if ever challenged he wouldn't be responsible for his actions. He also seemed to have eyes in the back of his head.

Tracy knew that he got these attributes from her. She was as sharp as a tack unlike his father – the useless lump. But she wasn't about to start winding herself up about him again by giving him any more time in her head. Markie seemed suspicious any time Tracy asked questions about his other businesses so she just listened and learned as and when she could. It was interesting and in another life it could have been her running something like this, if she hadn't had a load of kids and been a stay-at-home mum, she thought rather loftily. She headed into the office. There was no sign of Markie, but Tammy was kneeling in the middle of the office rearranging the entire filing system. She gave Tracy a weak smile. Tracy knew she couldn't expect anything more from her; she'd been nothing but a frosty cow to the girl since the first day she'd walked in the office. Today she decided it was time for a change of tack. And as Tracy was the boss's mother, poor old Tammy was just going to have to go along with it.

'Fancy a brew?' Tracy asked. Tammy, who was on all fours, looked around at Tracy like a dog that was slightly shocked to find another dog sniffing its bum.

'Me?' she said finally.

Tracy looked down at the girl. She wasn't actually that bad-looking despite Tracy's barbed comment to her the first time they'd met. She had dark brown shoulder-length hair, blue eyes and a button nose. Her lips were a bit on the thin side but nothing that a bit of lip gloss couldn't help. 'Who else?'

Tammy looked perplexed. 'Please,' she said.

Tracy wandered through into the kitchen area knowing that the girl was probably eyeing her intently, thinking that she'd never been near the kettle before. Tracy sang to herself as she made two cups of tea and arranged some chocolate biscuits she found at the back of the cupboard on a plate. She returned to the main part of the office to find Tammy sitting at an unused desk with the files arranged in front of her. The poor girl looked like she was barricading herself in.

'It's alright. I don't bite,' Tracy said, popping the tea and biscuits down. 'Alright, I do a bit but I won't bite you. Promise.'

Tammy laughed nervously.

'I think I might have got off on the wrong foot with you and I didn't mean to. You know how it is, you start a new job and you want everyone to think you know what you're doing. That's why I gave it the frosty-knickers routine. I'm not really like that; I'm sure our Markie's said.' She looked at Tammy, who seemed to be searching around her mental filing system to see if there was an example of when her boss had ever said that about his mother. 'Maybe not. He doesn't say much at work, does he?'

'Not a lot, no,' Tammy agreed, gnawing nervously on a chocolate digestive.

'Well, I was wondering if one night me and you shouldn't blow a bit of the petty cash and go into town and have a knees-up, what do you say?' Tracy asked. Tammy looked genuinely terrified by the prospect.

'Er … yes. That'd be lovely,' she said, her falsetto tone suggesting that she'd rather be dangled over a pit of crocodiles.

'Yes, it would, wouldn't it?' Tracy smiled. There was an awkward silence then Tracy looked at her watch and back at Tammy. 'Why don't you go have a long lunch? How does two hours sound? I'll man the phones.'

'Well, I don't know if Markie would be happy if he came back and I wasn't here.'

'Don't worry. I'll tell him you've just gone and then send you a text telling you to come back.' Tammy looked like a rabbit in the headlights. 'It's alright, you don't have to be scared. Look, I'm being straight up with you. I want us two to get along. We're the only girls in the office.' Tracy knew she was stretching the term *girls* but she quite liked it. 'And I think we should get on. So I'm just saying go have a long lunch as a treat.'

'If you're sure …'

'Course I am.' Tracy smiled genuinely. She was

sure. And whatever Tammy thought, she wasn't trying to stitch her up; she really did think that they should get on better. Because Tracy wanted an ally, someone she could trust in the office. She didn't want to spend the rest of the days marching the streets of Bradington extracting money; she wanted to learn about the business and make a great living like Markie did. If Jodie wasn't going to come along for the ride then she might as well get the hired help on side. And if it meant the odd piss-up and the occasional long lunch, then it was a small price to pay and one that she wasn't footing the bill for anyway.

chapter seventeen

Charly was alone again in her vast house. A week
had passed since she and Shirley had had their day
out together and Shirley had spoken at length about
what had happened to her when she had left. Charly
had mixed feelings about it all. She had never
suffered from depression so didn't think that she
was in any position to assume she knew what her
mum had gone through, but a little bit of her
thought that Shirley's love for her children should
have transcended any thought – or lack of thought
– for herself. Since their frank conversation, though,
Charly had felt better about her mum being around.
And she even found herself opening up to her
slightly. But not too much. She didn't want to get
too close to her mum only to find that she had
disappeared again.

Charly had had the usual stream of visitors

during the week, all of whom seemed anxious to stare out of the window and wish themselves anywhere but sitting opposite the morose, grieving widow. She felt sorry for them. She didn't want to be the person making people feel awkward; she wanted to be able to engage them in conversation and talk about something other than the obvious fact that Joel was gone and no one knew who was responsible.

But today Charly had awoken with a different feeling to the one which she had felt constantly since Joel died. Until today she had been utterly consumed by the blackness of her grief; of wondering how she was going to get by without Joel. Today, however, she was angry. She had entered the kitchen first thing that morning so full of rage that she had swiped the kettle from the work surface, forcing it crashing to the floor. She was angry at Joel for dying, she was angry at Joel for not saying goodbye and she was angry at Joel for how he had behaved with her: for never having the opportunity to right the constant wrongs in their relationship but instead being left with memories of being his punch bag rather than his partner. She was angry at the press camped outside her door every day, the public for their verdict of guilty by association that they seemed to have labelled her with and angry at whoever had taken Joel from her for putting her in this hideous predicament.

Charly wanted all of this to end. She wanted to be allowed a funeral so that she could stop living in limbo. And she wanted to know who had killed Joel and to see them tried and convicted. She couldn't believe that the police seemed to be no nearer finding a killer. He was one of the most high-profile footballers in the country and yet no one had seen anything that might point towards a killer. She had thought on a number of occasions that Kim or even Jodie might have had something to do with it. But both had been ruled out and were being used only as witnesses. Her mind had raced through everyone she had ever met with Joel, anyone she thought she could point the finger at and say 'You did it.' But the person she kept coming back to was her father and she couldn't even begin to think about the implications of such a thing. The police were doing their damnedest to find the person responsible. They didn't need the pressure of the media bearing down on their investigation any more than Charly needed it bearing down on her time of grief.

Carol, the liaison officer, had been great. She had listened and been patient with Charly and kept her as informed as possible, but Charly knew that she was just doing a job and that although she might care about what happened to Charly in the short term, it was still just her job and at the end of the day she went home to her family. Something Charly felt that she'd never again be able to think about having for herself.

Charly wished that her mind could settle on something else, even for a few moments, but it seemed unable. Even thinking about the most basic things, like what she should eat that day, in turn led her to think about what Joel would have eaten if he'd been here and then she was back thinking about what had happened.

'Hello!' a voice shouted from below. It was Terry. 'I've got a visitor for you.'

Charly shut her eyes and took a deep breath to steady herself; she wasn't in the mood for visitors today. 'I don't need any surprises. Who is it?'

'It's me, Charly. I just wanted to see you were alright.' Charly's eyes widened when she heard the familiar voice: Scott Crompton, her old boyfriend. She ran into the hall but seeing Scott, she stopped and smiled sheepishly.

'Hi.'

Scott stepped towards her. 'Our Markie said he'd seen you.'

'Did he?' she asked, worried as to what context Markie had given to their meeting.

'Yes. Didn't say much else though. That's why I wanted to come and see you. Been wanting to come and see you for a while.'

Charly saw that Terry was trying to weigh up the situation to make sure that she was safe. 'I'll leave you two to it,' he said, clearly realising that Scott did not pose a threat.

Charly smiled at him. 'That's fine, Terry. Thanks.'

Both Charly and Scott waited until Terry had left the house. Then they both spoke over one another asking how the other was. Charly smiled, embarrassed. 'Sorry. You first.'

'I've been dead worried about you. I know I'm probably a mug for being here but I still care about you and seeing all that shit in the papers, it eats me up, you know?' Scott said, looking into her eyes. He'd allowed his usually cropped blond hair to grow out into a shaggy mop. Coupled with his newly acquired stubble, Charly thought it suited him – he looked more adult somehow.

Charly nodded slowly. She did know. She and Scott had been together for what felt like years. They stood in awkward silence for a moment, then Scott looked down at the carrier bag in his hand as if he'd just remembered something. 'Oh, brought you something.' He handed the bag to Charly. 'You might not like stuff like that any more, but I just thought, you know ...'

Charly opened the carrier bag and there was a Mulberry handbag sitting in the bottom of it. She looked up at Scott and smiled. Not because this was just what she'd always wanted – she already had a wardrobe full of designer handbags – but because Scott used to buy her designer accessories that he'd just so happened to be standing near when they'd made their way off the back of a lorry. 'I can't take this, Scott.'

'Why not?'

'Because it will have cost you a fortune.'

'Come on, you know me. Ways and means to these things.'

'I know that these are a grand new and you'll have paid a couple of hundred quid.' She held the bag out for Scott to take back.

'I thought it might cheer you up.' Scott shrugged, looking like he was now out of ideas.

'I don't want you wasting your money,' Charly said, looking at the floor. She felt a massive pang of guilt. When they had been together that was probably all it seemed she wanted from him. He'd bought her a pedigree dog that she had paraded around in a handbag for a time until the vet's bills had become a problem and they'd had to give it back to the breeder. He'd kept her in fake J12 watches, designer shades and handbags and she had even convinced Scott to part with his hard-earned cash so that she could have a boob job, something she'd ended up changing her mind about once she started working with Leanne and realised that her own breasts were an asset not a problem. Poor Scott, Charly thought now. He'd put up with a lot. Only to be unceremoniously dumped for a footballer. And yet he was still here, with no apparent hard feelings.

'There's something you could give me,' Charly said quietly. She was trying to weigh up if what she was about to request was appropriate. Scott looked at her hopefully. 'A hug?' she said quietly.

Scott stepped towards her and took her in his arms. And suddenly she felt closer to anyone than she had since Joel's death. Although if she was completely honest with herself she felt closer to

Scott than she had to anyone long before Joel's death.

*

Scott ejected the DVD they had been watching and looked at Charly. 'I'd better get off.'

'Do you have to?' she asked before she had time to check herself and not sound so needy.

'I'm on nights this week, got to get back and changed.' Scott worked in a factory and his shifts rotated every week.

Charly wanted to say something but was finding it hard to put the words in such a way that they would make sense. 'I just wanted to say sorry for ...' She paused for a moment, thinking about everything that she was sorry for. 'Everything,' Charly said finally.

Scott shrugged. 'It's OK. We just weren't meant to be,' he said without meeting her eye.

Charly really needed to confide in someone about how she felt and Scott seemed like the perfect person, but she knew that it was wrong. Knew that Scott shouldn't have to listen to anything she had to say about Joel. 'I feel terrible at the minute. What do you think about everything that's happened with Joel?'

Scott looked at the floor. He didn't seem too comfortable with the question himself. He finally looked up, meeting Charly's eye. 'I can't pretend I'm sorry about what happened to him, Charly, because I know how he was treating you.'

Charly suddenly felt angry again. 'You know. Do you? How do you *know*? How does anyone *know*?'

'People talk,' Scott said simply.

'What, you mean that lot at the factory read the papers, jump to conclusions and then spend all day gossiping.'

'No, I mean that a friend of mine, his missus is a nurse at the hospital and she saw the state of you. I was going to call then but I didn't. I knew that if we spoke and you said yourself that he'd laid a finger on you then I wouldn't be responsible for my actions.'

'Some nurse! That's good of her. Thought that they were meant to keep that buttoned,' Charly said, pointing at her mouth. 'And anyway, what does she know? What went on between me and Joel went on between me and Joel. It's nobody else's business.'

'OK. But if he was hurting you then you can't blame people for being concerned.'

'We hurt each other, alright?' Charly snapped, wanting the conversation over and done with.

'Did he or did he not put you in hospital?'

'I don't have to answer that.'

'What a low-life piece of shit,' Scott spat.

'That's my husband you're talking about,' Charly shouted.

'Some husband. Knocking you around and thinking it's alright?'

'It's complicated.'

'Sounds it to me.' Scott was shaking his head in disbelief.

Something suddenly occurred to Charly. 'Have you been questioned by the police?'

'Yes.' Scott put his hands to his face. 'What you suggesting? You think I did it? Well, I didn't, more's the pity. That bastard got everything he deserved by the sounds of it.'

'You can't say that!' Charly shouted. Getting out her anger felt strangely fulfilling. She had wanted to shout and scream at someone for a long time. At least with Scott she could be herself without having to tread on eggshells, even if she was insinuating that he was capable of murder.

'I can and I have.' Scott turned and headed for the door. 'I'm going, Charly. I didn't want an argument but you're obviously not going to listen to anything I have to say.'

She let him go. He opened the hall door without looking back and slammed it forcefully behind him. She didn't want to think that Scott could have had anything to do with Joel's murder but she really couldn't be sure. She wanted an ally in Scott, a friend for life. But she couldn't have a nagging doubt about his innocence at the back of her mind and expect him to be her confidante. She heard a car screech off in the distance. Should she call the police? Charly walked back into the lounge and collapsed on the settee. No, she wouldn't. If the police were going to find whoever was responsible for Joel's death they didn't need her help. And if Scott had had anything to do with it, she was fairly sure that he wouldn't have had the nerve to show his face. But really Charly just didn't know what to think about anyone or anything any more.

*

Swing was at the end of his tether. For too long now he'd been mugged around by Mac and Markie. He did everything that was asked of him and got little in return. He felt that he had no life; wherever he was he had to drop everything for Mac. Not any more. He was standing outside Markie's office. He knew he'd be in there now. He was going in to straighten things out between them once and for all and if Markie wasn't willing to listen he was going to make him listen. He'd spent long enough jumping when Markie said jump. When they'd been younger they'd been equals: a team. But since Mac had come along the last decade had seen Markie go all starry-eyed about business and forget who his friends were. Swing knew that he only had himself to blame for Markie cutting him off after he'd slept with Mandy. But it wasn't something that just happened out of the blue. Swing had been fed up to the back teeth with the way he'd been marginalised by Markie. Today he was going to set the record straight.

It was 8pm and the light to the office was on. No one else would be there at this time, Swing had guessed – and he was right. When he opened the door to the office, Markie was sitting behind his paper-strewn desk, looking through the drawers. Markie looked up. When he saw it was Swing he looked back into his drawer and carried on his search. The only thing that gave away the fact that he was slightly rattled by the prospect of being in the presence of his old mate was the vein that twitched in his neck. Swing knew Markie better than he knew himself, and the pulsing vein was a dead giveaway.

'Well?' Swing said.

'Why can you never find a fucking stapler when you need one?'

Swing looked at him. He felt like finding the stapler for him and driving some staples into Markie's thick stubborn skull to make him see sense. He didn't respond, he just dragged a chair across to Markie's desk and sat opposite him, waiting for him to stop pretending to be distracted.

Markie looked at him witheringly. 'Sit yourself down.'

'I have, thanks,' Swing said. He was fed up of cowering, being frightened of what could happen next because he was in Markie's debt. They used to do everything together when they were kids. Swing had taken countless beatings for Markie and made sure that he'd dished countless out. And what for? To be treated like a leper when they were grown men? He didn't think so.

'What d'you want?'

'To stop acting like kids. To get back into the

action instead of having to do everything through Mac. What use is he anyway? Hiding away like a fucking kid.'

'He's got his reasons.'

'I know his reasons inside out, don't I? I've been doing his dirty work for him.'

'His dirty work is your job.'

Swing shook his head. There was a lot he wanted to say but he didn't think it would do any good. 'Right,' he said.

Markie stood up. 'You don't get any privileges any more. Not after what happened.'

'Who are you, Markie?' Swing asked angrily. 'The fucking Godfather?'

'I'm your boss.'

Swing couldn't believe the words had just come out of his mouth. There had been a time when Markie knew better than to treat Swing like a mug. 'Used to be my mate.'

'Well, we know who fucked that, don't we?'

Markie glared at Swing. Swing got to his feet, maintaining eye contact with Markie. 'I'll get off, then,' he said. Both men knew this was a stand-off.

'Yeah, make sure you do.'

Swing left the office and walked down the stairs. Once outside he found the nearest lamppost and punched it. His skin ripped and blood began to trickle down his hand. Swing didn't feel it. He walked off in the direction of the gym. That was the last time Markie Crompton was going to make a fool of him.

chapter eighteen

Len and Shirley were sitting in the living room on one of his rare nights off. There was so much that he wanted to say to her, even now, but he couldn't find the words. As she flicked through *Take a Break* magazine, Len found the silence deafening. Although she had explained about her life away, Len wanted to know what Shirley felt about her life now. Now that she was back in Bradington and waking every day in her old house with her old husband.

'How's the job then? You've not said,' Len ventured. Shirley had recently started work on a fruit stall in the market. The last time Len had seen Shirley get a job it had been the beginning of their life unravelling.

'Good. I like it. It is what it is. Bagging up apples for little old ladies who don't trust Tesco's and have been coming there for years. Nothing earth-shattering to tell you. It's a job, you know.'

'I bet you get some right characters coming in the market.'

'Yeah, I suppose you do,' Shirley said, but she was more interested in the article she was reading about a woman who had a cyst cut out of her that weighed thirty pounds.

Len didn't know what else to say. He'd have *liked* to have said, 'Are you happy, Shirley, now you're back? Do you want to stay? Will you ever be in love with me again?' But he didn't have the courage so instead said, 'Fancy a cup of tea?'

'Go on then,' Shirley said, not seeming to be paying attention.

Len went through into the kitchen. As he fired the tea bags into the cups he felt Shirley standing behind him. 'Len …' she said tentatively. He turned around. 'I'll move out if you want. If I'm, you know, getting under your feet.'

'You're not getting under my feet at all.'

'It's just that we never talk and I really wish we did.'

'I've just been sitting in there thinking the same thing,' Len admitted. He felt utterly relieved that Shirley was feeling as he was.

'I feel guilty about everything. Like I should apologise all the time.'

'Don't be daft,' Len said, filling the kettle, anything to distract from meeting Shirley's eye. He felt shy around her sometimes.

'I'm not being daft. So what do you want to talk about?' she asked.

'I just want to know ...' Len didn't get a chance to finish his sentence. There was a hammering at the door that made them both jump out of their skin. Shirley went to open it. Four police officers were standing there, and didn't wait to be invited in. The one at the helm was holding a piece of paper. 'We've a warrant to search the premises.' Len watched as if everything was in slow motion as he was handcuffed by one of the officers. Another went over to Shirley and began to handcuff her too.

'Len Metcalfe, we are arresting you on suspicion of murder ...'

'Shirley Metcalfe, we are arresting you for perverting the course of justice ...'

Len stared at Shirley. She looked back at him in alarm. It looked like their conversation was going to have to wait.

*

Tracy and Tammy were on their much-talked-about night out. Talked about by Tracy, at any rate. Tammy had seemed to just worry about the prospect of having to spend the evening with her colleague and mother of the boss. Tracy had arranged for them to go to the Glasshouse and sit in the VIP area sipping lethal cocktails. Personally she'd never understood the attraction of champagne. Everyone banged on about it but it wasn't much use for getting pissed as a newt. That's why Tracy liked Long Island Iced Teas. Any cocktail with five different spirits in was a friend of Tracy's.

So far the night had gone to plan. Tracy and Tammy were getting along famously and the girl wasn't too bad when she had a few drinks down her neck and relaxed a little. 'So, how long you been working for our Markie now?' Tracy shouted to Tammy over some racket that the DJ seemed insistent on playing.

'A year. Since Leanne left.' Leanne Crompton had been Markie's office manager for a time before she set up in business on her own.

'How much is he paying you?' Tammy looked shocked. Tracy looked at her as if this was a totally reasonable question.

'Er, sixteen grand a year.'

'If I was running the place I'd have you on more. Give you some incentive.'

'Right,' Tammy said slowly.

'I mean, you need to know when you've got good staff and sometimes I think that our Markie hasn't a clue. I think you should be on at least twenty grand.'

'Do you?' Tammy said cautiously.

'Yeah, but what do I know?'

Tammy smiled nervously and sucked back a large strawful of her drink.

'You any idea what level three means?' Tracy asked innocently.

Tammy looked at Tracy, slightly taken aback. 'In what context?'

Tracy was getting a little sick of the dancing round the handbags routine, but she persevered. 'Well, if our Markie was to say to you, "We had to go to level three on that", what would he mean?'

Tammy looked at Tracy as if this was a trick question. 'It means apply force, doesn't it?'

'What sort of force?' Tracy probed.

Tammy looked like she'd said too much. 'I don't know if I'm right, it's just what I've sort of ... gathered.'

'Yeah, that's what I'd sort of gathered too.' Tracy nodded. 'Have the police contacted the office again?'

'Again?' Tammy asked, confused.

'I just mean that they had Markie in for questioning and they were round my house. Thought they might have been in the office, that's all.'

'Not that I know of.'

Tracy nodded. She wasn't sure why she was putting herself through tonight, but she knew that it was probably better to have Tammy on side than not and if that was all that came out of this evening then it was an evening well spent.

Tammy went to the toilet and Tracy checked her phone. She thought that Markie might have called to see if everything was to their satisfaction but he probably couldn't care less whether his mum was having a nice night out. Sometimes she felt as if she bent over backwards for her kids and got nothing in return. She had four missed calls. There was a voicemail message. It was from Mac.

'Hi Tracy. I'm just calling for a chat. Give me a call. Back on the old number now.'

Tracy dialled his number. What was going on? she wondered. Why hadn't the police arrested him? Maybe they had and they'd let him go. They were a useless lot, she thought; she should've been a copper herself, she'd have got more done.

'Hello, stranger,' she said, walking over to the

foyer of the club where she could just about hear herself think.

'Tracy, fancy meeting up? I owe you a kiss and a cuddle and a sorry.' She'd rather have poked her own eyes out than kiss and cuddle this sap after his disappearing act but she wanted to know what was going on.

'Where are you?'

'I'm in the library.'

'Renewing your books?' Tracy joked.

'Very funny. The hotel.'

The Library was Bradington's new boutique hotel. Tracy didn't rate its chances for longevity. The good people of Bradington were more your thirty-pound-a-night kettle-nailed-to-the-wall lot but it was nice to see that someone thought the city was worth sticking a few quid into.

'I'll be there in half an hour,' she said, swigging her drink.

Tammy came back from the toilet. 'Same again?' she asked.

'No, love, I'm going to hit the sack if you don't mind.' Tracy knew that this was an early exit for someone who had been bleating on about their night out for so long but she'd rather get to the bottom of things with Mac.

'Oh, OK.' Tammy actually sounded gutted.

'Come on, love, when you're my age you need your beauty sleep. Tell you what, give one of your mates a ring and get a couple of bottles of champagne in, my treat.'

'Really?' Tammy asked, genuinely grateful.

'Course.'

Tracy walked behind the bar and whispered to the barman, 'Two bottles of champagne, and tell our Markie I've stuck them on the work tab.'

'There isn't a "work tab",' he said rather haughtily.

'There is now.'

*

The only way to describe the Library for Tracy was *posh*. The reception area was tastefully decorated with dark Edwardian colours that perfectly complemented the grand old building. The windows were swathed with purple velvet curtains and the huge mirror that hung at the back of the small reception area was an understated gold antique. It was the sort of taste that Tracy wished she had, but she knew that she couldn't walk past an ornament of a cat playing cymbals without buying it and sticking it on her cluttered mantelpiece, so the chance of her house ever looking anything like this was remote.

She asked for directions to the room where Mac was staying and felt curiously nervous. She couldn't quite place the reason for the nerves. She didn't think that it was because she would soon be seeing Mac again. She didn't think it was because she was in a hotel that she felt sure she was about to be thrown out of because she didn't look like she should be anywhere near somewhere this classy, and she certainly didn't think it was because she had betrayed Mac, because Tracy didn't think for a minute that she had. He'd let himself down, if anything. Maybe it was a combination of all those things that was making her nervous. Or maybe it was none of the above and Tracy was sensing something that she didn't even know about yet.

She knocked on the door of room five and waited for it to open. Mac was standing there looking slightly dishevelled but good for it. 'Come in, sweetheart,' he said, standing back to allow Tracy into the room. He didn't grab her as she thought he might. He simply stood there looking at her. Tracy looked around the room. She was going to sit on the bed but then opted for the chair in the corner.

'Nice gaff.'

'Not bad for round here, is it?'

'A lot of weather we've been having,' Tracy said, half-smiling.

'We're not good at bullshit small talk, are we?'

'No, so let's cut it, shall we? Where the fuck have you been, if you'll pardon my French,' Tracy asked, trying to keep her voice as neutral as possible.

'Look, Trace, I know we were messing around and you probably thought that I was a right tube for going off like that, but I swear I had good reason.'

'Did you kill Joel Baldy?' Tracy asked outright.

Mac didn't flinch. 'Now, Tracy, you know me and I'm not going to start going into the arse of things with anyone. Even you.'

'Especially me.'

'Why d'you say that?'

'That's what it sounded like you were driving at.'

'I don't drive at anything, I come straight out and say it. Anyway, Len Metcalfe's been arrested for killing the Baldy lad, so I think it's fair to say the police have got their man and I'm free to come back.'

'Len?'

'Thought you'd be pleased.'

It wasn't exactly what Tracy had been planning but it *was* good news. She thought that the police had exonerated Len since the prodigal wife had returned.

'How do you know?'

'I've got someone on the inside at the cop shop.'

Tracy felt the colour drain from her. Maybe this was why there had been no mention of the file she had sent to the police. She wracked her brain, trying to think if anything she had sent directly implicated her. She could always pin it on Tammy if she had to. 'Really?'

'Really.' Mac was eyeing Tracy closely. She shifted uncomfortably in the chair. 'Poor old Len, eh? They found some fingerprints at the hotel, apparently. Waiting for the forensics to come back. Three people who were staying at the hotel that night picked him out in photos they were shown and he had the best reason in the world to want him dead.'

'Do you think he did it?'

Mac laughed loudly for a few moments and stopped abruptly, looking at Tracy with what she knew to take as serious hatred burning in his eyes. 'Do I think that fat little Len Metcalfe murdered a strapping lad like Joel Baldy in his hotel room?' Mac asked, looking around the room that he was staying in as if he'd just realised that this too was a hotel room and what an amazing coincidence that was. 'I think it'll have taken someone far stronger than Len to pull that off, don't you, Tracy?'

Tracy got up from her seat and headed towards the door. Mac got up and pressed his hand hard against the door. 'Sit down,' he ordered. 'Me and you have got some talking to do.'

Tracy did as she was told. She had no choice. She was terrified.

*

Len was sitting in the interview room staring blankly at the wall. He was going to have to come clean with the police this time, tell them everything. He'd thought that by trying to keep himself out of the frame initially he'd be doing not only himself a favour but more importantly, Charly. Now he knew what it must look like to the police and he was wishing that he could turn back time and hold his hands up to what he had really done on the night that his son-in-law was murdered.

Two police officers came into the room. One sat down and without saying anything looked at Len witheringly. The other one threw his files on the desk and said, 'Could have saved us and yourself a bit of time, Mr Metcalfe, telling us from the start what happened.'

'I'm saying nowt till that thing's turned on.' Len nodded at the tape recorder on the table.

The officer looked at his colleague and raised an eyebrow. '10.48pm …' he said, pressing record and going on to state the date, Len's name and what he was being arrested for.

The officer sat back in his chair and eyeballed Len, obviously thinking that he and his colleague were here for the long haul and were going to have to drag the truth out of Len. Len didn't envy these men. The one doing the talking, his eyes were grey and sunken, his skin pallid from spending too many days in interview rooms with little light. Len sat forward and placed his hands flat on the table as if he needed all the ballast he could get to support what he was about to say.

'You don't need to do all that probing questions and whatever else it is they teach you at training college. I'll tell you everything.'

The police officers leaned forward. This was obviously a turn-up for the books.

*

Markie was at Pandora's, a massage parlour that he owned in Manchester. He was sitting in the foyer drinking a beer while the girl on reception nervously counted out the week's takings. He didn't visit this place often. There was a time when he utilised the services of the girls here, simply because they were on offer, but now he was bored by the idea. He didn't like the look of Sharn in her tacky silver hot pants and barely-there top. He knew she was nervously eyeing him up. A lot of the girls here did that, as if Markie was somehow going to take them away from all this. Fat chance of that; he had enough on keeping his head above water without worrying about an ex-hooker for a girlfriend.

'I think it's all here, Markie,' she said, putting the money in an envelope. A door at the other end of the corridor opened and a busty woman in her late thirties wearing a trouser suit and sky-high heels walked out.

'Bloody hell, stranger,' she said.

'Now then, Trish, how's it going?'

'Alright. Had some nob-head do a runner the other night but Swing caught up with him and gave him a kicking.'

Markie's jaw clenched at the mention of Swing.

That lot, he really needed to haul them all in and make sure he was keeping track of them. Trish walked towards him, and helped herself to some water from the cooler next to Markie. 'Business is good at the minute. Load of new Polish builders in town for them flats they're slinging up up the road.'

'Poles, eh? Anything specific?' Markie always found it funny when people had certain fetishes. Trish had often said that priests were the worst; they always wanted punishing. And often their idea of punishment knew no bounds.

'Not really. Men are men, aren't they? Whatever country they're from they just want to get their end away.'

Markie smiled at Trish. To the punters she was Pandora, although her own name was far more suited to her hard-faced reality than Pandora was.

Markie's phone began to ring. It was Charly. He answered it, but didn't want Sharn or Trish to hear his conversation with her. 'I'll call you back in a minute, yeah?'

Charly said yes, but Markie could hear that she was crying. He took the money from Sharn as he pocketed his phone. 'Nice seeing you, ladies,' he said and headed out of the door, passing a shady-looking man in the stairwell who couldn't have looked more like a first-time punter if he tried.

'They're bloody good,' Markie said to him, amusing himself. The man nearly jumped out of his skin at being spoken to.

Once outside, Markie grabbed his phone and called Charly. 'Everything alright?'

'No. Dad's been arrested.'

Markie checked the time. It was midnight. 'Where is he?'

'Bradington. They're questioning him there but they might move him to Manchester. I don't know how these things work.'

'I'm in Manchester now. You at the house?'

'Where else would I be?'

Markie knew it was a stupid question; she barely left the house. 'I'll come and get you and then we can go to the police station together. What about your mum?'

'She's there too; she's being done for providing a false alibi.'

Brilliant, Markie thought as he hung up the phone. He was sure that Len hadn't done this, and he had a good idea who had.

*

Mac rummaged in a bag next to him. 'What do you call this, Tracy?' He produced photocopies of the original documents that Tracy had given to Mac. They must be the ones she had sent to the police. Her jaw fell open; she quickly shut it again.

'I don't know,' she lied. 'Them papers I got from the office for you?'

Mac slammed them on the bed and pushed his face up to Tracy's. 'Don't give me your shit, Tracy. You know what these are because you sent them to the coppers.'

'I didn't do anything of the sort. I don't even know how to work the photocopier. Tammy does all that.'

Mac sneered. 'Fuck off, Tracy, don't play dumb. You wouldn't let a silly little thing like a photocopier stand in the way of stitching me up.'

'Why would I want to stitch you up?' Tracy asked, alarmed. She was looking around the room for a way that she might be able to get out and get to Markie so that Mac couldn't harm her.

'No point in thinking you're going to do a bunk. You're staying put.' Mac walked over to the door and made sure it was locked. 'Why would you want to stitch me up?' he pondered. 'Because you're ruthless and you're fucked off with me? I don't know, you tell me.'

'I didn't send anything to the police,' Tracy reiterated. She was just about to blame Tammy again but Mac interrupted her.

'So why are your fingerprints all over it?'

Shit, Tracy thought. If he had someone on the inside then they would have access to her fingerprints. She'd been done for shoplifting a few years ago. If she'd known a Curtis Steigers CD was going to lead to all this she wouldn't have bothered nicking it.

'I didn't do it!' Tracy said again desperately. She quickly thought of something that might save her. 'I stuck some paper in the copier the other week. I don't know; my fingerprints will be all over the office, won't they? I work there now.' She wanted to kick herself; she should have put gloves on. But then again she didn't think that she'd be faced with Mac accusing her of shopping him to the police.

'Bollocks, Tracy. You had the hump because I'd gone underground. Do you know the shit this could have got me in if someone hadn't got to them first? What am I saying? Course you did – why else go to the trouble of trying to hang me out to dry?'

Tracy threw her head back and stared at Mac. She wasn't getting out of this so she dropped the damsel-in-distress façade and spoke in the slow measured voice of the bitch that she was. 'So, you do it then? You knife the poor little bastard? And for what? Twenty-five grand? Aren't you the big man, Mac?'

'You think that if I had anything to do with Joel Baldy being stabbed I'd be sitting here chewing the fat with you about it?'

'Get over yourself, Mac, you nob,' Tracy said disparagingly.

He turned around, gathering all of his strength before lunging at Tracy, grabbing her by the throat. 'You're out of your depth, Tracy. Markie gave you a job because we needed a bit of help. Then you have to go biting the hand that feeds you.'

'When our Markie finds out about this he'll fuck you off and then where will you be?' she hissed.

'Are you serious? Do you think any of your kids give a flying shit about you? How long would it take, Tracy, before anyone noticed you missing?'

Tracy looked at the lamp on the bedside table. It was just within her reach. Maybe Mac should have chosen a less salubrious hotel after all, one that glued its lamps down. Tracy leaned across and, before Mac realised what she was doing, grabbed the lamp, pulling it quickly in one sweeping motion towards him, smashing it into his face, sending him reeling backwards. Tracy knew she had little time to stand around and watch Mac come back for more. She ran to the door, twisted the lock and ran out of the room. She could hear Mac following her but she didn't look back. Seeing the fire exit ahead she ran for it, not knowing if she was going to get out of this alive. But right now, she didn't have a choice but to keep running.

*

'I was at the hotel the night that Joel Baldy died,' Len said, looking directly at the interviewing officer for his reaction.

'Which hotel?'

'Heartbreak Hotel. Which bloody hotel do you think? The Hilton, the one he was found dead in,' Len snapped.

'Alright, Len, no need to lose your rag,' the accompanying officer, who had been sitting silently at his colleague's side until now, piped up.

'I'm not ... I was there about the time you lot say he was killed.'

'Murdered,' the interviewing officer corrected.

'Murdered ... And my car was in Manchester at

the time that it was spotted and Shirley was just trying to help when she said she'd been with me all night but she hadn't. I wanted to find Joel and make him pay for what he'd done to my Charly, but I didn't kill him.'

'We know you were there that night, though, Len.'

Len hung his head. If he kept denying it, hoping to call their bluff and see exactly how they knew what they said they knew, then it could backfire on him. Anyway, he was tired of pretending. He nodded slowly, not being able to raise his head to meet the copper's eye. 'I know. I followed him back to her room. I hammered on the door but he didn't answer. He knew it was me, so I just left.'

'Just left?'

'I wasn't going to kick up a stink, was I? There were people asleep – it was a hotel. I'd had enough of being in the papers the weeks before he was done in; I didn't need the press camped on my doorstep for causing a ruck in some swanky hotel.' The irony wasn't lost on Len that the press were camped on his doorstep regardless of whether he did or didn't do anything wrong.

'Mr Metcalfe, do you expect me to believe that

on the night that Joel Baldy was killed in cold blood, you were there, but after you had followed him to the room where he was awaiting a young model coming back to spend the rest of the evening with him, not only didn't he answer the door, but you just walked away?'

'That is exactly what happened. I knew that I needed to calm down and I wasn't going to get anywhere banging on the door so I came home.'

'Yet until tonight you never thought to tell us any of this? Thought that a shonky alibi from your ex-wife would see you through?'

'It's not like that – you're painting me in a bad light.'

'I don't need to paint you in a bad light, do I? You've done that yourself well enough in the past. Two years inside for GBH?'

'You can't be seriously suggesting that an isolated incident decades ago is the mark of who I am now,' Len said, but really he was surprised that it had taken the police this long to bring it up. 'I served my time. Never put a foot wrong after that.'

'Maybe you did before it, though.'

'What's that supposed to mean?' Len asked, glaring at the copper. The police officer brought out some notes that he had at his side. 'I'm now showing Mr Metcalfe notes taken in this police station on December 10th 1974. You were accused of rape, weren't you, Len?'

Len sat bolt upright in his chair. 'No, I was not,' he said, horrified.

'Sorry,' the copper said, sounding like he really wasn't, 'actually the allegation was dropped. The alleged victim didn't want to go through with pressing charges.'

'What alleged victim?'

'I couldn't say. It's just that your name isn't as clean as you like to pretend it is.'

Len was racking his brains. Who would have said something like this about him? And why had he never known about it? 'You lot'd have hauled me in for that. You're winding me up, aren't you?'

'Why would we?' The police officer leant back and looked at his colleague as if to say, *We've got a right one here*.

Len could feel his blood beginning to boil. He wanted to grab this smarmy sod by the throat but he didn't think that would exactly help his case.

'Who's this person, then, who made this claim all those years ago? Come on.'

'Like I said, Len, I can't say. Anyway, getting back to the job in hand …'

'Tracy Crompton,' Len said.

The officer folded the notes away. 'Come on now, Len. After you tried the door and Joel refused to answer … what happened next?'

'Tracy Crompton,' he said again, shaking his head. Is that what she'd thought of him all these years, that he was a rapist? He felt sick.

'Len!' the copper barked. He'd obviously asked him a question that Len hadn't heard. Len looked up and tried to think what had happened after he had left the hotel room.

'Nothing happened. I went home.'

'Right. Let's go over this again, shall we?'

Len wasn't getting out of there any time soon – he could tell that much – but when he did there was one person he needed to get something straight with and that was Tracy.

*

Tracy ran down the concrete stairs of the fire escape, taking them three at a time. One thing she had on Mac was that she was as wiry as a whippet. She reached the fire door that was the only thing standing between her and freedom and kicked it. It didn't budge. She could hear Mac closing in on her.

She looked at the handle – above it was a bolt encased in glass, she smashed it with her bare hands, drew it back to open the door and ran out into the street. Tracy didn't have a clue where she was running to, just that she needed to get to where Mac couldn't harm her. She ran towards the main drag, knowing that the bars would be busy, but as she ran she panicked – maybe the bars were a bad idea. Mac would know the bouncers on every door and she hardly had the time to start explaining that she was Markie's mum and that Mac was a psychopath who wanted to silence her. As she headed down the main hill into the city centre, she could see the police station next to the town hall. She quickly changed her trajectory. Never would Tracy Crompton have thought that she would voluntarily run into a cop shop. But there was a first time for everything. The heels she was wearing were beginning to hurt but she didn't have time to bend down and take them off to run in her bare feet.

She charged across the road and made the mistake of turning round. She could see Mac, flagging slightly but still hot on her heels. 'Come here now!' he shouted. Tracy didn't even waste any of her precious energy telling him where to go, she just kept running. She heard a sudden thud, then a skid and a crash and looked round to see Mac in the middle of the road on his back and a Transit van with a concertinaed front end against a pedestrian island in the middle of the road. Mac was struggling to sit up. The driver of the van got out, rubbing the back of his neck, and shouted, 'Where the fuck did you come from?'

Tracy didn't wait to hear Mac's answer; she could see him getting to his feet. She began running again. Away from the road where Mac was and around the back of the town hall, bringing her out onto the main road that ran through Bradington. She ran across the city square and saw a car come round the corner that she was sure she recognised. The driver didn't see her but the lights at the crossing changed and the car slowed to a standstill. Tracy couldn't believe her luck. It was Markie with some girl at his side. As Tracy ran towards the car and banged on the passenger window, she saw that the girl accompanying him was none other than Charly Metcalfe.

*

Charly looked up to see Tracy hammering on the car window. She nearly jumped out of her skin.

'What the fuck?' Markie said, pulling the car over

to the kerb. 'Where the bloody hell have you come from?'

'Let me in,' Tracy demanded, wild-eyed.

Markie popped the central locking and Tracy scrambled into the back. 'Drive!' she demanded like a woman possessed.

'No. We're off there,' Markie said, pointing at the police station. 'I'll take you home in a bit.'

'I don't want to go home!' Tracy shouted. 'Alright, don't drive. Just get me in there without Mac seeing me.'

'Mac?'

'Will you stop fucking around?' Tracy said, slapping the seat in exasperation. The lights had turned green. Markie put his foot down. 'Not that way, that way!' Tracy said, pointing behind her.

'Alright, Miss fucking Daisy, give me a minute.' Markie put the car into reverse and turned around to go the long way to the police station. Tracy leaned back in her seat. Charly peered around at the woman who'd never so much as given her the time of day. She looked exhausted.

'You alright, Tracy?' Charly asked.

'Do I fucking look alright?' Tracy panted.

'Jesus Christ,' Charly mumbled, folding her arms and facing forward. She didn't need this.

'What's she doing with you?' Tracy asked as she tried to catch her breath.

'She's got a name,' Charly said.

'I wasn't asking you.'

'Well, she's telling you,' Markie said, indicating that Tracy would be better off buttoning it.

'What is *Charly* doing here?' Tracy asked, drawing sarcastically on Charly's name.

'My dad's been arrested.'

Markie pulled the car into an empty parking space and turned around to look at his mum. 'When she says her dad she means *our* dad.'

Charly looked around to see Tracy's reaction. Her face had drained of colour and she was speechless.

chapter nineteen

Markie knew it was only a matter of time before he
had to confront his mum about this. He'd known
something wasn't right for years. He didn't look
anything like Paul, his supposed dad. He wasn't
anything like him in temperament either; not that
that was an immediate indication of someone's
paternal link but Markie had never felt like his dad
was his dad. He'd never been able to put his finger
on it.

When Markie was about sixteen he'd heard Tracy
and Paul arguing – there was absolutely nothing
new in that, they argued all the time. But as Paul
was saying that he could walk away with the kids in
the morning and the Social wouldn't bat an eyelid (a
tired threat in their house and one that was never
followed through), Tracy had snapped and told him
that he couldn't take Markie because he wasn't his

to take. The conversation had become heated and Paul had screamed at Tracy that she couldn't say things like that. Rather than sticking around to listen to the outcome of the conversation, Markie had left the house and headed for the youth club that he used to go to as a kid. He had downed a bottle of cider and tried to forget that the conversation had ever taken place.

After that he'd always just assumed that what his mum had said was true. His dad wasn't Paul. He didn't look like him and he certainly didn't act like him. But at the same time Markie didn't really want to know who his dad was. His mum had always been the mouthiest woman on the estate, but she wasn't someone who had particularly played around when he was younger. Then again, he'd thought, who really knew what their parents had been up to before they were born. He could hardly think that of all the kids born to someone else other than their supposed dad he couldn't be one of them. Tracy was hardly the Virgin Mary.

So Markie had decided that he wasn't going to say anything. It was too much of a can of worms and Paul never mentioned it, so why should he. And since being a teenager he hadn't really thought about it until six months ago when he'd been

approached by Charly. She had asked to meet him
in a bar and said that she didn't really know how to
explain what she had to say but that she thought
that they were brother and sister. Len had invited
Charly to come to a night at the club and she had
obliged but gone alone as she hadn't wanted the
awkwardness of inviting her famous boyfriend to
the grotty club where her dad had worked. Len had
got smashed at the end of the night. He began to
talk about how much he missed her mum, then he
got onto the topic of how Charly was faring with
Joel and this in turn led to him saying that he'd
always liked Scott Crompton. By this time it was
three in the morning and Len was falling into a
drunken sleep when he said, 'Good job he wasn't
mine like the other one – I'd have had to put a stop
to that.' Charly told Markie that she'd bolted up in
the chair and demanded to know what her dad was
talking about but Len had opened his eyes, blearily
trying to focus, and had looked at her as if he didn't
know why she was kneeling at his side trying to get
some sense out of him.

Charly hadn't been able to broach the subject
with Len in the cold light of day. She found it too
hard. There were too many unanswered questions
for her, she later told Markie. If her dad thought

that he had another son out there living around the corner, why hadn't he ever done anything about it? Why had he brought the twins up as his own but couldn't extend the same courtesy to his own son? Could she even be sure with such scant information that Markie was her half brother? But Markie hadn't walked away as Charly had assumed he might. He said he was in no doubt that Len was his dad. He just didn't want the hassle of unravelling it all now in his adult life. Markie looked like Len. Len was a fat shadow of his former self, but the Roman nose was there, the prominent brow. The dark hair where the rest of the Cromptons were light in colouring. Markie told Charly that he wasn't interested in building bridges with Len – suddenly going to the football with him and acting like something out of a Gillette advert. But he and Charly found a lot of common ground as they talked and Markie found himself warming to the girl that he had always had down as someone who was out for whatever she could get.

Their friendship had built up over the months and Markie found himself becoming very protective towards her when rumours began circulating about Joel's infidelities and temper. Markie tried to persuade Charly to leave Joel, but his pleas fell on deaf ears. He had finally given up, suggesting that if she was going to put up with all that Joel threw at her, she might as well make sure she was financially stable should the volatile Mr Baldy decide that he'd had enough of her. Markie reasoned with Charly, saying that any relationship after Joel – something she refused to even think about – would always be tainted. It'd be like David and Victoria Beckham splitting up and Victoria trying to get herself a date. She would always be David Beckham's wife in the public eye and although Charly didn't think she was in any way on the level of the Beckhams, her public persona was as Joel's other half. So she had done as Markie recommended and made sure that there was some money in a bank account for her. She had told Joel it was to maintain their properties, and it was in her name. This meant that she wasn't high and dry. It also meant that the press was painting her as the black widow who had squirreled her husband's money away for herself.

Markie was sitting looking at his mum, waiting for her to say something. Tracy, it seemed, had totally shut down. Charly was staring at him; he knew she was willing him to say something else. It was as if they were all suspended in time.

'What you on about?' Tracy said finally.

'You know what I'm on about. Who you running from? What's going on?'

'No, smart arse. Don't sit with Little Miss Prissy Knickers here and start saying shit to me. If you want to ask me, you can ask me on my own.'

'I'll leave you to it,' Charly said, opening the car door.

'You don't have to …' Markie began.

'She does,' Tracy said pointedly.

Charly got out of the car. 'I'll see you in there, Markie.' She threw a look at his mum. There was no love lost between them.

'Happy now?' Markie said, wishing his mother for once could just rein in her temper and not let everything that was rattling around in that mad head of hers spill out of her mouth uncensored.

'Not really. What you driving at?'

'My dad's Len Metcalfe, isn't he?' Markie said levelly.

'And you and her have been scheming and plotting, chatting on about this behind my back, have you?'

'No, Mum. We haven't. We don't all approach everything like it's an episode of *Dallas*.'

'You calling me dramatic? That's rich. You've just dropped a bombshell like that and *I'm* the dramatic one.'

Markie wasn't in the mood for his mum's diversionary tactics. 'Is he? I'm not bothered. Paul's my dad, as bloody hopeless as he is – I just want to know what's what.'

Tracy's bottom lip began to quiver. 'He attacked me.'

'What?' Markie said. He could barely hear what his mum was saying.

'He attacked me. He raped me.' Markie looked at his mum. His eyes narrowed. He knew that when she was backed into a corner she'd squirm and wriggle her way out of it, but even he didn't think that Tracy was capable of crying rape.

'You two were going out though, weren't you?'

Tracy shook her head and looked out of the car window. 'Not when it happened, no. I'd started seeing your dad, Paul.'

Markie knew if anyone else in the world was saying this he'd believe them without a second thought and it made him angry at himself that he didn't immediately trust what his mum was saying. But Tracy was capable of swearing that black was white so who knew what the truth of the matter was.

'I knew when I was pregnant that you'd be his. I prayed that you'd be Paul's but you never looked like him or acted like him, did you?'

'Fucking hell,' Markie said, taking in what Tracy was telling him. 'Why didn't you tell anyone what had happened?'

Tracy laughed bitterly. 'Who'd have believed me?' she asked quietly.

Markie looked at his mum sadly. *She has a point*, he thought.

*

Tracy felt awful sitting here now having to pour her heart out to Markie. She didn't want him to find out this way. She didn't want him to find out at all. She and Len had always had a volatile relationship but towards the end they had both been drinking all the time and were arguing and fighting constantly. When Tracy announced that she was leaving Len he had become psychotic. He punched the windows through at Tracy's mum's house and then lay in the middle of the road waiting for the next car to come along to run him over. It was hard to believe now but of the two of them, Tracy had been the more level-headed. But she knew how to goad him. And she couldn't have done any better in the goading stakes than going out with Paul Crompton, a good-looking hard lad from school. Len was working as an apprentice joiner at the time and didn't know the people that Tracy was at school with. He heard about Paul second-hand and once he'd waited at the school gates for him and beaten him to a raggy pulp then headed off to look for Tracy. Even though there was only two years' age difference between Len and Paul, Len still looked like a deranged bully, beating up a school kid.

He turned up at Tracy's mum's stinking of booze and ready for a fight. He pulled Tracy upstairs and tried to get her to explain why she was determined to carry on with this no-mark Paul fella. When Tracy told him in no uncertain terms to leave, Len had forced himself on her. Trying to kiss her, telling her that no one else should have her, that she was his. Tracy tried to fight him off but Len was too strong. When Len finally finished his sordid business, he stood up and looked through her, his eyes black. Tracy remembered thinking that he looked as if he wasn't even there.

Afterwards she had gone to the police but knew that they thought she was wasting her time. Tracy got the general feeling that they thought this was a lovers' tiff. What was she complaining about? Also she'd left it far too late for them to take any physical evidence from her. So Tracy had tried to forget about it. She rarely saw Len. He tried to make amends once or twice but the terrible thing, Tracy quickly realised, was that he didn't seem to remember what had happened.

When she found out she was pregnant she was alarmed. She didn't have the first idea how to look after a baby, and she wasn't sure she wanted to learn; what she was sure of was that the child was Len's. Tracy papered over the fact and announced to the world that she and Paul were having a child. They got a council flat together and made a go of things, but Tracy knew that they were both too young for the responsibility they had. Len found himself in Strangeways not long after Markie was born and Tracy couldn't have been happier. She'd had little to do with him or his lot until Scott announced to Tracy a few years ago that he had a new girlfriend and then presented Charly Metcalfe to her. Tracy couldn't believe it.

She explained as much as she could to Markie. She was usually prone to histrionics when it came to anything where she wanted to get people on side, but Tracy was past caring. She'd had a bad enough day as it was without having to turn the waterworks on about something that in her opinion needed no fanfare.

'Do you think he knows what he did?' Markie asked after listening to what his mum had to say.

'Well, you'd bloody hope so, but who knows. He always acts as if nothing happened, but that's all I think it is – an act.'

'I don't think he does know. Charly says he was always quite nice about you.'

'Must have been a bit of a shock for her to find out that I was horrible then, eh?' Tracy half-laughed. 'Look, Markie,' Tracy said, being as honest as she was about anything, 'I'm sorry you found out like this that your dad's a wanker and a fat wanker at that, but there you go. I didn't tell you when you were younger because I didn't think it'd help anyone.'

'You're probably right,' Markie agreed.

'Do me a favour, don't tell your dad. It'll kill him.'

'Paul?'

'And don't start calling him Paul like you're some lefty social worker. He's your dad, right?'

'Jesus. Alright.' Tracy could feel Markie looking at her.

'So, you going to tell me what the big rush was or do I have to guess?' Markie asked.

*

Charly was sitting in the grubby foyer of Bradington police station. The foam from the chair she was perched on was exposed where someone had picked at the fabric and someone had graffitied *Derek Shags Convicts' Wives* across the cork pin board that had a host of police hotline numbers tagged to it. The policewoman behind the desk hadn't been overly helpful. Sometimes, because she was now a famous face, some people seemed to take a certain pleasure in being obstructive towards her.

The door opened and instead of the steady stream of miscreants that had trickled through as she'd been waiting, Markie and Tracy walked in. Tracy was holding a file in her hand, and marched towards the desk.

'I believe you're holding that twat – pardon my French,' she corrected herself, 'Len Metcalfe.'

'Don't call my dad a twat,' Charly said, jumping to her feet.

Markie walked over and put his hand on her shoulder to calm her.

'Steady, Princess,' Tracy said, shooting her a look.

Charly let Tracy talk, even though she sensed that she was only there to cause trouble. She spoke to the officer behind the woman at the counter. 'I need to talk to the person leading the investigation into the murder of her boyfriend,' she said, nodding at Charly.

'Husband,' Charly corrected.

'Whatever.' Tracy waved a hand.

'I'm afraid that won't be possible right at this moment.'

'Tell him I know who did it. Then we'll see what's possible, won't we? And here's a clue. It's not her fat dad.'

The woman frowned at Tracy; she'd obviously had a long day and didn't need this spiky attitude. On the other hand, Charly could see she was thinking that if Tracy had some information on their high-profile case then her superiors would be all ears.

'Could you wait there a moment? I'll just go see if Inspector Jowett is free to speak with you.'

'Jowett? Is he running the investigation?'

'No, but he's involved with the case.'

'Don't I know it, love. From what I can gather he's up to his neck. He's bent as a nine bob note. Who's in charge?'

'Detective Inspector Hannigan. Excuse me a moment.'

The woman disappeared through a door at the back of the reception area. Charly didn't dare say anything. Markie and Tracy also stood in silence. The policewoman came back a few minutes later. 'He'll be here in twenty minutes. Can I get anyone a coffee?'

'She's changed her tune,' Tracy said, not caring that the policewoman had heard her. 'Right, now you're listening, you need to get to the Library hotel. The bloke who killed Joel Baldy is booked in there. He's probably done a flit now but it'll be worth trying. It's Mac Jones.'

Markie was holding his head in his hands. He didn't want Mac stitched up for this, but he didn't want Len stitched up for it either. He wanted to save Mac's skin but Tracy had told Markie exactly how Mac had been with her and he knew that although Mac was his business partner his loyalty had to lie with his family and he meant his mum. The jury was very much out for Markie with regard to Len. If what his mum was saying was right, he wanted Joel dead.

The door swung open and a harassed-looking middle-aged man walked through the door. 'DI Hannigan,' Markie said.

He was followed by two burly officers manhandling Mac through the door.

*

Len felt as if he had been in the interview room for hours. This Jowett fella was making his life a misery and he felt that he wasn't going to let him go until he had a written confession. There was a knock at the door. Jowett terminated the interview and went across and answered it. The other officer sat there staring at Len. Len looked back at him nonplussed – he was only doing his job. Unlike his colleague, who seemed to be getting personal joy from trying to get him to confess to a murder he hadn't committed.

Len looked across and could see the colour draining from Jowett's face. He nodded and turned to look at Len. 'We'll continue questioning in the morning. It's late.'

'You can't keep me here if you've nothing on me,' Len said, sensing a shift in the room.

'We've got fingerprints on a door handle, Len. That'll do for now,' Jowett said wearily. Len didn't know what to think, but whatever the woman who had come to the door had just said had shaken the interviewing officer and he'd run out of all enthusiasm for grilling Len.

*

Tracy watched Mac as he took in the people in the foyer. He looked at Tracy, but she quickly looked away. 'Where's that cunt Swing?' he shouted at anyone who'd listen. Markie looked at Charly and Tracy. No one seemed to know why he wanted to see Swing and why he was so angry with him. Surely it was Tracy that he wanted to kill in all of this? Mac was struggling and shouting. Tracy got up from her chair. 'I'm not listening to this shit, I'm off out for a fag.'

The door leading through to the main part of the station opened and an officer stepped through. When he noticed Mac, he looked as if he'd seen a ghost.

'Jowett,' Mac said, still struggling. The copper didn't meet his eye, Tracy noticed. This was interesting. 'Barrel-scraping, you lot, aren't you? What've you got on me?'

Jowett looked at his boss. DI Hannigan looked at Mac. 'We've got the lot, sunshine. Enough to throw the book at you.'

'Some fucking paperwork that that silly bitch photocopied. Put me down for twenty-five years,' Mac said sarcastically, still pulling at the two men who were holding him in cuffs.

'No.' Hannigan looked at Mac blankly. 'Your shoe covers, false passports you have in your name so that you looked to be everywhere at once, your gloves and the clothes you were wearing on the night that have Baldy's DNA all over them. I won't go on.' Hannigan looked like he'd *love* to go on. 'So you need to tell us what happened that night instead of pretending you were sunning yourself in Spain.'

Tracy was speechless. She looked at Mac. Just as she was thinking who had led them to all of this stuff and that it had to be an inside job, Charly flew at Mac. She was too quick for anyone to stop her.

'I hate you!' she screamed, pulling her nails across Mac's face and drawing blood. As he was handcuffed he was unable to defend himself. But Hannigan leapt into action and pulled Charly away.

'Right. Let's break the party up, shall we?' he said, holding Charly off the ground as she kicked out, trying to get free to have another go at Mac.

chapter twenty

The cemetery was situated on a bleak hillside overlooking Manchester. Joel had been advised to make a will – all young footballers were, Charly had recently found out – and one of his requests had been that he be buried rather than cremated. She thought this an odd choice for Joel. She would have thought he'd have favoured a grand gesture – having his ashes scattered across the main stand at Manchester Rovers, or being given a Tibetan sky burial. For a footballer the whole thing was very understated. But this is where he had chosen. Apparently he had been walking here one day on his own and liked the quietness and solitude. Charly found it hard to believe that this was the same Joel who needed prising away from his PlayStation. But maybe the other side to Joel that she had always suspected was really there. She just wasn't the person he was ever going to share it with.

Charly had been in two minds whether to go. The last few weeks since Mac Jones had been charged with Joel's murder had seen Charly's emotions put through the wringer. The full details of what had happened that night had yet to emerge, but Mac had followed Joel and in what could only be a premeditated attack, had stabbed him. He was claiming that it had all happened in the heat of the moment. That he was there to pick money up from Joel and that Joel had attacked him with a knife, but Mac had gone to great lengths to make sure that no one knew he had been in the room that night: plastic shoe covers, gloves. Hair covered, clothing that wouldn't shed telltale fibres. His two mistakes had been bribing a policeman who was now himself being brought to trial and forcing the disgruntled Swing to do his dirty work for him. Swing had turned grass and gone to the police telling them everything. How Mac had got him to fly to Spain with a passport that was in Mac's name but with a picture of Swing the afternoon before the murder took place. He then sent him back to Manchester with yet another false passport the following day to go to the lock-up where Mac had left all the evidence from the previous evening and then bury it on the moors. Mac thought that he could trust Swing, but it seemed that Swing thought that he was being taken for an all-round mug by both Markie and Mac and was willing to take what was coming to him, which wasn't as bad as it could have been as his lawyers had cut a deal due to the evidence that he had provided. Charly couldn't forgive him. Not that she knew him and he'd be losing any sleep over it, but he had known who had killed Joel and kept it to himself for weeks.

Throughout the past few weeks Scott Crompton had been a rock. As had Markie. They had both been present at the church service today; quietly watching on in the background to make sure she was OK. Charly had asked Markie that he not tell his other sisters and brother about his link to her and he had agreed, assuring both Charly and Tracy that he was going to respect their wishes and keep it quiet. Charly had been waiting for Tracy to finally confront her dad with her accusations. If there was truth to Tracy's claims of rape then she couldn't blame her. Charly, however, couldn't help thinking that secretly Tracy would have made more of this years ago if her father had really attacked her. And that as Tracy had a history of dramatics and crying wolf, this whole episode smacked of the same.

Charly walked over to the grave. Holding her up to one side was her dad, to the other her mum. She was angry. Charly found that her feelings towards Swing and Mac were slightly more ambivalent than they were towards her deceased husband. Looking back over the time since Joel's death until the police arrested Mac, Charly knew now that she had been in shock. She was only now emerging into the cold light of day, an angry young woman. Joel was dead and both her parents were tainted by this hideous turn of events. Len had been cleared, but his reputation had been tarnished and Shirley had been charged with providing a false alibi and was currently awaiting a decision from the police whether she would stand trial or not.

Joel's dad was at the other side of the grave crying. Charly couldn't even look at him. She knew they were crocodile tears and that he was secretly delighted that his son had left the bulk of his money to him. He was welcome to it. She had been doing a lot of thinking about her time with Joel and had come to realise that what she had put up with was abuse. Shirley had been gently trying to bring her around to this, suggesting to her that the way that Joel had treated her hadn't been normal or acceptable. She'd found it hard to see at first. But now she could. Any dealings on this level with her mum were difficult however. Taking advice about how you should allow yourself to be treated from someone who deserted you as a child was hard to take. Charly knew that she might be upright and holding it together but she was fraught.

She looked into the hole in the ground where the coffin was being lowered. She was barely aware of the crowds that had gathered at the cemetery; there was nothing to stop people attending a public place like this and they'd turned out in force. She could see people holding up their camera phones and the thought briefly entered her head that she couldn't quite believe that they wanted a photograph of a funeral. Who were they going to show it to? What sort of down-the-pub banter accompanied such a picture? But then she knew that anyone with a camera was a potential paparazzi. A picture of Charly crying at her murdered husband's funeral could probably earn some hard-up kid a hundred quid. But she wasn't going to cry. She could tell. There was nothing about this whole day which was going to make her shed another tear. She felt that she had cried enough and now just wanted to get this over and done with.

The vicar had finished his speech, none of which had meant anything to Charly. His talk of a talented young man snatched in the prime of his life was fair enough, but the whole devoted husband bit had been way too much. They'd only been married two minutes and Charly was most definitely coming round to the realisation that Joel had been nothing short of an unremitting shit.

Charly took the vicar's cue and bent down, scooping a handful of earth and throwing it in on top of the coffin. Opposite her Joel's dad did the same thing and then let out a sob and shouted, 'My beautiful boy.' If anyone caught Charly's face on their camera phone at that precise moment they would have made themselves more than a hundred quid. It was a look of pure disgust. For what she had married, for his father's crocodile tears, for being a victim of her own starry-eyedness and – she had to finally admit to herself – her greed.

Charly turned to walk away, her mum and dad still linking her arms. As she walked to the car where Terry was waiting for her, aware of the stares she was drawing from all around, she saw Tracy standing by a tree glaring at Len. Charly walked straight over to Tracy and grabbed her by the arm.

'What d'you think you're doing?' Tracy asked indignantly.

'Not today, Tracy. Of all days, not today.'

Tracy looked down at her arm as if to indicate that Charly should think about letting go right now. 'I'm here to pay my respects.'

'Well, that's good of you. Your lot are over there.' Tracy could see Markie and Scott heading over to them.

Tracy watched her sons approach and then turned her glare back to Len.

'I want a word with you,' she said, her voice cracking. 'But not here. Your lass is right. It's no place for what I've got to say.'

Charly was shocked but tried not to show it. She never thought she'd see the day when Tracy Crompton was actually respectful of someone else's wishes when they contravened her own.

*

Tracy marched toward the Metcalfe house. It was the day after the funeral and the country's press seemed to have finally had their fill of Len's daft head and had decamped to hound some other unsuspecting poor sod. The fact that Tracy hadn't been allowed to say what she wanted to say the previous day rankled, but even she knew that kicking off at a funeral with a load of photographers waiting in the wings to dredge up her previous history with the papers wasn't the brightest idea she'd ever had. She'd been ready for him yesterday, though. She hadn't felt sick or guilty like she had in the past; she was genuinely ready to tackle Len about what had happened between them years ago.

She hoped that Shirley wasn't there but if she was she was going to ask her politely to leave.

Tracy knocked on the door. Len answered it, the door pulling tight when the security chain reached its limit. 'Oh,' he said when he saw that it was Tracy.

'Can I come in?' Tracy asked flatly. She wasn't about to start begging this idiot on top of everything else.

Len quickly undid the lock and stepped back into the house to let Tracy through the door. 'No Shirley?' she asked.

'No. She's at Charly's.'

'Well, just so you know, Kent's waiting in the car for me, so I won't be long.' Tracy was lying. She had tried to contact Kent a number of times but he had refused to take her calls. She had even gone to the radio station to meet him from work but he had walked straight past her, refusing to even look at her. This had enraged Tracy but there was little she could do about it. She didn't want Len thinking that she had come here on her own.

'I wanted to talk to you, too.'

Tracy looked at him. What could Len possibly have to talk to her about? 'Did you tell the police I'd …' He seemed unable to say the words that he wanted to use. '… attacked you back in the seventies? There's a note on my file.'

Tracy was amazed that that was still there. She thought that Bradington police force would have screwed that up and put it in the bin years ago. 'Raped,' Tracy said boldly. 'I told them you raped me but I knew they'd make me out to be the town bike so I withdrew my statement.' She was looking directly at Len, bravely staring him down. His face fell in horror.

'I never did anything of the kind! I loved you.'

'Ha!' Tracy laughed bitterly. She couldn't believe that he was denying it or, worse, that he obviously had no recollection of the events of that day. 'You were pissed out of your mind and you couldn't stand it that I'd got someone else – Paul – so you came round and wouldn't take no for an answer.'

'That's not true,' Len said, shaking his head as if this would somehow shake the truth of that day into his consciousness. 'You went off with Paul, rubbing my face in it, and I just had to put up and shut up.'

'Bollocks,' Tracy said angrily. 'Whatever you think now, or whatever rosy little picture you want to paint of yourself as jolly old Len, back in 1974 you were a mad bastard when you drank and I got the brunt of it that day.'

'No, you didn't. That never happened,' Len said. He obviously couldn't believe it.

'It did. And I've got our Markie to prove it.'

'Markie?' Len said, his jaw dropping.

'Come on, Len, even you're not that much of a numbskull. What d'you think him and Charly are all cosied up for? They worked it out. And it doesn't take Einstein once you look at our Markie side on and know the history between us.'

'Markie?'

'Yes, Markie,' Tracy said irritably. She couldn't believe she was having to spell it out.

'Oh God!' Len said, sliding into a kitchen chair and holding his head in his hands. 'I don't remember ...'

'It happened, Len. And then you got slung away for GBH, remember that?'

'Course I remember that.'

'Well, there you go. Why is it such a shock to you that you're a nasty bastard?'

'I'm not a nasty bastard, Tracy, I'm not. You knew me better than anyone. Tell me I'm not a nasty bastard.'

'I can't do that, can I, Len? What I'm telling you is that you are. Or at least you were.'

Oh God,' Len said again, beginning to sob. 'I'm so, so sorry.'

Tracy looked at him. He seemed small and pathetic and as if he couldn't harm a fly. A strange feeling came over her. Tracy was a woman who could hold a grudge for years over absolutely nothing. But she didn't want to hold this against Len any longer. It was done. He knew about Markie; what he did was up to him. And as fearful as she had been about Len in the past, she knew now that she needn't have been, that he couldn't hurt her now. He wasn't the violent drinker he had been when she had known him, he was a fat little ball who ran the local club and liked to keep his nose clean and tell himself that he was a pillar of the community. She was done. She turned and walked out of the house. As she opened the door, Len said again, 'I'm so sorry.'

'So you've said,' Tracy said quietly. 'And so you should be.'

*

Charly was sitting in a curry house in Tooting with her mum, looking out at the road with its furniture shops and assortment of cut-prize frozen food emporiums. 'So this is it. Nothing much to it, is there?' Shirley asked.

Charly shrugged. 'I suppose not,' she said, dipping her poppadom in the mango chutney and taking a bite. 'I've made a decision.' She looked at her mum.

'Right …' Shirley said slowly, waiting uncomfortably for this to have something to do with her.

'I need to get off my backside and do something.' She looked at her mum. 'I've been waiting around scared to death of what's going to happen next. Scared to death of when you might leave …'

'I'm not going anywhere.'

'Maybe not, but I can't affect whether you stay or go, can I? I've just got to lighten up and start to get back on my feet. I'm sitting around worrying about you, about when something else bad about Joel is going to come out. But what else can come out? He's dead and he's not coming back and the simple fact is, he was horrible to live with. How long would I have gone on putting up with everything he threw at me? I could be the one that's dead. And yet I'm bleating on about how much I loved him. What does that say about me? I'm pathetic.' Charly sighed, angry with herself again.

'You're not pathetic. You need to give yourself a break. I've a feeling that if I'd met Joel he'd have got a pasting off me to beat the one he got from your dad, but that doesn't mean to say that you could have done anything other than what you did at the time.'

'I should have stayed with Scott.'

Shirley laughed. 'Come on, love ...'

Charly smiled as the waiter placed her chicken tikka in front of her. She and Scott were good friends but should never have been anything more. He was a gentle, lovely guy, but he wasn't what she needed in a boyfriend. In fact, she knew that the last thing that she needed for a long time was any sort of boyfriend. She needed to be on her own and to get her life in order. 'Maybe not,' she said. 'Tell you what I wouldn't mind doing after this ...' Charly shredded some chicken and popped it into her mouth. 'House hunting. Well, flat hunting.'

'Here?' Shirley asked, surprised.

'I've been thinking a lot about this and I think I need a break from the north. I can go back to modelling, get Leanne to get me work, most of it's done down here anyway. Might as well put my notorious name to some use.'

'But what about your dad? What about Jimmy? What about your friends?'

Charly didn't want to point out to herself let alone her mother that she didn't really have any friends. 'Well, Bradington's only two hours on the train,' she said.

Shirley pushed her hair self-consciously out of her face. Neither said anything but Charly knew exactly what her mum was thinking: she had spent ten years being only two hours away from her real life.

'Well, I think that it's a big decision, but no one could blame you if you did decide to move. I know this might sound like a stupid question, but how are you fixed for money?'

'I've got some. Not as much as people probably think but, you know, enough to get by for a bit.'

Charly had decided that she wasn't going to kick

up a fuss about anything that was in Joel's will. His dad was to receive the lion's share of anything that he had saved and he was welcome to it. The effort that she had gone to to make herself financially secure before Joel's death seemed shallow now. She might have a document saying that she was his wife and was entitled to half of everything but legally they hadn't been married for long enough for her to make any claim stick and she didn't want to. She had a car that was paid for, and Joel's dad had said that he would make sure that she was taken care of. Until now this had meant making sure that the house was still paid for every month, and he had promised to transfer an as yet to be agreed sum to Charly. He had mentioned thirty thousand pounds; her lawyers weren't happy. They felt there was far more money that she was due but to her that was the means to starting a new life somewhere else and worth far more than a million pounds only to be left sitting rocking in a mansion with no idea what to do next.

'Where would you live in London?'

'God knows. I don't know anywhere, really. I've only ever been to parties and hotels in the West End as far as I remember. But I don't think I'll be able to afford anywhere within shouting distance of there, will I?'

Shirley laughed. 'You could always move to Tooting.'

'I wouldn't mind being a bit nearer the action.'

'If you want action Streatham High Street's only up the road. It's all going on there.'

Charly smiled. She wasn't sure if moving to London would make a difference to how she was feeling but at least she would be doing something. And doing something on her own. Without the help of Joel, without the help of Scott, even without the help of Markie, who had stepped into the role of Lord Protector recently. And Charly knew that if she could make a life for herself without relying on anyone else, especially a man, then that in itself was progress.

*

Tracy was standing in the office with Tammy, who was still dining out on the notoriety of her colleague Mac Jones. Every time the phone rang she assumed it was the press and took great delight in refusing to make any comment or letting them speak to Markie. Tracy was glad that she had aligned herself with Tammy. The girl was great at her job and with Mac out of the picture she was being as helpful to Tracy as she was to Markie.

Tracy was tiring of her rounds but with Mac gone she was going to talk to Markie about getting someone else in and that someone else was going to be her daughter Karina. She hadn't been having the best time of late. She spent most of her time with Gaz and was looking thinner by the day but Tracy knew that a few weeks with her mum and she'd sort her out. Karina was mouthy enough to be good at collections and skint enough to need a job. She was also, if rumours were to be believed, spending too much time with the curtains drawn watching bad daytime TV and keeping herself topped up with coke when Izzy wasn't around. Tracy didn't understand the point in getting hooked on things. She enjoyed getting wellied with the best of them but her central belief had always been that when it stops being a party and starts being just what you do to get out of bed in the morning, something's got to give. The fact that Tracy had got out of bed on some mornings in the past and had a tumbler of vodka and a line of coke the thickness of a millipede wasn't the same. She had made sure there were other people around and that the day turned into an all-day session – justifying to herself that she was just a partyer, not a drunk or a cokehead.

It was beginning to feel like a family business. 'Who'd have thought it, Markie, eh?' she said. Markie was looking out of the window distractedly onto the street below. 'The Cromptons. It's like *Dallas*, isn't it.'

'What the fuck?' Markie said quietly.

'What?'

'The old bill.'

'What about them?'

'I don't know "What about them". They seem to be heading in this direction.'

A moment later the door opened. DI Hannigan walked into the office and came towards Markie. Tracy knew that this must have something to do with the Baldy case, or at least Mac, if Hannigan was doing the arresting. He was flanked by four other police officers.

'How many coppers does it take to change a lightbulb?'

The look that Hannigan gave Markie suggested that he wasn't in the mood for any of his smart-arsed jokes. 'Markie Crompton, we are arresting you for kidnapping and extortion. You have the right to remain silent but anything you do say will be taken down and may be used against you in a court of law.'

'I've got something to say, alright,' Markie said as one of Hannigan's flunkies slapped the cuffs on him. 'What the fuck are you on about?'

'Your mate, Mac. He's not going down quietly. Seems you and him had some little sideline, lending people money and then when they couldn't pay up you sold their houses from under them and pocketed the cash. Well, when you were keeping them in a lock-up against their will and beating the living shit out of them for days on end, what did you think you were doing? Because where I come from, that's kidnapping and extortion. And thanks to your mate not wanting to see out the rest of his life in the nick, he's told us a few things about you.'

'Fuck off, I don't believe you.'

'What you believe doesn't really come into it, does it?' He turned to the other officers. 'Get him in the van, lads.' Tracy and Tammy looked on, speechless.

Tracy finally found her voice. 'You can't take him away!'

'Why not, Tracy? Not like he's any stranger to the nick, is it, love?' Hannigan said as Markie was bundled out of the door. Tracy could hear him talking to the coppers, telling them they'd better have their story straight. But Tracy knew Mac. He was a vindictive bastard and he might have kept things ticking over when Markie was inside, but there was no way he was going to rot himself and leave Markie a free man. Not when he could get his sentence reduced.

Tammy was staring at Tracy, waiting for her to suggest what to do next. Tracy looked back at Tammy. 'What?'

'What now?'

Tracy thought for a moment. Markie was her son and she loved him dearly, or so she told herself because that's what mothers were supposed to think, but recently she'd have happily seen him strung up. All that stuff with Charly Metcalfe, ducking around behind her back and wanting to find out who his real daddy was like some sad case off *Surprise Surprise*. And even when everything came out she was sure that Markie believed Len's version of events over hers. Pathetic. And then there was this all-the-lads-together thing with Mac. Markie knew that he was up to something when he was away but he protected him – well, more fool him. She looked directly at Tammy and smiled. 'Looks like I'm in charge,' she said.

*

Charly's new flat was tiny compared to the luxury she had been used to. She was standing beside one of the many tea chests that Scott had brought in the van from Bradington for her. 'Look at you, eh?' Scott said. She could tell he was trying to sound upbeat, but his voice was tinged with sadness. 'All grown up in London.'

Charly walked over to him and hugged him. He held onto her, both standing in silence for several minutes.

She had chosen a flat in an unassuming area near Islington. It wasn't the best flat she'd ever seen in her life, but it was near central London and that's where she wanted to be. There was private security and the car park was gated. Charly knew that wherever she went, if the press wanted a story on her then they'd follow her. Living in a gated mansion hadn't stopped them so she chose to look on the bright side and think that it meant she could live where she wanted.

'Will you tell Markie that I'll come and see him the next time I'm up?' Charly asked. Scott nodded. Yesterday she had tried to visit Markie; he had been remanded in custody after his arrest. Len had asked if he could accompany Charly and she had told him in no uncertain terms that if he wanted to do some bridge-building with his new-found son then he could do it on his own. But Markie hadn't wanted to see Charly, let alone Len. She was worried about him. What the police had on him didn't look good. Charly couldn't believe that after everything Mac had sold Markie out.

'Is there anything you need me to do before I go? Shopping or anything?'

'No. I want to go out and about and find my bearings when you're gone.'

'You'll call if you need anything, won't you?'

'Course I will, Scott.' Charly smiled tenderly at her ex. He walked to the door and turned around to look at her.

'You look after yourself.'

She smiled. 'I will.'

Scott closed the door behind him, leaving Charly alone. She walked through to the small living room. When she had lived in the large house in Hale and the flat in town she had always felt as if she was just being allowed to play there, that they weren't really hers. But standing here now, looking at this manageable flat, one that she could afford to furnish and pay for herself, for the first time since she'd left home at the age of seventeen she felt like somewhere was hers. She might have some ghosts that needed laying to rest but she was free to live her life how she wanted to live it. And although a strange feeling for Charly, it was a great feeling and one that she wasn't going to throw away again lightly.

Tough Love

Also by Kerry Katona

If you enjoyed *The Footballer's Wife*, you'll love Kerry's first novel *Tough Love*. Here's the first chapter …

EBURY
PRESS

chapter one

Leanne opened the paper and looked at the young blue-eyed, blonde-haired vision of tabloid beauty staring back at her, the pert breasts and happy-to-be-there smile. She threw it aside. She wasn't particularly interested in what Mel, 18, of Colchester had to say about the war in Iraq. She knew that the girl's problems extended only as far as whether the spray tan she'd had before the shoot was too orange and if her false eyelashes were alluring or, horror of horrors, made her look like Jackie Stallone. The Knowledge and Knickers speech bubble that the papers insisted on printing above the new breed of page-three girls' heads was always made up in two seconds flat by some hack in Canary Wharf – it had nothing to do with the models. 'That's not Mummy,' Kia, Leanne's seven-year-old daughter, said, climbing on to her mother's knee.

Leanne looked at her and shook her head. 'No, darling, that's a pretty lady.'

'Mummy's pretty too,' Kia said.

Leanne smiled at her daughter, grateful for the compliment. Leanne was pretty. She was five foot five with an hour-glass figure and her blonde hair and green eyes ensured that heads turned when she walked into any room. They had also ensured that until recently her career had been long and lucrative.

She had agonised over telling Kia exactly what she did. She didn't think it appropriate that her young daughter should know that Mummy made her money as a glamour model, but at the same time she was proud of her work, so why should she hide it from her? In the end the choice had been taken out of her hands by her less than thoughtful mother, Tracy: she had given Kia a locket with a picture of a topless Leanne in it. Mother of the Year Tracy wasn't.

In fact, Leanne had recognised Mel. She had been sitting in the waiting room at Figurz Management when Leanne was given what she could only describe as the Right Royal Boot. Jenny, her manager for the past nine years, had summoned her into her spacious office and sat her down.

Leanne had known something was wrong as soon as she got the call to go to the office. Jenny didn't usually do the office. She liked to sink a couple of bottles of Pinot Grigio and go over the proofs for whatever men's magazine Leanne had been starring in that week. The office meant bad news.

'I suppose you know why I've asked you here...' Jenny, with her vicious bob and her black-rimmed glasses, had lit a cigarette and leant back in her chair, inhaling hard, then letting a plume of smoke out of her nostrils. Leanne's throat had dried. She had an idea of why she was sitting there, but she wasn't sure she liked it.

'You and me, Lee, we go back a long way.' Leanne hated it when Jenny called her Lee. 'And I've always said I'd be straight up and down with you, haven't I, girl?' Leanne winced. She wanted Jenny to get this over and done with, whatever she was going to say. 'And I've always said, "Tits is tits," haven't I?'

And I've always wondered what the fuck that's supposed to mean, Leanne thought but didn't say. She wouldn't. She was terrified of Jenny, if she was honest.

'Well, tits is tits, but there's younger tits coming through that door, if you know what I'm saying.'

'Look, Jenny,' Leanne's voice wavered, 'I offered

to get a boob job and you said no, natural's what everyone wants.' She didn't really want one. Her boobs were big enough as it was. She didn't need ginormous plastic orbs bobbing around so she couldn't see her feet.

'That's true, sweetheart. Natural is what everyone wants, but so's young. And you might be young to some bloke in his fifties, but twenty-five's over the hill to an eighteen-year-old brickie who wants a quick lump in his trousers while he's eating his corned-beef sandwiches. You get where I'm coming from?'

Leanne got where Jenny was coming from – loud and clear. She was telling her that her lucrative career as a glamour model was coming to an end. Leanne would have liked to think that in this situation she would stand up and tell Jenny exactly where she could shove her Eric Morecambe glasses, but she didn't. When it came down to it, she avoided conflict at all costs. With a mother like hers you didn't need to look for a fight – they came to you.

'What about my fan base?' Leanne had asked meekly.

'They're a fickle bunch. They move on quickly, and that's what I'm here to spot.' Jenny looked at Leanne, who was fighting back tears now. She could have kicked herself: she didn't want to break down in front of the hard-faced witch. 'I'm not saying you won't work again, sweetheart, just that you might have to do it with your top on.'

Leanne had stumbled out on to the street near Battersea Bridge. She got well away from the office before she fell in a heap and started crying. She'd had such a nice life for the last six years – parties, premières, free holidays if she put her name to the travel company – and now Jenny, the number-one glamour agent in the country, was telling her it was over. What was she going to do?

She stood up, tears streaming down her face, and looked around for a taxi. Typical! There wasn't one in sight. Leanne walked on with her thumb out like a hitch-hiker, until a cab pulled up beside her, splashing mud up her leg. Brilliant! Could today get any worse? she wondered aloud.

As she climbed in, the driver stared at her. 'You're that Jodie Marsh, ain'tcha?' he asked.

Yes, she decided. It could.

*

'Get out here and fucking talk to me!' a man's voice screamed.

Tracy turned up the volume on *Jeremy Kyle*. She'd rather listen to someone else's problems than confront her own. Suddenly there was a loud banging on the back door, something she was well used to.

'I said, "Fucking talk to me!"'

Tracy raised an eyebrow and stuck a spoon into the tub of Dairylea she had grabbed from the fridge for breakfast; she had nothing else in and she was damned if she was going outside the house to get an ear-twisting from her ex-husband. Just as she was about to find out the result of the paternity test on TV an almighty whack put paid to her morning of loafing around. She turned to see a foot sticking through her boarded-up back door.

'For the love of God, Paul!' she shouted, jumping up from the settee and heading over to the door. The foot was waggling around. Its owner was obviously trying to free it.

'Let me in, and we'll have this out once and for all.'

'I'm calling the police. You're not allowed anywhere near here,' Tracy reminded him.

'This is my fucking house!'

'It's the council's fucking house. Get your facts

right, dickhead.' Tracy stood back and kicked the foot as hard as she could.

'Ow!' the disembodied voice wailed. 'You bitch!' The foot disappeared.

'Now, fuck off, or I'm calling the police and you'll end up back in the nick!' Tracy returned to the settee. This wasn't the scene of domestic violence she liked to paint but it was how she and Paul were with each other since they had split so acrimoniously. She was used to the frequent ructions and bored with them.

Paul and Tracy had been together since they were teenagers. He had always fancied himself as a bit of a hard man around the estate, but his hard-man credentials didn't stretch much further than thumping people when he'd laid into the Stella Artois a bit harder than he should have. When they'd first met, Tracy had believed the hype. He'd been the tough lad at school, the one everyone fancied, but a few years with him had soon put paid to any romantic notions she'd had about him. He was a lazy waster who prided himself on not having had to get out of bed before ten o'clock since he'd left school. Something of a feat in itself, Tracy had often thought, seeing as they had five kids together.

Tracy loved her kids, she really did, but she often thought they didn't understand what she'd gone through, what she'd given up, to raise them. She'd been a looker when she was younger, could have been a model like Leanne, but instead she'd ended up sitting out her life in Bolingbroke Estate, Bradington's number-one problem area, so they were always being informed. Leanne didn't know she was born, Tracy thought. Granted, she'd had to go out and work when she was fourteen, but there was nothing wrong with that, Tracy told herself. Bit of grafting to pay some board had done none of her kids any harm.

The rot had set in between her and Paul years ago. He'd thought that having children meant giving up. He'd soon stopped looking at Tracy as anything other than the mother to his kids, and she'd wanted more. She'd wanted some romance in her life, but there was a slim chance of that when she had five kids in tow and the only place for a night out was the Beacon, a dump of a pub where the men were men and the women looked like men.

Three years ago, on Tracy's forty-fifth birthday, Paul had produced the straw that finally broke the camel's back. He'd been promising to take Tracy out all year. They'd go into town and have a proper knees-up – they'd even go to a club. Tracy had bought a new outfit, courtesy of some cash that Leanne had put her way, and then Paul hadn't come home. She'd waited all night for him and in the end had gone into town on her own and got blind drunk. She couldn't remember what had happened, but her youngest daughter, Jodie, had informed her that when she and her mates found Tracy she was draped round some thirty-year-old and had been sick down her top. Eventually Paul came home all apologies but Tracy had known things had to change.

Along with *Jeremy Kyle*, one of Tracy's pleasures in life was *The Late Nite Love-In* on Bradington Community Radio. The voice of the DJ, Kent Graham, was enough to make her go weak at the knees. After Paul's no-show and the subsequent arguments, in which he had defended going on a three-day bender, Tracy had decided to do something for herself for once. Never mind sorting her rabble out. She was going to look after number one. She had picked up the phone and rung the radio station, then asked to be put through to Kent, saying she was an old school friend. When she finally had him on the phone, she put on her best, most seductive voice and asked him out. And Kent, to her utter amazement, said yes.

What followed was a whirlwind romance. At first, Tracy thought he might only be interested in her because she was Leanne's mum. Her daughter was the local celebrity and everyone, as far as Tracy could see, wanted a piece of her, and if that meant going through her mother, then so be it. But it soon became apparent to Tracy that Kent wanted her for herself.

A month later, Paul had found out. Tracy soon tired of hiding her new love and became more and more brazen in her choice of venue when meeting him. She wanted Paul to see that someone else was more interested in her than he was in the bottom of a pint glass. She was finally spotted by one of the locals from the Beacon, being pushed on the swings in Bolingbroke Park by Kent. She had thought Paul would realise that this spelled the end of their marriage. The kids were all grown-up now: Jodie still lived at home but was working at the Beacon; Karina had moved in with Gaz; Scott and his girlfriend Charly had a flat on the other side of the estate; and Markie was in prison but was due out any time now. Leanne, of course, little Princess Tippy Toes, as Tracy liked to call her, if not to her face, was off setting the world alight. They didn't need a mum and dad – she and Paul had done their bit, Tracy thought rather grandly. She didn't understand that her 'bit' couldn't be considered first-class parenting.

Paul didn't take it well. He broke every window in the house and posted a lit rag through the door. The whole thing got dragged through the papers because someone on the street saw a quick buck to be made. It was good reading: the page-three girl, the psycho dad and the DJ. Tracy had played the injured wife, but the truth was that she enjoyed winding her ex-husband up. She'd even got the police to install a panic button in case of violent attack. Paul had laughed at this, thinking it was a joke, when he had come round to have his monthly Shout-at-Tracy-from-the-Garden. She had pressed it, and he'd found out the hard way that it was anything but a joke. He had spent the night in Bradington Bridewell with his belt and shoelaces confiscated.

As for Kent, he'd stuck with Tracy through thick and thin. He felt he'd met his soulmate. He'd say, 'I feel like I can tell you anything.'

Tracy would reply, 'Me too.' But there were a few things she thought it was best not to let him in on, such as that when they'd all ended up in the tabloids she had grasped there was money to be made. Ever since, she had been anonymously drip-feeding the papers stories about Leanne to make herself a nice bit of coin on the side. Now if she could only get Leanne to spill the beans on who Kia's dad was, which she had been tight-lipped about from day one, Tracy'd have two weeks in La Manga and a plasma-screen telly sorted. She had an idea who it was, though. And if it was who she thought, then it was tabloid dynamite.

Tracy liked to think that what stopped her finding out more was that she was concerned about Kia: she didn't want her dragged through the papers like the rest of her family had been. But she knew she could rationalise it, if push came to shove and a large cheque from the *News of the Screws* was winging its way in her direction. Her other, bigger, concern was that she didn't think Kent would be very understanding about her on-the-side income. He could be a right uptight sod sometimes, she thought. She'd sit schtum on that one for the time being.

With Paul still shouting outside, Tracy wandered over to the panic button and pressed it. A few minutes later the police were at her door. She prepared herself for another Oscar-winning performance.

'Thank God you came so quickly, officers,' she said, fighting back crocodile tears – they came so easily to her. 'I thought he was going to kill me.' If there was one thing Tracy loved more than *Jeremy Kyle*, it was a good drama.

*

Lisa Leighton looked out over the beautiful blue crystal waters of Lake Garda and snapped the magazine shut. Ever since her husband Jay had moved to Milano Atletico she had had the weekly gossip magazines shipped out from the UK just to see how many column inches she and her beloved had notched up that week. It had been Lisa's idea to move to Italy three years ago. Jay's reputation had been getting slightly out of hand back home but she knew that if she could get him away from the hangers-on they might be able to get on with their lives in the way she wanted. For the most part her plan had worked. The move had seen the Leightons go from being the UK's golden couple to a European phenomenon.

Lisa based herself in Italy and London. She quite

liked Italy, but found the language barrier tough. Also, everyone went on about Milan being the fashion capital of the world but the place was an overgrown industrial estate and the clothes were like something her mother would have worn out for a night on the tiles in Essex, all gold lamé and appliqué clowns.

It was strange to be so famous, but Lisa felt she had the hang of it now. She had grown used to being photographed everywhere she went, and so had Jay. But that was more to do with the fact that she let the paparazzi know where she was going to be than their popularity.

Since the move her own career had rocketed. When they had lived in the UK she had been a TV presenter. She'd started off on a music channel but had soon been noticed for her good looks and bright on-screen personality. The main channels had snapped her up. Now she had her own column in a weekly glossy, her own fashion show on UK Lifetime TV and her own perfume, Suggestive, by Lisa Leighton. It actually smelt of turps, but she wasn't wearing it: her loyal public was and that suited her fine.

Even now, ten years after she and Jay had first got together, she knew she could expect to see herself and him on the front cover of at least one of the weekly magazines with a couple of mentions from Rav Singh or the 3 AM. girls thrown in. But this week there was nothing. All anyone was interested in was Leanne bloody Crompton. There were pictures of the glamour model getting into her car with her face screwed up – she was obviously asking for privacy – and the rest were old reruns that Lisa had seen a thousand times.

Did people really fall for this? she wondered, not for the first time. If the press didn't have a picture, or a story for that matter, they would delve into their archives and use an old one. Lisa should know: they'd dined out for months on Jay's alleged affair with a Manchester Rovers female physiotherapist, using the picture of her massaging cramp out of his leg at the FA Cup final over and over again. Lisa knew that she'd massaged more than his leg, but she wasn't about to let the mask of her perfect marriage slip any time soon. She knew she and Jay were worth far more together than they were apart, and so did he.

Just when Lisa had thought that Leanne Crompton might drift into obscurity she'd reared her not-so-ugly head again. Even when she was papped with a scrunched-up face she looked all right, Lisa thought grudgingly. She herself daren't go out of the house without having every one of her long auburn tresses in place, her green contact lenses in and her Fake Bake professionally applied. She knew that if the paps caught her first thing in the morning they'd jump out of their pasty skins, shortly before snapping their shutter lenses and making themselves at least ten grand for the picture. She was naturally pretty, Lisa, but not naturally stunning. That bit took work. But years of eating only protein and constant high-end professional grooming had made her the svelte size eight über-redhead she was today.

Lisa didn't mind reading about Leanne when it was bad news. In fact she enjoyed it. Leanne, it appeared, had finally been dumped by her agency. The magazines were talking about it being the end of her. But Lisa knew that if Leanne was smart it could be the making of her. She could turn her hard-luck story into a lucrative rags-to-riches, riches-to-rags story. But Lisa didn't have Leanne down as smart. She had her down as Bradington scum. And people like her, Lisa knew, didn't think to look at the bigger picture and plan a career. They spent money when they had it and panicked when they didn't. And if Leanne started panicking,

God only knew what would come out of her mouth. Well, Lisa wasn't about to take any risks.

She picked up the phone and dialled Jay's number. It went to answer-machine before she remembered he was having one of his tattoos lasered off. He'd had it for three months and thought it read *'my country, my life, my heart, my wife'* in Sanskrit. But it had turned out that the tattooist had been a Manchester City fan and apparently it read *'I flick turds for a living.'* She wouldn't mind but he hadn't played for Manchester Rovers for years.

Lisa rose from her sun-lounger and walked across the balcony of the villa they were renting from George Clooney. They'd never met him but that didn't matter – she knew they would now be associated for ever with him in the public's consciousness. For a moment, she wondered what to do, then picked up her phone and called Mike Atkinson, their head of security.

'I think we might have a little problem that needs attending to,' she said, splaying her free hand and checking that her perfectly manicured nails didn't need a touch-up.

*

Leanne walked along the Thames by the imposing Tate Modern with Kia, looking at the sky-line. St Paul's Cathedral rose up on the other side of the river and the buildings in the Square Mile vied to be noticed too. Leanne loved and hated London. She had worked in the capital since she was sixteen, moving in a year later, but she had always felt like an outsider. She envied the Sloaney young women in the coffee shops around Regent Street who could order a double mocha choco skinny latte and not feel they had to apologise for their pain-in-the-arse order. She still felt grand when she asked for a cappuccino.

She had come for a walk to clear her head. She lived in a house in Greenwich. The rent was astronomical but until last week Leanne hadn't cared. She'd always had money coming in and spent it accordingly. But this morning she had sat down and opened the credit-card statements she usually tossed to one side to discover that she was in trouble.

She glanced down at Kia, who was wearing her favourite Dolce and Gabbana trainers with her Matthew Williamson for Kids jumper, and her heart sank. Her poor little girl had grown used to having the best of everything, and Leanne had grown used to assuming that she could give her the best of everything.

She took out her mobile phone and rang Directory Inquiries. 'Can I have the number for Pink Models, please?' Pink Models were Figurz Management's biggest rivals.

The operator put her through. 'Hello, can I speak to Meagan Richards, please?' Meagan had been Jenny's arch enemy.

'May I ask who's calling?' the receptionist asked, in a nasal voice.

'It's Leanne Crompton.' She felt nervous to be ringing up and asking for work, which she hadn't had to do since she'd first done the rounds in Bradington, looking for a cash-in-hand Saturday job.

'One moment, please.'

The receptionist must have pushed the wrong button. Instead of Meagan's polite business voice, Leanne heard, 'Leanne Crompton? Ha! She gets dropped by Hag Features and thinks she can come crawling to me? Let her sweat. Tell her to call back tomorrow. She's old news, anyway.'

Leanne clicked the phone off, feeling sick. She had a strong suspicion that she and Kia were in for a rocky year.

*

Karina was off her head. Gaz, her boyfriend, had been dealing coke for a year or two but had suddenly landed a massive stash, and while he was off working as a bouncer at Bradington's current number-one night spot, Cloud Nine, she had been charged with dealing it up and hiding it. Never one to pass up the opportunity to test Gaz's wares, Karina had tucked into the coke like a kid in a sweet shop. She was now on day two of a paranoid bender, which had started with her being Queen of the World and was ending with her scrabbling around on the floor, taking the coke out of the settee cushions and sewing it into her two-year-old daughter Izzy's teddy bears. Which was a good idea, as it turned out, because when she heard a loud knocking at the door, it wasn't just her paranoia at play, it really was the police.

'We've a warrant to search the premises, Miss Crompton,' the police officer said, and barged past her.

Karina reverted to the cocky madam she'd been at school and started telling the police what she thought of them.

'Nothing better to do? Haven't you got some

tom you should be shaking down for free blow-jobs or something?' she asked sarcastically.

'Good afternoon to you too,' the police officer said.

Karina was trying her best to act normal, but she had no way of knowing whether she was pulling it off. She flattened herself against the wall and looked on as the police tore the flat apart.

'What you looking for, then?' she asked, aware that her eyes were like saucers.

'I think you know, don't you?' The police officer stared at her, raising an eyebrow, as his colleague upturned cushions and rifled through drawers. 'Mind if we look in the bedrooms?'

'No, go ahead. You'll do what the fuck you please anyway,' Karina said, trying to pretend that she wasn't completely bricking it.

'No need for the bad language. What did your mother teach you? Oh, that's right, nothing – your mum's a scumbag.' The two coppers fell about laughing as Karina scowled at them.

'Don't bring my mum into it.'

The copper looked at her. She knew that he knew she was as high as a kite.

She began to scratch. She wasn't itchy, just felt that she needed to get out of her skin. Her mind raced. They were going to find the stuff and all Gaz's hard work would be down the drain. She'd be put in prison and Izzy would be taken into care and it would be all her fault. Karina was trying to keep calm, but her already racing heart was thumping in her chest.

The coppers swaggered back into the living room where Karina was standing, sure that this was the moment when she would be arrested. 'Well, looks like it's your lucky day,' the copper said. 'We can't find anything.'

Relief flooded through her. 'I told you,' she said defiantly.

'Anyway, say hello to that lovely sister of yours, won't you, from all the lads? Can't have her posters up any more – the political-correctness mob's gone mad. But she's up here.' The copper tapped his temple.

'You make me sick,' Karina said, as the coppers let themselves out, smiling. But it wasn't just them who made her sick. Her sister, bloody Leanne – Leannecrompton, everyone said it as if it was one word, like Madonna – made her nauseous too. With her fancy clothes and her smart life and her bleating all the time about being down-to-earth. She could afford to be, Karina thought. I'd be down-to-earth if I had a Mini Cooper S and four holidays a year. *Bloody Leanne*. She felt the stab of envy she often experienced when she thought about her sister. Not that she'd tell her. Leanne was too good a meal ticket for Karina to start falling out with her now.

*

Jodie leant over the bar and made sure that her low-cut top gave Dave, one of the regulars, a good look at her ample cleavage. 'And your own, love,' he said, as he always did. Jodie got the best tips at the Beacon. There was a fight every night and there were more boards than windows on the outside of the building. She didn't particularly like the place, but it was a good stopgap for the time being – and she got the attention from the male regulars that she craved.

She had worked there for a year but knew she wouldn't have to stay much longer, not if Brian Spencer had anything to do with it. He had walked into the pub a week ago and asked the manager, Val, where the lovely younger sister of Leanne Crompton could be found. Jodie had shimmied across to him, swung her long blonde hair over her shoulder and announced, 'You're looking at her.'

He had managed two seconds of eye contact before his gaze came to rest on her chest. Jodie didn't mind. She knew, as her sister had found, that they were going to be her fortune. Brian had slid his business card across the bar. 'Call me. I think I could represent you,' he had said, then ordered a Campari and soda. Val had taken the ancient bottle down and sniffed it slyly. Nobody had ordered Campari at the Beacon for at least three years.

Jodie had looked at the card with delight: Brian Spencer Management. She had tried and failed before to get someone to take her seriously as a glamour model. When she was younger she had thought things would be as easy for her as they had been for Leanne, who'd been an overnight success. But when Jodie had sent her amateur pictures to Leanne's horrible manager she had been told, 'Yeah, love, I see where you're coming from but you're not the full package like your sister. You're a bit of a barrel and your features are too clustered. Don't get me wrong, sweets, you're a pretty little thing, you just ain't Leanne.'

She had shelved her ideas of fame and fortune and instead had gone on an extreme diet, slimming down to a size six. Her mum had noticed that she was often sick in the middle of the night, but Jodie had passed it off as a bad stomach, and as her mum didn't think about much other than herself for any length of time, she carried on being sick. Every time someone told her how good she was looking, Jodie thought it was all worth it. She could see in the mirror now that her once-chubby face had been transformed. Her eyes were huge and blue and her cheekbones were sharp. Her hair had been brown when Jodie had sent her pictures to Jenny, but now it was blonde, well coloured and styled – she had made a deal with JoJo at the hairdresser's: JoJo did her highlights for free and in return Jodie shoved her as many Bacardi Breezers as she could get down her face on Friday and Saturday nights at the Beacon.

Until Brian had walked through the door, Jodie had been annoyed with Leanne. She thought her sister could have helped her more. OK, she'd taken Jodie to celebrity parties where she'd met Calum Best and Duncan out of Blue, but so what? She was still living at her mum's and pulling pints at the Beacon. Leanne should have made Jenny take her on, or at least give her a chance.

Anyway, she was going to show that Jenny. She was going to go all the way with Brian Spencer managing her. She didn't know whether Brian could manage a piss-up in a brewery but that didn't matter to her. She wanted the kudos of having a manager. And that was what Brian was.

'Val says you've got yourself a manager,' Dave said, still staring at her boobs.

'Yeah, that's right. He's got an office in town. I'm calling him soon to get some pictures taken.'

'Want me to take some pictures for you?' Dave leered.

'Why don't you pop off to the toilet and have a wank, Dave? Get it out of your system.'

Val looked on and smiled approvingly. She didn't want to lose Jodie as a member of staff. She might not be the sharpest knife in the drawer but her tongue was like a razor.

More exciting new fiction coming soon from Kerry Katona

GLAMOUR GIRL

Tracy Crompton is having the time of her life. She's gone from sitting around in her velour tracksuit all day to helping run her son Markie's mini-empire while he's inside.

Meanwhile, her daughter Jodie is fed up; she can't believe that she is now working for her mum, fronting the advertising campaign for new poker syndicate, Ladies of Leisure. That is until she meets Ben Ridley, the suave millionaire head of the Turquoise Property Company. He quickly sweeps Jodie off her feet and she's enjoying herself far too much to ask any questions about his past.

Turns out that Ben and Markie go way back. Ben's been running money through Markie's companies for years. So with Markie in prison, Ben has to go it alone and he quickly comes unstuck. And it's down to Jodie to try and sort out the Crompton troubles once and for all …

To be published October 2008

To find out more about Kerry Katona's amazing life read

TOO MUCH, TOO YOUNG
My Story of Love, Survival and Celebrity

'You'll be moved by this rags to riches story' *Glamour*

By the age of 11 Kerry Katona had lived in countless different homes and attended 8 different schools. By the age of 13 she could beat grown men at pool and knew how to look after her mother during a breakdown. By the age of 15 she had lived in women's refuges, the heart of London's East End gangster-land and several different foster homes. By the age of 18 she was a pop star ...

Too Much, Too Young is the moving, gripping – yet often very funny – account of one child's unique upbringing, and a woman's journey through pop stardom, motherhood and marriage heartbreak to a new beginning. From the backstreets of Warrington to the smoky pubs of the East End, from the shelters where victims of domestic violence hide, to the exclusive hotels where international pop stars party, this is an extraordinary read.

Better than fiction, more dramatic than the tabloids, more emotional than the soaps and funnier than a reality TV show ... welcome to Kerry's life.

Also by Kerry Katona from Ebury Press

SURVIVE THE WORST AND AIM FOR THE BEST

'*I've made mistakes. I've struggled. But I'm still here. I know it's not over and that there will be lots of tough times ahead, but you have to keep trying. Even when it seems horrible there is always something to look forward to. Remember you're not the only one. I've learned that everyone has their struggles and you just have to keep going because it's worth it. What makes it worth it for me is my kids. If I can make sure they have it just a bit easier than me, then I've done my job OK.*' Kerry

Kerry Katona knows what it's like to have to grow up fast. At just 26 years of age, she's experienced more than most people, including domestic violence, depression and a very public break-up.

In *Survive the Worst and Aim for the Best*, Kerry shows how she has used some of her worst experiences to learn positive life lessons. Her ability to keep going when times are tough will strike a chord with anyone who has struggled. Through her own experience, Kerry shows us how to remain positive, not to rely on others to help you, be proud of who you are, not to bear grudges, and not to be too judgemental.

Above all, Kerry shows us that the struggle really *is* worth it. And that the things that really matter are often those closest to you.

**Order further Kerry Katona titles from your
local bookshop, or have them delivered direct
to your door by Bookpost**